Finding Fairy Tales

Kate Ramsey

www.TalesMustBeTold.com

First Edition

ISBN: 0-578-45578-1
ISBN-13: 978-0-578-45578-5

Editing by LH Editing

Book Cover Design by ebooklaunch.com

To Molly and Arden, who were practically babies when the story started. Sorry I told you Molly was a princess.

CONTENTS

PART I

〜

"Since it is so likely that they will meet cruel enemies, let them at least have heard of brave knights and heroic courage."

C.S. Lewis

1

A SURPRISE VISIT

The Town Just West of the River, like all other towns, had a schoolhouse. It was an ordinary little school house – droopy outside, dingy inside, and imminently practical. No unnecessary embellishment breached the bareness of its walls or doors. No decorative plants, or paintings, no showcases of student art, no personal touches on faculty desks. It was an ordinary facility, to be used for strictly ordinary purposes.

Inside it, ordinary boys and girls with dim expressions stared at a severe little woman who told them in ordinary tones how to multiply fractions and subtract negative numbers.

The ordinary children sat in neat rows, flanked by grim plaster interrupted only by an ordinary door and three grimy windows. Outside the first two windows, ordinary people were doing very, *very* ordinary things.

Outside the third window, however, a highly un-ordinary pirate ship happened to be sailing by.

Its hull was square, like the foundation of a house. It did not fly the jolly roger flag – or any flag at all – and no mermaid or maiden graced its bow. In fact, you might not have recognized it as a pirate ship at all. It resembled a house in nearly every way, except for the violent bursts of color that comprised its exterior paint, and the ambitious eyes of the pirates peering out of its windows. That, and of course, the fact that it was floating, which is always a dead giveaway that something is not a house.

The reason this pirate ship was so unlike those more orthodox vessels of popular lore, was that a very un-ordinary girl was imagining it. Molly Morris had never learned about pirate ships. She had never learned about any kind of ship, in fact. In those days, only a few people remembered that ships had ever been real.

Molly had never heard of pirates either, so these pirates were not quite the swashbuckling rogues you might be familiar with. They wore top hats with flowers in the bands and patchwork capes, but they were still brave adventurers on the high sea as surely as Redbeard's beard was red.

Had she grown up where you did, Molly might have had clearer notions about what these marauders and their vessels should look like. She might have asked a grown-up, or read a book that cleared things up. But Molly grew up in Druinor and she could not do such things. She could not even tell anyone what she saw sailing by the third dirty window. In Druinor, the mere possession of a book (other than school books of course) was a crime punishable by death, or worse.

Molly knew that she was different than the other children. She was prone to daydream (and even night dream from time to time!) but she had learned at a very young age not to talk about her dreams to anyone. On the few occasions she had tried to describe them to other children, she had been met with blank stares, while her parents seemed frightened and hushed her quickly. At first Molly thought there must be something wicked about dreaming and had tried to stop. But as anyone who is familiar with dreams could tell you, not to dream after one has learned to do so, is nearly impossible.

The police in The Town Just West of the River were very diligent and were quick to notice civil violations of all varieties. If a man dropped his hat too close to sundown, or a child said their letters wrong too many times, they were as likely to spend the night in jail as at home. But the fiercest and swiftest punishment was reserved for those who employed their imaginations for any purpose deemed inappropriate or unnecessary. Citizens of that whole country were allowed to imagine only in very small quantities and even those exercises that were necessary for survival were placed under a heavy tax. The emperor's henchmen prowled the cities and towns, monitoring every person's behavior, expression, and productivity for any sign of excessive imagination. Large numbers of the regular citizenry could be counted on to fulfill this role as well, always watchful of opportunities to label their neighbors "anti-progs" and turn them in to the authorities. No one could remember how these things came to be. The progress wars and the glorious rise of Emperor Marlowe were long past. What remained was only unquestioning obedience, fear, and ironclad imagination sanctions. Still, Molly could not help but dream.

She saw things no one could see, or ever had seen. While the teacher instructed the other children in slow detail about the ins and outs of onion cultivation, Molly watched parades of fantastical characters wander by one after another: fairies with hummingbird wings, warriors painted head to toe in bright colors, and something that bore only a little resemblance to a tiger.

By the time you and I came across her, Molly had learned to love her inner worlds in silence and was nearly always in them, even when she was helping in the kitchen or the onion fields. She had plenty of time to herself, since most of the townsfolk found her presence inexplicably troubling and avoided it instinctively. Only Seamus knew the truth. But of course, the house cat always does.

Molly, at the beginning of our story, was very close to graduating the seventh grade. The seventh grade in The Town Just West of the River was even more frightening than the seventh grade in *your* country, which is saying something. What made the seventh grade so frightening was that it was the year that most children turned twelve, when they would be sent off to the Institute for Societal Transition. Professors always spoke of the Institute as if attendance there was a very impressive achievement rather than a universal mandate. They made each child feel proud to have successfully reached the age of twelve, but they never said anything else about it. Parents never spoke of it at all. No adult ever remembered anything about their time in the Institute. That was, perhaps, for the best. I will not yet describe the horrors that took place there, but since *you*, reader, are allowed to use your imagination, I ask you to do so now.

∽

The town's onion crop had been very poor that year and no one could imagine why. Since onions were Town West's main export, this was not good news. It was this shortage that had Mr. and Mrs. Morris so worried on that fateful Tuesday afternoon.

Upon returning from school, Molly had found her parents talking earnestly together at the kitchen table. It was rare, in that region, for any conversation to last long, since there was so little to say. Glad for any change of pace, she had looked on with interest for a while, but soon felt she was being intrusive. As Molly was a polite child, she eventually went outside and sat down to try to remember her nightdreams.

She had her eyes closed tightly, or she certainly would have noticed the unfamiliar boots approaching the house. Her hands were over her ears to help her concentrate, otherwise she most assuredly would have heard them. A child like Molly would never have overlooked such a momentous event as an unexpected visitor. It would have caused her small heart to race with delight. However, for the aforementioned reasons, it wasn't until the caller rang the bell, dripping water on her nose as he did so, that she took any notice of him.

Looking up with a start, she was utterly flummoxed to see the stranger looking back down at her. He had long, dark hair and a rather large nose. Worry lines traversed his face and his were the most penetrating eyes she had ever seen.

Molly instantly went cold. Dripping wet or not, there was no question that this dark-clad, serious stranger was a government agent. Molly knew as well as anyone else in Druinor what the punishment for excessive imagination was. When she was 6, she had made up a story about talking cats and told it to her mother. Mrs. Morris, visibly frightened, warned her daughter about the imagination laws, and emperor Marlowe's long reach. That night Molly had lain awake, trying with all her might not to imagine what would happen if she was found out, convinced that the emperor himself would come and carry her away to prison or worse. In the intervening years, however, her fears had not been realized, so she had stopped trying to suppress her imagination, and eventually grown lax in her efforts to conceal it.

Too lax it seemed.

Before she had time to say anything, the door opened and an astonished Mrs. Morris gaped at the dripping wet visitor on her front porch. It would be prudent to point out at this time that it was not raining in The Town Just West of the River. In fact it hadn't rained there, at least not *properly*, for many years.

"My name is Arthur Holcombe, Madam," he announced stiffly.

Mrs. Morris stared aghast for another moment, then found her voice and inquired, "And what is the meaning of this, Mr. Holcombe?"

"I have no idea. I inherited it from my father, Roger Holcombe," he replied.

"I don't mean your name. Why are you sopping wet?"

"I'd like to see *you* swim across the river and not get wet," he answered.

This was highly unexpected behavior for a government official and Molly could do little more than gape.

Mrs. Morris took a deep breath and donned a strained smile.

"And *why*, if it's not too much to ask, would you swim across the river when there's a perfectly good bridge?"

Mr. Holcombe looked mildly affronted. "Why, Madam," he said, "would I want to use a bridge, when there's a perfectly good river just under it?"

Mrs. Morris had just decided this was not the sort of thing that a child should be exposed to and was ushering

Molly inside when Mr. Holcombe said brightly, "I suppose I should tell you why I've come."

Unnerved, Mrs. Morris urged him to be quick about it.

Mr. Holcombe stood up straighter. "I'm a member of The Council for the Enforcement of Restricting Fiction, which, as you must know, works closely with the Office for the Taxation of Excessive Imagination. I've come about Molly Morris," he said, in a very official sounding voice.

Mrs. Morris' eyes widened and Molly saw her own desperate fear reflected in them.

Her mother was suddenly very anxious to get Mr. Holcombe inside the house and out of sight of the neighbors, so she invited him in and offered him some coffee.

As Mr. Morris and Mr. Holcombe shook hands, Mrs. Morris nervously shooed Molly outside and told her to wash the onions. Molly thought this was rather unfair. After all, it was on her account that the peculiar stranger had come.

Despite her terror, Molly felt a curious anticipation, although she did not know what the feeling was, having never felt it before. It's the way you and I feel when we know there's something grand just around the corner. It was most unfitting for the situation, she told herself.

The conversation seemed to last for ages, but it was really only a few minutes before the door opened and her mother, now beaming proudly, summoned Molly inside. Apprehensively, Molly obeyed and found Mr. Holcombe waiting for her. His demeanor was stiff and formal and her trepidation increased.

"I'll see you tomorrow Miss Morris," he said. This was the first time anyone had called Molly "Miss" anything, and she smiled in spite of herself.

"Why?" She asked. Then, remembering herself, she

added, "That is, what for Sir?"

"We're going for a little journey. Pack warmly. I've given your mother very strict instructions so see that you both follow them carefully." And without another word he turned and strode out the door while the Morris family watched, astonished.

‿

Molly could hardly sleep that night, despite Mr. Holcombe's instructions to rest well. She had never been on a journey of any kind, so both her anxiety and her anticipation had good reason. Mrs. Morris refused to tell Molly where she was going, but assured her it was not to prison. Mr. Holcombe had left a list of instructions so strange that Molly knew this was not to be an ordinary journey. Not like the occasional trips her father took over the bridge, or to The Town Slightly Farther West of the River. Those trips, though not rare, were so shrouded in mystery to her that she often begged to go along and danced about excitedly while he packed his onion cart. Molly could hardly believe that she was about to embark on a *truly* mysterious journey with an unknown destination.

Mr. Holcombe's instructions had been both very specific and entirely nonsensical. Mrs. Morris read the long letter he had left her and proceeded to follow each step with a fearful precision that seemed absurd in light of the far-fetched nature of the commands themselves.

She insisted on utmost adherence to each edict, even as they progressed from sensible *(Make sure you only pack one bag that can be easily carried)* to odd *(Each time you enter or exit the house, do so by a different method than the last)* to downright silly *(Pack one pair of brown stockings and one black. Then quickly unpack one pair, not looking to see which it is, and throw it in the fire).* After Molly clambered through three or four windows Mrs. Morris told her she might just stay in the house, if it was all the same.

All this seemed to Molly the most remarkable way a journey could possibly begin and it took her quite a long time to drop off to sleep.

❧

Mr. Holcombe was telling the truth: he did work for the government. However, his activities that day were a bit beyond the scope of his duties. It had been in the interest of avoiding detection by a group of passing colleagues that he had been compelled to hide, along with his horse, under the bridge during his approach to Town West. Seeing that no other government agents were in the vicinity upon his return, he left town by way of the bridge, the use of which Mrs. Morris had so strongly advocated.

Mr. Holcombe was in fairly high spirits. He felt he had pulled off his first meeting with Molly quite well, considering how long he had been waiting for it. However, his business for the day was not yet accomplished. He began to head east, but instead of going back the way he came, he swung his horse slightly south and paid a visit to another town that day.

❧

It seemed as though Molly had only just closed her eyes when she was awakened by a noise she could not immediately identify. Sitting up to sleepily survey the room, she saw nothing out of the ordinary and would have quickly dropped off to sleep again, but for a small movement in the corner of her eye which caught her attention.

Glancing out of the window, Molly was first frightened,

then curious to see the large, bulky figure of a man looking in at her. She stared back for a moment, her thoughts still sluggish from sleep, when the figure spoke.

"Molly!" he hissed. "Open the window, child, and be quick about it!"

Instantly, Molly remembered the afternoon's unusual visitor and her feet hit the cold floor before her eyes had managed to completely open themselves. Running to the window, she raised it and stuck her head out to examine Mr. Holcombe, for of course it was he lurking outside. He wore a black traveling cape with the hood pulled up so that it concealed nearly all of his face. In the dark he was even more disconcerting than he had been that afternoon.

"Well? Are you coming then, or shall we stand about gaping at each other 'til dawn?" he asked, but not unkindly.

Molly was still half convinced she was about to be taken to the capital to be tried for imagination crimes, but seeing that she had no other choice, she picked up her satchel and began to clamber out of the window. With one leg swung over she stopped.

For reasons that Molly could not quite define, she suddenly thought about Seamus, but as she opened her mouth to protest, Mr. Holcombe cut her off.

"No time for goodbyes, Molly. Besides, Seamus is long gone by now."

Molly blinked in surprise. Finding no appropriate response to this revelation, she swung her other leg over and dropped to the ground.

"I thought you weren't coming 'til tomorrow, sir."

"It *is* tomorrow, child. Nearly an hour past midnight and we've very little time."

Molly, whose understanding of time consisted chiefly of knowing she ought to be at school shortly after breakfast and in bed shortly after dark, would have questioned him further, but he had taken her hand and was hurrying toward a horse-drawn coach that waited on the road. It seemed impossibly large to a child who had been on no grander a ride than her father's donkey-drawn onion cart. Its black curtains were drawn. The horses were, likewise, black and no bells hung from their harnesses.

Mr. Holcombe lifted Molly into the coach and shut the door.

"You must be awfully confused, and I would've liked to explain the whole affair to you on the way, but as we're traveling under the utmost secrecy, I couldn't go calling for a driver, could I?" And with that he was gone.

At the words "utmost secrecy," a delicious thrill ran down Molly's spine and she repeated them to herself several times. It wasn't until the coach started moving a moment later that she realized that she wasn't alone.

2

THE JOURNEY BEGINS

A boy slightly older than Molly sat across from her, regarding her with frank curiosity. He was pale, with unruly hair and awfully dirty, but his green eyes were friendly and Molly liked him at once.

They continued to size each other up for a moment, before Molly offered cheerfully, "Hullo!"

The boy grinned amiably and announced, "I'm Hatch. Who are you?"

"I'm Molly. What an odd name."

"Yes," the boy agreed. "Where did you get it?"

Molly laughed. "I meant yours, of course."

Hatch shrugged, laughing too. "Well, it's not so odd to me. I've had it all my life, or at least all of it I can remember."

"Say, have you any idea where we're going?" Molly asked.

Hatch grinned wider. "Not at all!"

He seemed very pleased about this, and Molly saw that they were kindred spirits. This was unusual for Molly, who was shunned by the children in her own village, and she realized that Hatch felt the same, for they fell to talking about their adventure with great enthusiasm and quickly became fast friends.

Molly knew instinctively that the boy (who had grown up in The Small Village East of the Bridge) would not laugh at her if she told him about her day and nightdreams. Indeed, he listened solemnly, and she was not surprised to learn he had them too, though they were not the same ones.

Hatch told her how he had been behind his house the previous evening when he had seen a stranger approaching from the fields behind the town. No stranger had ever approached town on foot from such a direction, so the novelty of that small act had intrigued him. But oh, what an impossible wonder when it became clear the stranger was deliberately approaching *him*! The stranger, of course, had been Mr. Holcombe.

"He knew my name before I told it to him," Hatch breathed, still awestruck. "I thought for sure I'd been reported as an anti-prog, or something of the sort, and he was come to arrest me."

Mr. Holcombe's encounter with Mr. and Mrs. Holland had been much the same as his visit to the Morris house. He was met at first with fear, followed by confusion, and eventually timid pride, though Hatch was unable to tell what precipitated any of these shifts.

"Oh! And he left us the strangest instructions!" Hatch said, and his eyes sparkled.

"I can imagine," Molly replied, and instinctively lowered her voice on the final word. "But... you weren't afraid?"

"Utterly!" Hatch said, as if this only added to his enjoyment of the event. "I thought the government must be onto me, and they'd sent him to have me hanged."

Molly was a little awestruck by his apparent nonchalance.

"I still wonder if that's not the case," she said, but Hatch shook his head dismissively.

"Why not take us right then? Why leave cryptic instructions, and then come in the dead of night?" he asked.

He then told her how his parents had closed the shutters of their home to repel any possible attention from the neighbors as the family conducted the most enjoyable evening they had ever had together.

The strange list of instructions had kept them occupied, both in mind and body, as they attempted to comply with its odd demands (*#14: remove everything from the cupboards of the boy's room, organize by color and size, and replace exactly as you found it*).

"But you know what's strange?" Hatch asked after relaying the story.

"Other than every moment since yesterday?" Molly grinned.

"It may have been nothing," Hatch said, before hastily adding, "never mind, I'm *sure* it was nothing."

"I very much doubt that anything about this is nothing," Molly said (quite correctly, too).

Hatch flushed, though it was too dark for Molly to tell. He was still accustomed to feeling embarrassed of his mind. "Well it's just... we had such a strange and delightful evening, but I noticed a few times that Melody – she's the cat, you know – she was looking at us almost as if she understood everything that was happening. I was almost hesitant to leave her behind."

To his relief, Molly didn't laugh, or even seem surprised. "I felt quite the same about Seamus!" she exclaimed. "He's our cat of course."

"Anyway," Hatch said, "there's just something about this Holcombe fellow... it doesn't *feel* as if he wants to have us hanged. Don't you feel it?"

Molly supposed she did.

The children went on like this for quite some time, and found they had no end of things to talk about. In fact, they had quite worn themselves out by the time the coach rolled to a stop a few hours later and were sound asleep as Mr. Holcombe carried them one at a time into a small cottage, shrouded in foliage (and a little magic) so that it was nearly invisible from the road. He laid them in soft, warm beds where they dreamed happily until late morning.

3

~⁀

STARTLING REVELATIONS

Molly opened her eyes to find the sun streaming through the window of the simple, but not unpleasant room in which she found herself. She felt perfectly happy, except for a slight pain in her back – the kind you might feel after having slept in the car for some time. She sat up and stretched, not wanting to get out of bed.

"I believe that's the nicest bed I've ever slept in," said Molly, who had only ever slept in one bed, and had never even heard of a down mattress. They didn't have such things in Town West. It wasn't practical.

She found Hatch in the kitchen, eating the breakfast of apples, cheese and bread that had been laid out for them. You may think this simple fare, but for Molly, who had never had a meal that didn't taste at least slightly of onion, it was very nice.

"Where's Mr. Holcombe?" she asked.

Hatch held up a hastily scrawled note. "Said he'd be

back this afternoon and not to leave the cottage."

This suited the children just fine, as they had never slept in a house other than their own and were content to explore it. Eventually they found a tub of clean water, chilly but just under a sunny window. This was where they very nearly had their first quarrel, for Molly suggested they take turns bathing, and Hatch felt that mundane tasks like bathing would take all the fun out of such a jolly adventure, and Molly said it wouldn't be so much fun if they couldn't stand the smell of each other.

It might have gone on for some time if Mr. Holcombe hadn't settled it on his return by insisting they take turns bathing immediately, for he had much to tell them. Both were so excited to hear what Mr. Holcombe had to say that they forgot the argument and were scrubbed clean in no time. Even so, it was some time before the children got to hear the story.

Mr. Holcombe cleaned and cooked several fish he had just caught and produced more bread, along with some butter and coffee. After the three were well-fed and comfortable he reached into his pocket and withdrew a pipe, which he lit with some satisfaction.

"Heaven knows, you two've gotten no proper history lessons in school, so this will take some time," he remarked. Thus, the story commenced.

"First thing's first," Mr. Holcombe began. "From this moment forward you will no longer call me Mr. Holcombe. You will call me by my real name, which is Eldon."

"I knew it!" Hatch exclaimed. "You're not from the government at all! Are you... are you an anti-prog?" he asked, awestruck.

Mr. Holcombe laughed. "I suppose in a sense. Though there isn't really an 'anti-prog' movement you know. That's just what the government calls anyone who disagrees with them. Marlowe likes to encourage this, in fact. It gives folks reasons to have one another hanged and imprisoned." he paused, smiling sadly at the children's shocked expressions. They had never heard anyone casually refer to the emperor as *Marlowe* before.

"So yes, I suppose I could be classified as an anti-prog. Though I'm not actually opposed to real progress by any means. In fact, I believe for the first time in a long time, the country has a real chance of making some.

"The truth is, I'm not a citizen of Druinor at all. I come from the land that lies north of here, and it is only by years of hard work and strong northern magic that I have gone thus far undetected. In fact, I have become quite trusted ..." Mr. Holcombe, or, as we too shall now refer to him, Eldon, saw the children's blank expressions and sighed.

"Let me start over. You children have grown up in the cold southern lands, which its rulers refer to as 'the modern lands,' and which we in the north call 'Druinor.' In our storytelling language that means, 'land of the sleepers.' It is a long journey between here and the northern land, called Arden, where you will soon go. But I will get back to that.

"Arden, you will find, is quite different from Druinor. The people are just and kind and happy. The country is warm and beautiful. Life can be difficult in some ways, but we get along quite nicely, or we did when last I saw my fair homeland. Arden is ruled by King Mardius, a merry, wise fellow and the tenth of his line to possess the throne since King Torus gave it up. Torus was not wicked, but he was ambitious and a little foolish. It is largely because of him that Arden and Druinor have long been enemies, though they used to be one and the same."

"You mean Druinor was part of Arden?" Molly asked.

"Sort of. The land itself belonged to Arden, but it's separated from Arden proper by a vast wasteland," Eldon said. "Everything south of The Wasteland was uninhabited for hundreds of years, because legend held that some sort of dark magic dwelt here."

"There's no such thing as dark magic," Hatch scoffed.

"That's where you're wrong," Eldon said, looking fondly at his pipe as he spoke. "Although Torus took your view, or something like it. He hated to see land go to waste, and sent some intrepid settlers here to see what it was like. It seemed alright and the land was plentiful, so they stayed. Only the legends were right. There *was* a dark magic here. It's just that nobody recognized it."

"How do you recognize magic?" Molly asked.

"Exactly," Eldon said. "The Ardenians are a romantic people, you know. They're fond of legends and mysteries and all that. A little *too* fond, in fact. They heard "dark magic" and thought they'd find wraiths and ghosts and mysterious deaths after dark. What they found was much more subtle, and insidious.

"It started slowly. Things that people once delighted in failed to spark their interest, their affections cooled, and their better natures gave way to those faults of character against which they had once battled. It's easy to see now, from an academic standpoint, of course, but it was much harder for those in the midst of it. Whatever spell infected this country went to work quietly, drawing out the worst in people and subduing their nobler inclinations."

He went on to tell them how Marlowe, at the time a young wizard full of greed and ambition, had taken advantage of the unpleasant circumstances to seize power for himself. He had intentionally fostered the divide between the north and south, calling the southern lands "progressive" and the northern people "superstitious friends of faeries" until everyone began to feel they could no longer stay united with their old-fashioned northern neighbors, and decided to officially secede. They became obsessed with machinery and new inventions. They abandoned the old languages and adopted newer, "more sensible" terminology.

The problem was that no one had a clear grasp on what the term "progressive" actually meant. Fierce debates raged over what counted as *truly* progressive and factions began to form, each trying to outdo the others with newer, more monstrous machines. Some even claimed that their new technologies were so powerful that they could do away with magic altogether. In the midst of this, Marlowe claimed that he alone could lead them into the modern era, and they were only too happy to put someone in charge, so they crowned him emperor of Druinor.

"Apparently the dark magic that dwelt here wasn't quite potent enough, though," Eldon said. "Once it became clear that Marlowe meant to rule by oppression and fear, people began to talk about Arden fondly again. So Marlowe had to take more drastic measures. He sent his minions out to whisper among the people that the northern lands were a lie, a work of fiction designed to spread discontent among the people. It may seem amazing to you that they would believe such nonsense, but by this time there were very few people alive who remembered Arden.

"Not long after this, Marlowe outlawed fiction altogether. But where there is imagination, stories will exist. Long after the books had all been burned and the songs forgotten, children continued to be enchanted by stories of the adventurous people and the faeries of the northern lands. The very air of secrecy in which they were told made them all the more marvelous for Druinian children. So that's when things got really bad."

Eldon leaned forward in his chair, caught up in his own narrative. "Summoning the darkest magic he could conjure, Marlowe tracked down Fiction herself, and imprisoned her in a secret location in the cold western mountains."

The children didn't entirely understand what Eldon was saying but Molly looked stricken nonetheless. "Poor Fiction," she said with a shudder.

"Well, that's not quite right, actually," Eldon corrected himself. "It wasn't Fiction exactly. It was her daughter Fairy Tale. Fiction could never be entirely contained, and in fact her other daughter, Falsehood, is still quite free in the southern lands."

This speech made even less sense to Eldon's listeners than the previous one had. Seeing their puzzled expressions, Eldon shook his head and was about to begin again when the story was interrupted by a sound at the door. It was after dark by now and Eldon extinguished the lamp quickly. The children waited in breathless silence as they heard him go quietly to the door. After a moment Eldon returned and relit the lamp. He was accompanied by a large white cat and slightly smaller Tabby.

"Why it's Seamus!" Molly exclaimed as the Tabby settled down comfortably in front of the fire.

"And Melody!" Hatch cried and the white cat leapt into his lap with a purr.

"What?" asked Eldon, looking up from his pipe and glancing at the two cats. "Oh yes, well, I'll get to that later. Where was I?"

"Fairy Tale's been imprisoned in the mountains," said Hatch. "But I don't understand. What does all this have to do with Molly and me?"

"And our cats!" Molly added.

23

Eldon smiled compassionately. "Yes of course. This must all be terribly confusing for you."

The truth was, neither of them minded very much. Perhaps they should have, but this was their first adventure, and it still had the delightful feel that many adventures have in their earliest days.

"Haven't you ever noticed that you are not quite like the other children in your towns?"

"Yes!" Molly exclaimed, as the excitement rising in her belly threatened to choke her. *At last!* she thought, feeling as a ghost might feel on meeting someone who could finally see her. "Why? What is it?" she asked breathlessly.

"Don't you see?" whispered Hatch, eyes wide. He glanced at Eldon as if afraid to continue, but Eldon nodded encouragingly. "We don't belong in Druinor at all, do we?"

"Excellent deduction, my boy!" Eldon roared his approval. "You're even sharper than I'd hoped, and I had very high hopes! Indeed, you are not. You, Hatch Holland, and you as well, Molly Morris, are children of Arden. I've been waiting nearly twelve years to come and fetch you!"

This declaration, of course brought on a great number of questions from the children, some excited shouts, and not a few tears. Even you would probably be surprised by news like this, so imagine what it must have been like for them. The gist of the story was this.

In the early days of Marlowe's rule, he had gone on an aggressive campaign to stamp out all imagination and storytelling, all inspiring tales of nobility and woe. At first, he tried powerful enchantments to suppress imagination *entirely*, but this had disastrous results. What he had failed to realize was that people cannot function without imagination. A man will not plant seeds and care for them properly if he cannot imagine something growing several months later. A woman will not feed her children properly or give them medicine if she cannot imagine what the results of her not doing so might be. Indeed, without *any* imagination, people simply gave up doing anything at all, since they could not imagine why they ought to. Famine and sickness ravaged the country before Marlowe could put a stop to it, but the damage was already done to the population.

For many years afterward, that wicked emperor had sent spies and thugs north to kidnap Ardenian children to replenish the population, as his questionable policies provided for a fairly high mortality rate. Marlowe hated the north with a passion that was only surpassed by his hatred of children, with their bright innocence and inquiring eyes. The theft of young ones from northern families was a favorite of his government programs.

Of course, King Mardius sent raiding parties into Druinor to rescue as many children as they could and return them to their families. With each mission Mardius gave instructions to rescue any other Druinians who could be persuaded to come along as well. Many of the children, and even a few Druinians, were rescued, but many were not. Those unfortunate children were placed in Druinian homes, where Marlowe delighted to see them stripped of their natural curiosity and childlike exuberance. Later, they were sent to the Institute, where such terrible things happened to them that, if they survived, they emerged as full Druinians, their souls having forgotten the richness of their homeland entirely. Arden built up heavy defenses along its borders, but Marlowe had black magic on his side, and his men still occasionally managed to sneak into homes and take children in the night. That is, until something stopped him forever: the Wasteland Wall.

Molly and Hatch, the last two children of Arden to be snatched, had been taken that very night. Molly's mother was the first to discover her daughter's empty bed. Within minutes a squad of seven men, including Molly's father and several neighbors (some of whom Eldon didn't even know) was in hot pursuit of the kidnappers. They might have caught them too, had it not been for the magic. As they tore across the wasteland, one of the men saw what appeared to be a tidal wave rushing toward them in the darkness, blocking the light of the low hanging moon. Spurring their horses on faster, now to escape the oncoming blackness, the men reached the edge of the Wasteland at nearly the exact same moment as the black mist. Two of the men burst into the woods beyond the wasteland just in time to see their slower companions swallowed in the dark mist. They only paused a moment – long enough to see the mist dissipate as suddenly as it had appeared, leaving no sign of their comrades. The children and their captors were nowhere to be found. Their trail had vanished entirely. The two soldiers searched for days and could not locate the children.

It was only when Eldon – naturally you've guessed that he was one of the two – and his comrade began a weary and defeated return journey nearly a fortnight later that they discovered the wall. The dark mist of that night had not disappeared at all, but only hardened into glass. They could see clear across the Wasteland as it stretched out toward Arden's border, but could not return.

From that point forward, the two made locating and rescuing those two stolen babes the focus of their lives. They blended into Druinian culture as best they could and worked their way into government positions that allowed them to move freely. For years they searched, relying on rumors and hushed whispers for information, but eventually they discovered the whereabouts of Molly and Hatch. They watched the children from a distance as they grew, waiting for the right time to make a move, certain the Wasteland would become passable again before long. But it never had. Now the children were twelve and ready to be sent off to the Institute. Time had run out. The children had to be rescued now, before it was too late.

"But how?" Molly asked. "If we're cut off from Arden, I suppose we can't get back there?"

"Yes, I wondered about that too," said Hatch thoughtfully.

"Well," Eldon answered. "It's important that you understand that every story is part of a bigger story, and yours is no exception. I'm afraid that I must ask something quite unfair of you: you must help rescue yourselves. Before your rescue – as part of it, rather – there's a very important job we must do."

The children again looked bewildered.

"You see," Eldon said, "I have for eleven years been studying everything I could about the night the mist settled on the Wasteland. And I have discovered something fascinating. That mist came up at the very hour that Fairy Tale was locked up in the Western Mountains."

"We are convinced that the only way the wall will lift is if Fairy Tale is freed from captivity," Seamus said.

The children both gave a great start and Hatch screamed, then turned a blistering red and glanced at Molly. But Molly was too busy staring at her lifelong house pet to pay him any notice.

"What?" was all she could manage by way of words.

"Oh yes, sorry," Eldon said, gesturing distractedly at the cats. "I suppose you haven't properly met. These two have been your ever-present guardians for some time now."

The children gaped at him uncomprehendingly.

"Well, cats you know, they're all government agents. Spies really (begging your pardon, my feline friends). That's why every family has one."

The children stared, aghast.

"Only not us. We've defected," said Melody, Hatch's sleek white cat. Her voice was soft and velvety. "Sorry to have startled you dears, though I dare say Seamus did it on purpose," she added with a touch of reproach in her tone.

"You have these two to thank for the fact that you have not succumbed to Marlowe's magic, or been spotted by the imagination enforcers," Eldon added.

It took a few moments for the children to adjust to this new development. Eldon made them some tea to calm their nerves before resuming the conversation.

"As master Seamus was saying, we are all firmly convinced that the only way to lift the wall is to set Fairy Tale free."

"Why would setting her free lift the wall?" Hatch asked.

"You children might not understand this… at least not yet," Eldon said. "But that's the way it works in all the fairy tales. The details vary, but in every story about an imprisoned princess, or an evil enchantment or the like, some act of heroism by a brave adventurer lifts the enchantment. I feel certain this is the same."

"And *we* must set her free?" Molly asked. "Why?"

"Well…" Eldon paused. "Again, I must apologize. I can't expect you to understand all this. But there is an ancient Ardenian prophecy that predicted Fairy Tale's captivity. It was fuzzy on the details, of course (why can't prophets ever just be straightforward?) so I didn't understand what they were prophesying 'til after it had happened. Now I'm no prophetic scholar, but it seems to me that the prophecy foretells a task being undertaken to break Marlowe's curse, and indicates that it will be undertaken by two people — a male and a female."

"But... us?" Molly was incredulous.

"The unfortunate truth is that there is no one else." Eldon said. "Marlowe was careful with the curse he used to keep her captive. He designed it specifically so that it cannot be broken by any citizen of Arden or Druinor. You two are actually citizens of both countries, which means you are not citizens of *either* one, *or* the other." He shrugged apologetically. "It's a technicality, but it's the best chance we've got. Until the curse is broken, there's no possible escape for the people of Druinor from his oppressive reign."

"I'm afraid I don't understand why we'd want to," Hatch said. "I mean, I'm sure she's lovely, I'm not saying she ought to stay imprisoned. But isn't the wall a *good* thing? The way I see it, it protects Arden from Marlowe."

"That it does," Eldon agreed. "And conversely protects Druinor from Arden."

"Do you mean King Mardius wants to attack Druinor?" Hatch asked excitedly.

"Quite the opposite!" Eldon said. "He wants to save it. You're not the only kidnapped children, you know. Others must have survived, even if they *have* forgotten who they are. And if you go farther back then that, all citizens of Druinor are really Ardenians. They just can't remember."

"Chose to forget, more like," Seamus added moodily. "Stupid, hard-headed creatures you humans can be."

"True!" Eldon agreed, amiably. "Stupid and arrogant, the whole lot of us. But these Druinians are our kin, and even if they've forgotten their country, their country's not forgotten them. It's a rescue mission for the whole nation, not just the two of you, and it's been ongoing since long before the wall appeared."

"But how will we find her?" Molly asked. "Won't it be dangerous? What do we do when we *have* found her?"

"All in good time, dear," Melody's silky voice interjected. "We'll explain it all as we go. But now, off to bed! It's already late and we must get an early start!"

৵

Anyone familiar with plans knows that they rarely work out the way they are supposed to. If they did, they wouldn't be worth writing stories about. This plan was no exception and it started to go wrong very early on.

The departure of the children and cats was, of course, supposed to go undetected in their respective towns, for as long as possible. The children had departed in Mr. Holcombe's government coach in the dead of night, and the cats had filed their usual reports at the local municipal offices and slipped quietly away just afterward. Only Hatch's exit was not as discreet as Melody had hoped. A cat named Charlie, who lived with Mr. and Mrs. Wilson, had been hiding out near the Holland house the previous afternoon, waiting for the neighbor's cat, Ms. Primrose to appear. Charlie didn't have any particular ill will toward Melody, but was, as nearly all cats were, a staunch supporter and faithful steward of Emperor Marlowe. Beyond that he simply shared the natural proclivity toward villainy for which cats are universally known, even in your world.

Ms. Primrose, having already spurned Charlie's advances once, primly refused to come outdoors again that day, leaving Charlie in an especially foul mood. He stalked away to nurse his wounded dignity, and in doing so, narrowly dodged the still soggy boots of Mr. Holcombe, as he bid farewell to the Holland family.

"Pardon me sir," Mr. Holcombe said solemnly, accompanying his apology with a deep bow. Charlie opened his mouth to hiss something unpleasant, but Mr. Holcombe was already hurrying away, leaving the cat to scowl at his retreating back.

It might have ended there too, but for Charlie's having glanced behind him to make sure Ms. Primrose hadn't seen the incident. What he saw instead was Mrs. Holland peering out of her window with a very strange look on her face.

Charlie turned to head homeward, but paused. Cats have a sort of sense about things, you know. The whole encounter had taken a mere 10 seconds, but it didn't sit quite right with him. Having nothing better to do, he stole around to the back of the house and hid himself in the shrubbery, where he settled down to wait. Something odd, he was sure, was going on in the Holland house and he was determined to find out what it was.

Cats are very patient creatures. His wait would not be fruitless. When the government coach appeared in the dead of night and spirited away the Holland boy, Charlie Wilson watched it go.

4

~◦

PLANS GO AWRY

H atch thought he'd never be able to sleep again
now that he'd heard so many new and terrible
things. Nevertheless, he fell into an exhausted
slumber nearly instantly, as children who have faced a good
deal of excitement and are presented with a warm down
bed often do. Molly, however, truly couldn't sleep. She lay
awake for a long time, turning the wonders of the day over
in her mind. So it was that she became privy to the
unsettling conversation that followed.

After the children had gone to bed, Eldon leaned back
thoughtfully in his chair, watching the smoke from his pipe
weave its way toward the rafters. He thought to himself
that the children had handled the day's revelations quite
bravely. This was a good sign, as much bravery was to be
required of them in the coming days.

He was quiet for a long time, listening for any sound
from the bedrooms to which his young wards had retired.
Finally he leaned forward again, resting his elbows on his

legs and looked hard at the cats.

"Well?" he said, in a low voice. "Have we been found out?"

"We think not," Seamus answered. "It won't be long though. It was a mercy you took them just before our reports were due. We filed them under *Nothing of Interest* of course, but that will keep them off our tails for a few weeks at most."

"Will the parents give us away?" Eldon asked.

"It's unlikely," Seamus said confidently. "That was a stroke of brilliance on your part, telling them that the children were being promoted to the Institute early for their good performance. They've been worried about the children and their imaginations. Afraid they wouldn't get into the Institute at all. You put their minds at ease and they won't want to jeopardize the promotions by making a fuss about it, in case the other parents try and put a stop to it."

"The other cats will notice our absence though," Melody interjected. "I've made a show of being under the weather so that it won't raise any red flags if I'm not out and about for a few days. But they're trained to look for anything suspicious you know. It's only a matter of time before they realize."

"They'll report it straightaway of course," Eldon nodded. "I'll see what I can do on my end to buy you some more time. I'll use my connections in the Council."

Melody and Seamus were silent.

"What is it?" Eldon asked.

"Well it's just… we think you ought to come with us," Melody said softly. "It's far too dangerous for you in Druinor now. And we could use your help."

"You know I can't. You'll need me to cover your tracks. They'll be after us the moment they notice my absence."

"He's right, you know," Seamus said. Melody stayed quiet.

"We'll meet up with you as soon as we can," Eldon promised.

After another moment of silence, Seamus cleared his throat uncomfortably. "And… what of the other parts of the prophecy? The part you didn't tell them?"

Eldon shot him a sharp look. "There's no way of knowing what that really means," he said. "Would you have me risk letting them get sent to the Institute for a thing like that?"

"No…" Melody said slowly. "But it must mean *something*."

"Why can't the damned prophets ever just say what they mean?" Eldon demanded again, glowering at the ceiling.

"If they were the damned prophets, we wouldn't want to listen to them anyway," Seamus said mildly.

"Don't talk like that," Melody said. "Ealdor wouldn't like it."

Eldon only laughed. "Don't be so pious," he said affectionately. "That's the quickest way to forget what *actually* pleases Ealdor."

At this point, Molly must have made a noise, for the room fell sharply silent. It was several moments before the conversation resumed, but this time the voices were too low for Molly to make out any more of it, strain as she might. Molly slept very little that night.

༄

Before the sun was up, Eldon gently shook both the children awake. Molly was light headed from lack of sleep, but the excitement of the journey had yet to wear off and her mood could hardly have been better. She rushed into Hatch's room to tell him about what she'd overheard, but she found him engaged in casual conversation with

Melody. She marveled for a moment at how quickly he'd adapted to the presence of talking cats. It still made her own head spin. She hung around for a few moments hoping for a moment with him alone, but he didn't seem to notice. Before long the preparations for the upcoming journey put it out of her head.

Eldon poured coffee, served breakfast and packed saddle bags for the children, talking quickly as he did so. They had, he said, a hard day's work ahead of them. When he had finished, they all went out behind the cabin where two smallish gray horses waited. The children knew how to saddle a horse but had never ridden before. Eldon taught them patiently how to mount, how to speak to the horses and how to direct them. He showed them several different plants and berries and told them which ones they could safely eat. He made them repeat the plant names back to him several times.

Strangest of all for the children, Eldon taught them entreaties to recite for the blessing of Ealdor: The Entreaty for Divine Protection, The Entreaty for the Favor of the Elements, The Entreaty for Blindness of Enemies, and others. The children little knew what to make of these, but learned them all the same. They had to memorize a story to tell anyone who crossed their paths.

"Don't include too many details," he said. "The more details you give, the more you have to remember and the easier it is to catch you in a lie."

The children worked hard all morning, learning, repeating, memorizing, until their poor minds were exhausted. But Eldon wasn't finished.

"The most important thing is that you keep your minds and your imaginations sharp," he told them. "It's your main advantage over Druinians. You've both got very good imaginations, but they're undisciplined. They've run wild your whole life. You must learn to command them."

"To command them?" Molly asked, puzzled.

"Yes, put them to use! Apply them to problems. They're not just for daydreaming," Seamus said.

"An imagination is a wonderful tool, but you must learn to rule it and not be ruled by it," Eldon explained. "An imagination that's run wild can be a dangerous thing indeed, and the pictures it paints are never accurate. What you anticipate is never so satisfying and what you fear never so terrible as your imagination tells you it will be. That's why you must employ it, but never let it drive your decisions. Truth only must be your ultimate standard. The imagination is useful only insofar as it serves the truth."

The children did not entirely understand this, and Eldon dwelt on it for some time with dubious success. He told them they needed to do imagination exercises every day.

"Think about everything you do. Think of the most creative way to do it, the most effective, the quickest and the most surprising. Then choose based on what the situation calls for."

Molly blinked at him. "Is that why you left such odd instructions, that day you came to visit my house?"

"Very good!" he rewarded her with a warm smile. "You'll do alright, you know. You look like Druinians, but your minds aren't clouded by Marlowe's spells."

The sun was low by the time they sat down to supper. As they ate, Eldon told them he could risk no more time away from the capital without arousing suspicion. Though they'd known him only a matter of hours, the children already loved him fondly and were nearly in tears when he announced his departure.

"Will we see you again?" Hatch asked, as the dangerous

reality of the journey ahead began to settle upon him.

"Very soon I hope," Eldon said, and his broad smile put the children much more at ease.

The whole troop followed him to the door, where he knelt and whispered a few words to the cats before embracing Molly reassuringly and offering Hatch a sturdy handshake.

"I'll see you both in Arden!" he proclaimed (ah, but we must be careful with proclamations, reader!), and in no time at all, his black-curtained government coach was rumbling away from the cabin in the direction from which it had come two nights before.

"Well then," said Melody, taking care to keep her voice cheerful and carefree. "Off we go! I'm always ready for a good adventure."

Seamus said nothing.

～

The journey started pleasantly enough. Every difficulty or inconvenience they encountered was another exciting element of the adventure. The children chattered animatedly about the strange events of the past few days, the wonderful revelations about Arden, and the uncertain future. Molly wondered what the queen of Arden looked like and Hatch wondered whether Fairy Tale would be chained up in a dungeon when they found her and whether she'd be so glad to see them that she'd reward them with great treasure once they'd set her free. Their enthusiasm caught on, and the cats soon found themselves joining in the conversation. Seamus, who loved to know things, was delighted to show the children the wonders of the universe. He taught them how to tell time by the stars, told them the names of many of the constellations, and tales of the great exploits of King Mardius. Sometimes he talked about Marlowe too, telling them dark rumors he'd heard of the wizard – strange appearances and frightening encounters. Melody didn't like these stories very much but the children were fascinated by them.

"They say he can walk through walls," Seamus said one night as they relaxed around the fire. Molly, who loved Seamus' stories, leaned forward to listen. Hatch glanced up from a hunk of wood he'd begun to carve with his pocket knife – one of his imagination exercises. "He can't!" He exclaimed. "Can he?" Melody frowned and stared at the fire. "A fellow I knew used to run shipments to the capital and back," Seamus said. "At that time there were a group of rebels out to overthrow the empire. They'd been quietly gathering recruits and making plans. They called themselves 'the Damascus Guard' but everyone else called them the Maskies. My friend came across them one night. He was late with his shipment and tried to take a shortcut, but got hopelessly lost in the city's back streets. He was in an alleyway, when all of a sudden a door opened into it and out stepped the Maskies.

"Of course he didn't know it was them. But they didn't see him, and were talking to each other. One of them said, clear as day 'that's a matter to take to Damascus with us.' That's when it happened."

Seamus paused for effect. He needn't have bothered. Hatch had stopped carving and Molly was staring at him, wide-eyed.

"All of a sudden, there he was. Marlowe. Jack swears the wizard walked directly out of the wall. And there he was in the middle of the Maskies. Before they could say anything, he held up his scepter and shouted a curse, and they were all gone. Nothing left at all. Jack was alone in the alleyway, just him and the Emperor."

Melody said something that sounded like "humph."

"What happened to him?" Molly asked.

"Nothing," Seamus said. "It was strange. Marlowe just looked at him for a minute. Jack was so scared he couldn't move. Then Marlowe turned and walked back into the wall and was gone."

"Enough, you'll frighten them!" Melody said reproachfully.

"No you won't!" Hatch exclaimed. "Tell us more!"

But Seamus thought better of it and wouldn't be persuaded to tell another story that night. For all their bravado, it took the children a long time to get to sleep.

⌒

It was not long before the novelty of the quest began to wear off. Exhilaration was soon replaced by irritation and exhaustion as the children attempted to make fires and beds and meals with only advice from the cats for guidance. Hours in saddles and hours in the sun and hours on the stony ground turned the adventure into a chore very quickly. If you've ever had an adventure you know exactly what I mean. They're nowhere near as romantic in practice as in the retelling.

The children had made enthusiastic attempts to do their imagination exercises the first few days. Hatch tried mounting his horse from the wrong side, an exercise that rewarded him with a very bruised tailbone. Molly experimented with different food combinations for a while, with mixed results. She made a surprisingly nice soup of berries, chicken and leaves from the Tankernut Tree, but followed it up with an unappetizing mixture made of crushed Tankernuts and water, which she thought would be a paste sort of like peanut butter, but actually tasted more like wood glue. But continually thinking of new ways to do things that were already new in and of themselves, was exhausting. Before long the vast array of wholly unfamiliar tasks became taxing and without discussing it, they'd both given up their exercises.

The worst of it was that Molly's horse had quickly caught on to her lack of experience as a rider, and was enjoying himself immensely by traveling at whatever pace and in whatever direction struck his fancy. Hatch, meanwhile, seemed to have an excellent command of his mount. The difficulty made progress both painfully slow and miserably unpleasant, with much quarreling between the children. Hatch tried not to think more highly of himself for having mastered riding so much more quickly than Molly, but he didn't have much success. Why such bright children and wise cats didn't think to switch horses is anyone's guess. We'll be charitable and chalk it up to weariness. The cats did a decent job keeping the party on course, working in a sort of sheepdog capacity to corral Molly's stubborn pony. This made Seamus very irritable.

One day, as he was attempting to prod the horse away from a gangle bush he'd decided to eat, and finding himself steadfastly ignored, Seamus hissed in frustration and swiped a claw at the horse's hind leg, hoping to produce a reaction. A reaction is just what he got. The startled steed launched into action immediately and tore away into the woods as if lions were chasing him, a terrified Molly clinging desperately to his mane as he disappeared. Hatch didn't waste a moment. Wheeling his horse around with surprising skill, he shot after her. For the few, terrifying moments that followed, the two ponies and their small riders caused quite the stir in that quiet forest, crashing through the underbrush at a speed that must have surprised even the ponies.

Hatch instinctively leaned forward to keep a low profile and protect himself from the tree branches whipping across his face. Molly simply clung to her horse's neck in wide-eyed terror, letting out a little scream now and then as her bursting lungs allowed. The pony, by this time, seemed to be running for the sheer exhilaration of it, driven by some internal urge the source of which he'd forgotten entirely. After a while he began to dimly wonder what was happening, and slowed his pace to consider. The pony kept doggedly going in the same direction, but now at a trot. This gait was even more jarring for Molly than the full-on sprint had been, and it took a great deal of self-control to keep her seat. The change in speed gave Hatch a chance to catch up and he pulled up beside her, leaning over and deftly grasping the pony's reigns. This ought to have been enough to stop that headstrong horse, but he merely tossed his head and wrested them back, trotting determinedly onward.

At just that moment, both ponies and children suddenly found themselves in the open air, having emerged into a large grassy clearing. For Molly's mount, the change of scenery seemed to satisfy whatever instinct he'd been obeying. Deciding that this was what he had been meaning to get to all along, he stopped abruptly, dislodging Molly, who landed unceremoniously on her back beside him in the turf. Hatch slid down the side of his mount and helped her up. For a moment they stood wordlessly, attempting to catch their breath and assess the bodily damage. Molly was bruised and scratched from head to toe, with bits of branches and leaves clinging to her hair and clothes. Hatch was not much better off. It was in this disheveled state that the cats found them when they caught up a moment later.

"Thank goodness you're alright!" Melody shouted as she shot gracefully out of the forest, Seamus following a step behind. "You frightened us!"

Molly half laughed, half groaned in response. She was still quite shaken, but recovering her good humor as the relief of being alive set in. "I didn't think I'd come out of that in one piece. What on earth happened?"

"It was all my fault," Seamus said remorsefully. "I startled him. That confounded animal... what was Eldon thinking, saddling us with a dimwit pony like that?"

They decided unanimously to take a rest and regroup. Hatch tied the horses to nearby trees and Molly stretched out on the grass, groaning as she discovered new bruises and bumps.

"How far off course do you think we've gotten?" Hatch asked as he gingerly settled down beside her.

"Not far," Seamus said. "Anyway, it will be easy to get back to where we were. Those blasted ponies made a trail a blind baby could follow. We'd better hope the police aren't out looking for us yet. We might as well have hung a sign announcing our location."

"Then we shouldn't follow it back," said Molly. "What if they *are* looking for us? It wouldn't do to be found in the very spot they're sure to look."

This was an excellent bit of thinking on her part and Seamus made sure to tell her so before they set about the problem of getting back to where things had gone wrong, while avoiding any further disturbance to the landscape. Seamus didn't think it should pose much difficulty, as cats have an excellent innate sense of direction. They merely needed to be sure to keep their backs to the sun and steer clear of their previous route by a few meters. By his calculations they would be back on the intended route within fifteen minutes. After a rest and a drink of water, they clambered back onto the ponies (with considerable hesitation on Molly's part) and set out with the cats leading the way.

Molly's steed, having had enough adventure for the day, submitted cheerfully to her directions, and within a few minutes the outlook of the whole party had improved significantly. This revived exuberance was, however, short-lived. Half an hour into the journey, Seamus was becoming irritable, having clearly miscalculated how far out of the way they'd gone. Nothing around them seemed familiar and his normally keen instincts felt strangely off-kilter. Melody, too, was feeling oddly uneasy. Molly's stiffness was setting in something fierce, and Hatch was encountering that wave of exhaustion that so often follows on the heels of a departing adrenaline rush. Still, they plodded on as the minutes turned to hours.

Every now and then, Seamus would say, "Ah! Just as I suspected, that's where we went wrong," and adjust course. Everyone felt much better when he said these sorts of things, at least for a while. Eventually, even his aplomb began to fade, and he lapsed into silence. As you are no doubt aware, cats really do have an uncanny ability to know exactly where they are and where they're going, so it was with no small measure of bewilderment that Melody stopped in her tracks as the sun was setting.

"We are really quite lost," she said candidly.

Those words, spoken aloud in the forest, had a strange effect on her companions. Until that moment, all the travelers had entertained a lingering hope that there was still some chance of getting back on track. Now the truth seemed obvious. Whether through some momentary lapse on the part of the cats or because some strange magic lingered in those woods we may never know, but the fact was, the little weary group of children and animals was absolutely, without question, impossibly lost.

～

Molly and Hatch had been traveling for nearly two days and were already well on the way to muddling their part of the plan quite badly by the time Eldon arrived back at the capital. Knowing that the children would be discovered missing within the week, but counting on at least a few days before his connection to the disappearance became known, he drove his Council coach boldly into the city. The cats had urged him to sneak in at night, but Eldon knew that a government official breaking the law was least likely to get caught if he appeared brazen and confident all the time, a trick the government officials in your world discovered long ago. What he could not have known was that Charlie Wilson had reported everything he saw at the Holland house the day after Melody had filed her *Nothing of Interest* weekly report, or that news of the children's disappearance and his own part in it had reached the capital a full six hours before he did.

What he did know was that on entering the pub where he planned to meet his comrade – the other Ardenian soldier from the night of the children's kidnapping – he was met only by whispers and distrustful glances from the patrons. This was not unusual (he *was* a government agent after all), but it felt far more sinister this time. Eldon tried to tell himself that it was just nerves, sat down at the bar and ordered a beer. He was a lawman himself and knew that many a criminal had been caught simply because they got nervous and bolted too soon. The bartender, a man named Pudge, fetched the drink and set it down on the bar.

"Mr. Holcombe, isn't it?" he asked. "There was a cop in here to see you earlier."

Eldon took a draught of the beer and tried not to hurry in his response. "Oh? Did he leave his name?"

Pudge looked at the ceiling for a moment, trying to remember. "A Lieutenant Spencer, if I remember correctly. He was only here a moment. Left this note for you." He held out a sealed envelope he'd retrieved from his pocket. Eldon broke the seal and extracted a folded note:

Sorry, old pal. Rain check on dinner tonight. Got to get down to the garden before dark. Two of my saplings are in danger of getting caught in the frost tonight I'm afraid. Mr. H has everything prepared for your arrival home. Cheers! – S

Eldon glanced around the bar. Tossing a coin Pudgeward by way of payment, he stood up and strode out the door, chucking the note into the fire on his way. He must leave town immediately. The contents of the note made it clear he could not even stop at home. They'd be waiting for him there. Mr. H could only be the constable, Colonel Hampton Conway, as foul a man as any Eldon had met during his stay in Druinor. If he was at the house, Eldon and the children were already found out.

The street was empty when he exited the pub, and Eldon allowed himself an ill-informed sigh of relief. Leaving the coach and horses standing out front, he slipped into the alley next to the pub, where he was met by a full squad of the Emperor's Guard, including Conway himself, who greeted him with a greasy smile. Eldon didn't even have time to draw his sword, before a pair of gruff hands seized him from behind, pinning him against the wall. In the blink of an eye he found himself bound and deposited in the back of another dark-curtained government coach, bouncing along the cobbled roads into the heart of the city.

The jig was apparently up.

5

⁓

THE WASTELAND WALL

When Molly opened her eyes the next morning, for one delicious moment, all seemed quite well with the world. Her groggy mind drank in the warm sun and sweet scents of the forest. Then she attempted to sit up and discovered that her muscles were a hundred times stiffer and sorer than they had been the previous day. She let a sharp cry escape her lips, waking her weary companions in a very disagreeable fashion. Thus, the discouraged little group of adventurers began their second day as a miserably lost little group of adventurers.

They had a quick breakfast of bread and water (which on this day lacked all the delightful flavor of adventure it had boasted a mere 24 hours earlier). After more than a few sharp words and trodden on tails, the disgruntled crew took up their journey again, not at all sure where they ought to be headed.

"We've got to go *somewhere*," Seamus had pointed out,

"just sitting here waiting for the police to come marching in won't do."

They spent the better part of the day trudging along and making a brave effort to spare one another's feelings by keeping silent. Hatch was mildly encouraged to look up and see that nothing looked familiar. It wasn't evidence that they were back on the right track, but at least they weren't going in circles anymore, which marginally decreased their chances of being caught. Molly's thoughts were less cheerful, as she reflected drably that the mission had gone wrong remarkably early on. She wasn't familiar enough with adventures yet to know that when things look very bad, they often begin to look up in surprising ways (or that they usually get significantly worse first.)

It was a dreary sort of day, gray and damp, always promising but never delivering rain. The sun hung tiredly in the sky, looking half hearted, but still managing to burn the children's arms and foreheads infuriatingly. It was in this humor that our dear droopy heroes spent the morning and early afternoon. Molly's pony must have sensed the change in mood, as he allowed himself to be steered, though he still plodded along at a pace of his own choosing. Hatch was several yards ahead and just out of sight of his companions when they heard him say, "Oh!"

A moment later, the whole group stumbled out of the trees and found themselves staring across a vast expanse of desert. Each of them instinctively knew that they were in the one place they had meant to avoid. This was the edge of the Wasteland.

⌒

Eldon was surprised to find that he hadn't been hanged. Upon being deposited into the government coach outside the pub, he had taken it for granted that the gallows would be the next stop. The justice system of Druinor was highly efficient and hanging criminals prior to trial had been found to save much time and many legal fees. Even now, when Eldon awoke in a small cell many floors underground, deep in the capital city of Druinor, it seemed highly unlikely that his execution had been stayed. But Eldon's powers of deduction had always been strong. He reasoned that no version of Paradise could include such a vicious headache, nor quite so many sour smells, as he now encountered. Being a devout disciple of Ealdor, it never crossed his mind that his soul's destination would be any other place than Paradise, and thus he reasoned himself still alive.

Finding his expectation of certain death to be not quite so certain had an encouraging effect on his outlook, so that while any other man might have despaired upon waking in such a hopeless place, Eldon was downright cheerful. He felt his chances of saving the children, while still very small, were greatly improved by his continued existence. Realizing that this situation was at best temporary, he lost no time in setting his mind the problem at hand: escape.

Eldon began by conducting a thorough investigation of his surroundings. His cell was small, dark and damp. It was longer than it was wide, just barely accommodating the dirty cot along the back wall. At the front, a thick door sweated the grime of a hundred dark years in the bowels of an enchanted city. A small barred window in the door allowed him a limited view outside the cell. Peering through it, he saw that his cell was in the wall of a deep, rectangular pit. Directly outside his door was a narrow catwalk, dimly lit by torches placed at equal distances along its banister, and beyond that a wide chasm. On the opposite side, rows of cell doors, floor upon floor, stretched as far upward and as far downward as he could see.

Eldon instantly recognized the dreadful abyss in which he found himself. As a law enforcement officer, he was familiar with all the Druinian prisons, of which there were many. This one was Kalgren. It was famous for inducing despair in its inhabitants, who were kept in endless rows and columns of cells plunging deep into the earth. For added flavor, the guards were notoriously corrupt and violent. Eldon processed all this information coolly. He returned to the cot, closed his eyes and allowed himself a few deep breaths, as he waited for revelation. But none came.

⸎

Molly and Hatch were fascinated by the wall. Even with their practical upbringing and the heavy task placed on their shoulders, they were still children. Eldon had said it was glass-like, but that description did it no justice whatsoever. Far from being merely transparent, the wall was simultaneously invisible and fantastically obvious. Looking directly into it, one couldn't believe it was there at all. The children could see so clearly and so far into the wasteland, they could make out individual grains of sand., some of it ambling along in what could only be a strong breeze, though the air where they stood was perfectly still. The wall was nigh invisible head-on, but from the corners of their eyes, the children could sense it quivering and sparking with a tense energy. The feeling was like the one you get when you've forgotten someone's name, but you know it's lingering just barely outside the edges of your memory.

The wall was nearly buzzing with some unidentifiable force, as if it might burst at any moment. It seemed likely to give them a severe jolt if they touched it, and yet they could hardly resist doing just that if only to make sure it really existed. Whatever magic hung over that place, Hatch thought, a person would be wise not to linger there too long. Eventually Molly reached out her hand. She had expected the wall to be cold and hard, but found it was warm, soft but unyielding, practically alive. Before she had time to wonder at this, another surprise drew the children's attention.

While they'd been staring in wonder at the Wasteland, a figure had been approaching slowly, emerging from the tree line so silently that even the cats didn't notice him until he was nearly upon them. When he was close enough to reach out and touch Hatch, he cleared his throat and all four travelers visibly started. Melody even darted behind Hatch's legs.

"Apologies, friends," the visitor said with a deep bow. "I was certain you heard me approach and did not intend to frighten you so."

Seamus made a show of visibly relaxing but said nothing. In fact, he surprised the children very much by turning slowly in a circle, before settling down comfortably and appearing to fall asleep in the sun. Hatch stared at him in confusion. Molly, on the other hand, saw immediately that the encounter would be left up to the children to handle. If they still had a chance of passing themselves off as ordinary Druinians, it would only be preserved by their appearing to believe that the cats were ordinary pets.

She laughed a breezy laugh and curtseyed politely. "Our fault!" she said. "We ought to have heard you coming. Mother always says I'm *horribly* inattentive."

The man was very short – likely a dwarf, Seamus thought, though the children had never heard of those – and quite unsavory in appearance. His countenance was greasy and scarred, and he smelled of heat and sweat. The contrast between his rough, unwashed appearance and his courteous greeting was jarring.

"Fascinating, isn't it?" he said, nodding toward the Wasteland.

"Hm?" said Hatch, who had caught on at last. "Oh, yes that. I suppose," He said with a disinterested shrug. The children were quite used to behaving like dull Druinian children and slid naturally back into the role.

The visitor studied him for a moment. "Pardon me if I seem forward, young master, but what might bring two fine children such as yourself to these parts?" he asked.

Molly smiled disarmingly. "We're lost," she said simply. "Our donkey wandered off. Have you seen it?" Her performance was flawless and Hatch gave her such an admiring glance that it would have made her blush if she'd seen it.

The stranger seemed amused by her explanation, for he chuckled in a manner that did very little to put the children at ease. After a moment, he began to laugh outright, baring his noisome yellow teeth to the sun. The children glanced at each other, alarmed.

"Come now!" exclaimed the increasingly unpleasant dwarf. "Come now, children, what do you take me for?"

"I'm afraid I don't..." Hatch began, but the laughter had fled the dwarf's face as quickly as it had come, leaving in its place a menacing glare that stopped him short.

"Well isn't that perfect?" he sneered, dropping all pretense of courtesy. "Two good little children – dimwitted little Druinian pups - out here in the middle of nowhere. Isn't that just wonderful? No, no master cat, you needn't bother." This last bit he'd directed at Seamus, who had begun to rise. "I've no idea what your business is here, nor have I the slightest curiosity on that point, only I can see that whatever it is, you've gone to some lengths to keep it secret. And that means we're not likely to be joined by anyone else, are we?"

As he said this, the stranger snapped his fingers and a swarm of dangerous looking dwarves emerged from the forest behind him and descended upon them with astonishing speed. Molly felt herself shoved roughly to the ground while strong hands bound hers behind her back. With her face pressed against the earth she could just make out Hatch receiving a similar treatment from a brawny dwarf straddling his back.

For a moment the air was filled with the sound of the scuffle and angry exclamations from both the dwarves and the children. In the midst of it, the children heard the voice of the first dwarf, presumably their leader.

"After the cats, you fools!" He shouted. "They're getting away!" And several small dwarf feet pounded away into the wood.

Now securely bound, Molly was dragged to her feet again. A hand in her back propelled her forward until she was half running, though toward what she couldn't tell. The children could only just see each other as they were jostled and shoved in a crowd of dwarves, all laughing and talking merrily about their conquest.

"These two will fetch a pretty penny!" cackled the dwarf nearest Molly's ear.

"That they will!" came a cheerful response.

"Quite the catch, these young'uns. Quite the catch indeed!"

All the while the whole procession made steady progress

away from the Wasteland and into the woods.

After a while, however, the talking died down as the party trudged along. They continued like this for a very long time. So long, in fact, that Molly had to be prodded quite violently to keep her from falling asleep as she walked. Hatch tried manfully not to appear weak to his captors, and for some time marched with his head high, ignoring their jabs and taunts. But after many hours of this treatment, his feet aching and his eyelids growing heavy, even he began to wonder if he could go much farther.

They had been walking for many hours – all night in fact – when they finally arrived at their destination. They entered the mouth of what initially appeared to be a very small cave. But when their eyes had adjusted to the dim torchlight inside, they saw that in each wall there lay several more dark openings leading, presumably, to deeper caves and passages. It was down one of these passages that several of the dwarves headed with Molly in tow, whilst Hatch, much to the children's horror, was led down another. The cats were nowhere to be seen. The children were, Molly realized with a jolt, completely alone.

6

IN THE DWARF WARREN

Let us leave our dejected heroes for a moment, the one in prison, the others taken captive, and pay a visit to another gentleman, about whom you've no doubt been wondering. You know by now, reader, that Eldon was not alone in his 12-year quest, but accompanied by another soldier from Arden. That man's name was Brogan and he was a kind and honorable man. He, like Eldon, had worked in Druinian law enforcement, as a policeman by the name of Lieutenant Reuben Spencer. He maintained a low rank in the capital city's famously corrupt police force, allowing him to become privy to types of information a council-member, such as Eldon, would not have access to. By these means he had discovered that the plan had been compromised and attempted to warn Eldon, though his warning had come too late.

After leaving the note for Eldon in the pub, Brogan had proceeded to a predetermined meeting place – a flat near the outskirts of town. This neighborhood was not frequented by police and the flat was situated on a hill, allowing them to observe anyone approaching from nearly any direction. Here he had waited for his friend, alternately pacing and straining his eyes toward the streets until there could no longer be any doubt that Eldon had been taken. After that he waited an hour more, and finally, when wisdom would allow him to stay no longer, he made his escape. And a very narrow escape it was, too.

⁓

Colonel Hampton Conway may well have been the vilest man who prowled the streets of Druinor. But if he had competition for this title, it was in the person of Captain Steven Snyder, a policeman under his command. Snyder was a man of singularly unsavory character and appearance. He was known among cops and criminals alike as "the Weasel." No one knew whether this nickname referred to his behavior or his visage, which did bear an uncanny resemblance to that unpleasant animal. Most likely it was both. Either way, Snyder wore this nickname as a badge of honor. I have heard that the local weasel population, on the other hand, found the comparison highly offensive.

Snyder had been one of those present at Eldon's arrest outside the pub. He had derived great pleasure from it, tempered only by his disappointment at not having been allowed to beat the man to death, or to any degree at all. Snyder was both uncommonly clever and unimaginably cruel. Such a combination was not unusual in Druinor, as Marlowe's Imagination Tax was far more lenient toward those who used their imaginations to do harm. Snyder knew, therefore, that capturing Eldon was only a piece of the puzzle on the way to the emperor's true goal: apprehending the escaped children. He neither knew nor cared why these two might be important, only that whoever facilitated their capture would be in the emperor's good graces. He began, therefore, to turn his thoughts toward that task the very moment the prison coach pulled away from the pub.

There had been something strange, he thought, about the arrest, though it had gone entirely according to plan. It had been Snyder who had seen Eldon re-enter the capital, followed him and had sent word to Hampton in time to lay the trap. The traitor had fallen into the trap far more easily than any of them had imagined possible, and more quickly. That was the strange part. No sooner had they taken up their position, in fact, than Eldon rounded the corner and stumbled right into them. He had entered the city confidently, as if he had as much right to be out in the open as any other government official. Clearly he didn't think word of his treason had reached the capital yet. Why, then, had he come out of the pub so quickly after entering? He certainly hadn't been inside long enough for a drink. And why, upon exiting, had he ducked into an alley? They had assumed they would ambush him as he passed by.

The only possible conclusion was that someone inside had warned him. This idea gave Snyder a great deal of pleasure. If a co-conspirator was still inside, at least one interrogation would be required. There was nothing the Weasel loved so well as a rousing interrogation.

There were quite a few people in the pub, their faces all struggling to hide the fearful distrust that his presence generally inspired. He decided to start with Pudge, the bartender.

Pudge was an honest man and a good one, given the circumstances. He lived comfortably by minding his own business and not causing trouble. But he had been raised in

Druinor, and as such he knew very little of high ideals such as courage and nobility. It took very little work for Snyder to extract from him the information he needed. Despite his cooperation, Snyder delivered a few vicious blows to the poor bartender's head, without which he would have had a thoroughly disappointing afternoon.

Within moments he knew that Eldon's visit had been preceded by that of a policeman named Lt. Spencer, that Spencer had left a sealed message for the traitor, and that he had departed immediately upon reading its contents.

It just so happened that Snyder was familiar with Spencer and already bore him no small amount of ill will. Somehow, Spencer had managed to lead a successful career on the police force without ever engaging in extortion, violence, or any of the other criminal behaviors that were so common among Druinian police they were practically considered policy. This was irksome enough, but even worse was the fact that Spencer never showed the proper amount of fear (or any fear, for that matter) in the Weasel's presence. Snyder found this unnerving, and he was not accustomed to being unnerved.

It was, therefore, with great relish that he set out to find Brogan. Though he knew nothing of Brogan and Eldon's meeting place, he knew plenty about the roads in and out of the city. He sent officers to each of them immediately and, by pure coincidence, chose for himself the very road Brogan himself had taken.

As fate would have it, he missed Brogan by a mere two minutes.

❧

Molly spent a disconsolate night in the care of the dwarves. They propelled her into the depths of the caves, past winding passages and dark doorways. As the dwarves hurried her past a larger opening, Molly caught a glimpse of armed guards and a group of children huddled together. Their small dirty faces watched her with lackluster eyes as she passed. From this she surmised that this band of dwarves made kidnapping something of a profession. She had hoped to share quarters with some of the other children, and from them learn something more about the dwarves, perhaps even her whereabouts. Instead, she was deposited in an empty cell dug out of cold rock and left there alone. The corridor outside her door, like the cave itself, was entirely unlit. It took much longer than usual for Molly's eyes to adjust to the oppressive darkness, but when they did there was nothing to see but stony walls.

The long night's walk, coupled with the despair of capture and separation from Hatch, proved to be more than her small body could bear and she fell into a deep sleep, unhindered by hunger or the cold dirt floor.

Hatch, meanwhile, was having a very different experience. On his side of the warren there were no empty cells, so he found himself sharing a dimly lit space with bars across the entrance. It was occupied by three other children: two boys and a girl. He was as exhausted as Molly, but between the gnawing of his stomach and the added stimulation of torchlight and companions, he did not rest nearly so well as she. The other children were poor company, though. Being Druinian through and through, any vestiges of natural childish curiosity in them had long since been stamped out. Thus they were wholly uninterested in the newcomer. Indeed they barely acknowledged his arrival and, upon being heartily questioned by him, offered short, unhelpful responses.

"How long have you been here?" Hatch asked the boy

nearest him, whose name was Rob.

The boy only stared at him stupidly.

"In the cave I mean," Hatch clarified after a moment's pause. Rob glanced around the cave as if noticing it for the first time and shrugged.

"Dunno," he said in a tone that betrayed as much interest as if he had been asked whether it might rain on Thursday.

"What are they going to do with us?" Hatch asked.

"Who?" asked the girl, who was called Alice.

"Why those wretched little men of course!" Hatch exclaimed.

Alice looked mildly surprised, as if she had given this concept no thought whatsoever. "Dunno," she shrugged.

Hatch couldn't tell if these children were particularly unresponsive, even for Druinian children, or if he had simply grown accustomed to the sharp contrast of Molly's company in the few short days since they had met. At the thought of Molly, a sharp pang of fear pierced him.

He moved on to a question he felt sure they would be able to answer. "How did you get here?"

Rob looked at him as if he were the dull one and answered simply, "Through the tunnels."

Hatch stared at him in disbelief. Could it be possible that he had grown up among children such as these? How had he escaped madness? It occurred to him for a brief moment that maybe he hadn't – perhaps he was mad after all. But no, he could never have dreamed up someone like Molly.

"No, I mean..." he paused, searching for a way to frame the question that might result in its being answered. "Where were you when they captured you and brought you here? You weren't always here with... them. Were you? They must have brought you here from somewhere."

"At the Institute of course," said Ben, the boy who had not yet spoken. "Weren't you?" And in those few words Ben both provided the only remotely helpful answer presented thus far, and also demonstrated the first shred of curiosity about Hatch, thereby endearing him greatly to our hero. This one piece of information made the children infinitely more interesting to him, as he had never met anyone who had been in the Institute before (save for all the adults, of course, none of whom cared to recollect the details), and was supremely curious about it.

From that point forward, Hatch directed his questions solely to Ben, who seemed to be the brightest of the bunch. He was a far cry from clever, but showed a capacity for cleverness that his companions appeared to wholly lack. Hatch questioned him about the Institute and about his capture until Ben tired of the interrogation and, without warning, rolled over and went to sleep.

From the interview, Hatch formed a vague picture of the Institute being rather like a giant version of his village schoolhouse. He tried to determine if it was a very bad school, but Ben didn't understand the question. Indeed, Hatch gleaned more information from comments made in passing than any of Ben's answers themselves, but slowly he came to understand at least that punishments at the Institute were severe and almost entirely arbitrary. He discovered that his three cellmates had been outside the school grounds as a part of some sort of penalty (the details of which were unclear) when they'd been waylaid by the dwarves. As Hatch drifted off to sleep the thought crossed his mind that the children, despite being currently held captive by dwarves, had expressed no desire to be returned to the Institute.

So our friends passed their first night in captivity, little dreaming of the woes that would yet befall them.

〰

Like the cats, Brogan had tried to convince Eldon not to return to the capital. Fleeing alone now, he cursed his friend's obstinacy. For all his bravery, once an idea had entered Eldon's mind, he rarely allowed cooler heads than his own to prevail. Now he'd been captured and would surely soon be hanged.

Sometime in the middle of the night, Brogan reached the cabin in the woods where Eldon and the children had stayed and was relieved to find that the enchantments around it had not been tampered with. It was still, for the moment, safe from Druinian eyes.

It had taken him several days to reach it, though it wasn't far from the capital. Eldon's disappearance had made him wary, so Brogan had taken a circuitous route, waiting to approach until he was satisfied that he had not been followed. Upon entering, he immediately sat down at a rolltop desk in the living room, unlocked it and withdrew several stacks of papers – maps and government files which he and Eldon had secreted away from the capital. Most of these he used as kindling for the fire that evening, but he put aside a small portion of them to take with him.

Among those he kept was one that stood out from the rest. It didn't bear the emperor's stamp, nor was it printed on a crisp clean sheet from the government warehouse. Instead, it resembled a fragment of ancient parchment. It was nearly blank but for a few lines scrawled by a delicate hand, written in verse. This he placed in the satchel with the others, but gingerly for fear of damaging it.

He did not spend long in the safety of the cabin –

enough time to eat something and rest for a few hours – before setting out to find the children. Though he had little hope of seeing his friend again, he left a note written in code to tell him where he had gone. If fate willed it, Eldon would catch up to him soon.

⤚⤙

Molly awoke in the unnatural darkness of the cave. She had no idea how long she had slept or what time it was. She was aware only of being cold, sore, ravenously hungry and so very lonely. She longed to be reunited with Hatch. If they could only get a few moments to talk together, she was sure they could come up with a plan of some sort. The cave was so deathly quiet and her loneliness so intense that eventually she could bear it no longer.

She called out, hoping to draw one of her captors into conversation. She knew not what she hoped to gain by this, but any information would be better than none. It was only after multiple calls were met with hollow silence that she began to suspect she was quite alone. Her first bright blaze of hope at this discovery was immediately dampened when she recalled the thick maze of tunnels through which she had been led here, and correctly surmised that it was for this reason that her captors had felt confident leaving no sentry at the mouth of her cave. Still, she reasoned, it would be better to risk getting caught, or lost forever, than to die by doing nothing at all.

So, slowly at first, but with increasing confidence, she wandered the warren unmolested for quite some time. Evidently, the dwarves had no fear of their inmates escaping.

Molly could not remember how long it had taken to arrive at her cell exactly, but she guessed at about half an hour. She recalled passing many locked cells full of children on the way. So she was alarmed when hours of wandering seemed to bring her no closer to the surface, or even to an occupied part of the warren. It seemed that every tunnel entrance only led to endlessly more dark and empty tunnels. Molly was armed, however, with the natural curiosity and fearlessness that sometimes protects young children from being as frightened as a wiser person might be.

The truth was that the dwarves had simply opted for magic in lieu of physical restraints. They had enchanted the door of her cell so that even if she wandered out of it, the cave would continue to grow and expand inward toward the earth, but never toward the surface. The dwarves' cruel spell caused its victims to become more and more lost until they expired from hunger and despair deep in the heart of the earth. Of course, they could find her in an instant if they chose, using another type of enchantment. In this way, prisoners who were deemed valueless could be disposed of with little trouble, and those who might bring a profit could be retrieved with the smallest effort.

Much of the magic employed in those days was of a parasitic nature – that is, it fed off of and reflected the psyche of its intended target – and this enchantment was no exception. Its effectiveness was strengthened exponentially by the despair it induced in prisoners. Of course, the dwarves who cast it could not have anticipated its effect on a child who was immune to Marlowe's spells. Although she had been miserable when she had gone to sleep, Molly was not prone to despair. The same instinct that had motivated her to leave the cell had given her a sort of reckless confidence. As she wandered through more and more tunnels and caverns, Molly even found herself smiling as she imagined the dwarves' frustration, should they try to find her.

The enchanted prison had never encountered this sort of prisoner before and the magic began to weaken in the face of it. After a while, Molly began to wander up toward the surface after all. She felt the change in the incline of the floor and understood instinctively that she was headed in the right direction. As she passed out of the enchantment's grip, Molly felt as if a dark veil had been lifted from her eyes. Not long after that, she began to see actual light coming from one of the caverns ahead of her. As she approached, she heard a dim mumbling which soon materialized into voices and words. Pausing only to take off her shoes, Molly crept slowly toward the door of the lit cavern and stopped in the darkness just outside of it to listen.

"I tell you, there's something amiss about those two," said a voice that she recognized as belonging to the dwarf they had first encountered at the wall. "They're not like the rest of the little brats."

"So?" answered a deeper voice. "What difference does it make Dudley? A slave's a slave. You'll not get a higher price for their brains."

"Just the opposite," said a third dwarf. "As likely as not, you'll get no price at all. No one wants a slave what thinks for itself. That'll get the whole household in trouble."

From this exchange Molly saw clearly what was intended for the children's future.

"That's just my point, isn't it?" the first voice, presumably owned by Dudley, answered. "They'll be more trouble than they're worth at the market."

"Might as well kill them and get it over with then," remarked the second voice.

"We may still be able to turn a profit if we're sharp about

it." Dudley said. "Seems to me two kids with brains and 'magination would be of some interest to the Emp'rer."

"A reward!" roared the third dwarf, his voice thick with greed. "Well that's a good bit of thinking Dudley! We'll turn them in!"

This fate seemed even less desirable to Molly than the other. In the short time she had spent with Seamus and Melody, Molly had developed a healthy fear of the Druinian government and realized that she would have preferred to be in the hands of whatever sort of person bought children as slaves than in the emperor's.

One thing was clear: she must find Hatch right away and escape this place.

The dwarves talked for some time more, becoming more and more raucous as more and more beer flowed (this was the dinner time custom for dwarves) until one by one they fell asleep and began to snore loudly.

Molly waited with excruciating patience until she was convinced that none were still stirring and crept past the wide opening of the cavern. She paused just long enough to get a look at them, sprawled in unflattering positions all over the room like so many dirty socks strewn about her bedroom floor back home. Disgusted, she moved on.

It wasn't long before she reached the mouth of the cave where they had first entered the day before. The evening sunlight was streaming in, and Molly could smell the forest just outside: the fresh green scent of grass, the woody scent of pine and oak, and a cool floral breeze flowing between them. After a night and day lost in the dank passages below, this had a maddening effect on Molly, and for one second she considered running out to meet the fresh air. But not a moment could be wasted. She quickly found the passage down which Hatch had been taken and headed down it, peering cautiously into each door she passed looking for his blonde head. Hatch's cell was not nearly so deep in the earth as hers had been, so it did not take her long at all to find it. He and the three other children were sound asleep.

"Hatch," she whispered urgently. When he didn't stir, Molly tried again, raising her voice as much as she dared. "Hatch!"

Hatch still didn't stir. When boys go to sleep, they are quite serious about it. Alice, however, woke with a start and looked around. Seeing Molly's pale face looking through the bars, she jumped to her feet.

"Please," Molly started in a whisper, but it was too late.

Alice screamed, not so much out of fear as out of a general proclivity toward meanness. Druinians are taught from a young age to hate letting other people get away with anything.

"Help!" Alice screamed, ignoring Molly's pleas. "*Heeeelp!* There's a girl who got loose! Come and get her! Guards!"

By this time all the children had been aroused. Rob and Ben looked confused and irritated. Hatch sprang into action immediately, clapping his hand over Alice's mouth, but the damage was done. Molly could hear the loud *clomp clomp clomp* of half a dozen pair of dwarf shoes running down the corridor. Luckily, they were coming from farther inside the warren rather than the entrance.

"Run!" Hatch shouted as Alice writhed and spluttered in his grasp. "Molly run!"

And with one wild, pleading look, willing him to somehow free himself and follow, Molly ran. She ran like she had never run in her life before, nearly blind from fear and frustration.

In mere moments she burst forth from the cave's entrance into the warm twilit forest. She kept running, tears streaming down her face, cursing herself for having failed to rescue Hatch. The dwarves followed her but in the confusion she disappeared easily into the wood. Before long a fight broke out among them about who was to blame for her escape. None of them knew who threw the first blow, but dwarves love a good brawl. They quickly abandoned the search for Molly and fell to punching one another until they were all black and blue before sullenly disappearing back underground.

Molly did not stray far from the dwarf warren after her escape. She found a place from which she could see the entrance without being seen, and watched it closely. She spent the rest of that day and the cold night that followed watching futilely for any movement.

She had no idea what she would do if the dwarves came out with Hatch in tow. By morning Molly was so exhausted, frightened, and hungry that she felt she could not have moved if an entire horde of dwarves and wild beasts bore down upon her. Overpowering any one of them was certainly out of the question. Molly's small body was not accustomed to the punishment it had endured over the last few days. Nonetheless, leaving Hatch to the mercy of the dwarves was unthinkable. Where would she go, anyway, without him or the cats? So she waited.

Her wait soon came to an abrupt end. As Molly sat staring tiredly at the entrance to the cave, she began to nod off, only to be awakened by the sound of feet running toward her from the direction of the forest. Before she was fully awake, she felt cold, powerful fingers grip the back of her neck and lift her to her feet. Crying out in pain she struggled against her captor, but to no avail.

In a moment, Molly had been turned around and found herself facing a tall, severe woman, whose features were contorted with rage. She grasped Molly's shoulders and began to shake her, much to Molly's astonishment.

"*What* has gotten into you, you little brat?" screamed the woman. "Half the faculty has been out looking for you. Where are the others? What did you think to accomplish, running away? Did you think you would ever be able to escape *me*?"

Molly only gaped at her, wholly unprepared to address this meaningless onslaught of questions and accompanying spittle. But her silence only enraged the woman further.

"Answer me!" she screamed, digging her long fingernails painfully into Molly's arms.

"I... I don't know what you're talking about," Molly stammered. "I think you've confused me with someone else."

The woman stopped shaking her and stared in disbelief. For a moment Molly began to think she might escape this brutish interrogator, but quickly saw that the woman's incredulity was not at herself for mistaking Molly's identity. Rather, she was so unaccustomed to being corrected, so infuriated that any child would dare question her, that she had been momentarily stunned into silence. Quite suddenly, she drew her right hand back and slapped Molly hard across the face.

The shock and pain dissolved what was left of poor Molly's internal fortitude and she, very understandably, began to cry. She was, after all, still a child. It seemed that no behavior would appease this tyrant of a woman, though. Far from pitying Molly, she merely looked disgusted.

"I swear, you'll live to regret this day, Alice Green," she spat. Spinning Molly around once more with shocking strength, she hooked one arm around her waist, hoisted her up and began to march determinedly through the woods, away from the dwarf warren. As she marched, she shouted, "I've found the girl!"

In a moment she was joined by two rough-looking men, one of whom easily took Molly from the woman's grasp. He placed one large hand over her mouth as he carried her onward. In a few moments they came upon three horses tied up, awaiting their owner's return. The man set Molly down momentarily, bound her hands and feet, and laid her over the backs of one of the horses.

"You stay and look for the boys!" shouted the woman to the other man, as she swung herself up onto the same horse. In this way, Molly, squeezed uncomfortably between the terrifying woman and the saddle horn, began her journey toward the Institute.

7

TWO VERY INTERESTING INTERVIEWS

During the few days Eldon had been in prison, he'd had no human contact, save for the daily meals delivered by other prisoners. He always greeted these prisoners warmly, but his greeting was never returned. The first time one had appeared, Eldon had rushed to the door to meet him, hoping for the smallest sliver of information.

"Hello friend," he called. The man might have been deaf for all the notice he paid him as he slid the plate through a slot in the door and shuffled on.

Eldon had tried again that evening – it was a different man at the window this time – and again the next morning to no avail. On his fourth attempt, the man gave a start at the sound of his voice and looked fearfully over his shoulder before scampering on to the next cell. So when he awoke on the fourth morning to the sound of a key turning the in the lock of his cell door, Eldon regarded it with not a little interest. He had felt certain that an interrogation of some sort would be forthcoming, assuming the children had not been caught. From what he knew of this prison, it was not likely to be an experience he'd relish. Eldon sat up quickly, his muscles tightening, his stomach shrinking. Yet his demeanor betrayed none of this. He leaned forward, resting his elbows on his knees and stared coolly at the door.

When it swung open, an enormous man ducked inside, carrying a cruel-looking club in one hand. His expression was that of a man whose sole joy in life was derived from torturing creatures smaller than himself. If you've ever been in a situation that calls for extreme fear on your part, you know that it is often at these moments that inexplicably mundane thoughts choose to make an appearance. As he surveyed the leering countenance of his soon to be tormentor, Eldon mused that the man was lucky to have found an occupation so perfectly matched to his hulking frame and apparently natural inclination for violent problem-solving. *I suppose the Institution knows its business,* he thought.

To his great surprise, however, the man proceeded only two steps into the cell and, without acknowledging Eldon, stood off to the side facing the door as if waiting for a high-ranking official to enter.

Perhaps, Eldon thought, they've sent a member of the Council who they think might be able to reason with me.

The truth, however, was far worse. A cloaked figure detached itself from the shadows and entered the cell, bringing with it a chill that settled over the whole room and a stench of decay so powerful that Eldon's eyes began to water. Instantly he knew his visitor's identity, and his skin grew cold. It was none other than Emperor Marlowe himself.

Eldon, who was an extraordinarily brave man under

most circumstances, felt a knot begin to form in his stomach.

Marlowe removed his hood to reveal a face that was human only in the most technical sense of the word. It was deeply scarred, bearing the marks of a hundred years of whatever dark ceremonies the man had endured to prolong his life, but noticeably devoid of any human expression. He was, for all intents and purposes, alive, though not in any meaningful way. This, at least, satisfied Eldon's curiosity on that point. He had more than once suspected that Marlowe was long dead and that the other members of government had kept it a secret in order to retain their stranglehold on the population.

Yet here Marlowe stood, staring at Eldon, a thin smile resting on his lips. Eldon simply stared back, his face maintaining a resolve that his quavering insides belied.

After a moment Marlowe opened his mouth, proving it to be the primary source of the foul odor.

"Kneel."

His voice was soft and low. It was a voice that, on anyone else, might have been considered pleasant, but when he spoke, it conjured images of rotting flesh, maggots and all manner of crawling, oozing things.

Eldon felt a nearly irresistible urge to obey. For one terrifying second, he thought his body might rebel and do as it was commanded without his leave. With great care not to allow a single twitch of the muscle that might betray his struggle, Eldon remained seated.

Marlowe's head moved nearly imperceptibly in the direction of the guard, who effortlessly lifted Eldon by the throat and held him in the air for what seemed like several minutes, though it could only have been a few seconds, before helpfully depositing him on his knees at Marlowe's feet. The emperor waited patiently while Eldon gasped for air.

Finally, Marlowe spoke again. "Mr. Holcombe, you have not been the loyal public servant your emperor has always believed you to be. You are, in fact, a traitor to the crown."

"I have served the true crown since my youth and I am loyal to it still," Eldon answered.

Marlowe smiled without mirth. "Ah, but Mr. Holcombe, there is only *one* crown. *Mine.*"

"I won't answer your questions," Eldon said. "I've been trained in Druinian torture by your own government. You may as well save your time and kill me."

"I haven't asked you any questions," Marlowe said quietly.

This was not what Eldon expected. He waited silently. The emperor suddenly leaned down and pulled Eldon's head close, so that only he could hear Marlowe's next few words.

"I am certain you are as good as your word in that area, my dear Eldon, and that you would put up a very inconvenient resistance to any questioning. Yes, I know your name, you needn't look so surprised. I know that you are a soldier of Arden, that you came here in pursuit of two little brats on the night that the Wasteland Wall materialized, and that you've spent the past twelve years guarding them from my eye."

Eldon could not have spoken now if he had wanted to. How had Marlowe acquired such a wealth of secret information? *No one* knew these things, except Brogan. A spike of cold fear entered his heart at the thought of his friend. Surely Brogan had been tortured to give up this knowledge. But Marlowe was not finished.

"I know that you recently secreted those two children out of their towns and have sent them back to Arden. Of course, I didn't need to be told why you chose now to do so. I'm as familiar with your country's prophecies as you are."

A great wave of sadness assailed Eldon as he thought what his friend must have had to endure in the pursuit of this intelligence. The truth was much more straightforward. Marlowe had been notified of the placement of all Ardenian children in Druinor, and when Charlie Wilson's report had revealed the disappearance of the children, Marlowe had known at once which two children they were. The only real trick had been learning Eldon's true identity, but in the end it had taken only some simple police work, a few dark spells, and a few fresh marks on the old wizard's abused body to accomplish this.

But to the man who had spent more than a decade cleverly concealing these things, Marlowe seemed to have an impossible quantity of knowledge. Under the withering magic of the emperor's gaze, Eldon was sure in his heart of hearts that it could have been obtained through no other means than the torture of his trusted companion.

"I didn't come here to ask you any questions," Marlowe had straightened up, and now spoke loudly enough that the guard could hear. "I came only to assure you that your quest has failed. The brats *will* be caught. My men are crawling the hills and valleys of Druinor. There are only a few routes your small friends could have taken. Really, Mr. Holcombe, I don't know what you were thinking sending two children and two cats… yes, I know about the cats too… off on their own in the wilderness. What happens to them now is entirely your fault, you know. They were unfortunate to be given such a derelict guardian as yourself."

In that moment, with Marlowe's dark presence and rancid breath overshadowing every other thought, Eldon believed him. All his brilliant plans seemed foolish now. As he listened to Marlowe's words, the absurdity of sending the children after Fairy Tale washed over him painfully. Nonetheless, he could never allow himself to crumble before this villain's eyes.

"You know nothing," he scoffed. "If you were so sure of yourself, you'd have killed me already."

Marlowe smiled cruelly. "I haven't the slightest intention of killing you. A loyal subject of Druinor, murdered without a trial? For shame. You will live out your days here and I wish them to be long indeed. I will make sure your stay is not lonely."

And with that he turned on his heel, leaving a crestfallen Eldon and a delighted guard alone in the cell. The guard, it seemed, did not have any urgent tasks which needed attending. He closed the door behind him, having every intention, Eldon realized, of spending some time reminding him why Kalgren Prison had such a dour reputation.

What Marlowe had failed to take into account, though, was the surprising power of his own absence. So dreadful was his presence that the instant he left the cell, the air cleared and Eldon's spirits began to improve. Perhaps Marlowe's enchantment had a more lasting effect on his Druinian subjects, but Eldon was a soldier of Arden, after all, where the people were happy and free. He felt his courage resurfacing before the door had even closed behind the emperor. So relieved was he, in fact, at the wizard's departure, so suddenly did the world right itself, that something like a mad exhilaration rose up in him and, as he stared into the monstrous face above him, manifested in the form of loud, unrestrained laughter. Suddenly it seemed to him that Marlowe had come for the express purpose of delivering very good news: *the children hadn't been caught, and Marlowe didn't know where they were!*

The guard was accustomed to pleading and groveling, and this giddy outburst both perplexed and annoyed him. He began his work with the usual vigor, but found it far less satisfying than usual (the victim remained downright cheery throughout the course of it!) and he gave up sooner than was his habit. He left the cell in a very foul mood – plotting, of course, what tools he would employ to ensure more success on his next visit.

Despite his manic joy, the guard's beating had taken a toll on Eldon, in both body and spirit, and as the adrenaline departed, he fell into a restless sleep.

When he opened his eyes again, he groaned in pain. While failing to attend to the guard's emotional needs, the beating had nonetheless been fairly sound and left Eldon badly bruised. As soon as the groan left Eldon's lips, a sound very near him caused him to spring to his feet, despite the screaming agony of his muscles. Assuming a defensive stance, he stared wide-eyed at the man who leaned with arms crossed against the opposite wall.

The man was tall, lean but muscular, and dark from the sun. A three-cornered hat sat atop his head at a jaunty angle. At first Eldon thought he must be a new prisoner, captured and left there while he slept, but the stranger did not appear in the least distressed. In fact, he wore a jocular grin and maintained an entirely relaxed posture as he watched Eldon attempt to make sense of the situation.

Could he be another guard? A questioner? But this man's eyes bore none of the dull cruelty that marked all of Marlowe's servants. After a few moments, it began to dawn on him. This could only be a member of the elusive Damascus Guard! Eldon had heard a great many far-fetched rumors about them, but had long suspected they were only a myth.

"Good morning Eldon!" the visitor said cheerfully. "Or evening, rather. It all runs together in here I imagine."

"Who are you? What are you doing here?" Eldon tensed further at the sound of his true name from yet another strange set of lips.

"Percival, at your service sir," said the man, removing his hat with a flourish and bowing deeply with the same jovial air. "Captain of the Damascus Guard. I've come to rescue you." He paused, before adding politely, "Assuming you've no pressing engagements here?"

Eldon regarded him warily. "Why? How? Wha…" he spluttered, not having regained his usual presence of mind.

Percival laughed. "It's alright, friend, you've nothing to fear from me. All your questions will be answered in time." And as he said it, he sat down on Eldon's cot, leaning back against the wall and placing both hands behind his head as thoroughly at ease as if he had been settling down on his own couch.

Eldon felt himself relax as well, wincing as the adrenaline subsided once again and the ache of his abused body returned.

"I'm afraid I don't understand at all, but if you are really a friend and not a foe, you are quite welcome here," he said, with the dignity of a man inviting a visitor to his home.

"We don't have long to talk," Percival said. "The guards here are diligent, as you know, so you'll have to save most of your questions for later. As I mentioned, I'm a member of the Damascus Guard. Surely you've heard of us?"

"Of course!" Eldon assented. "Though until now I never really believed you existed. I thought you might be another made up enemy, like anti-progs."

This seemed to please Percival. "And you, a high government official! Well that's fantastic. We're never sure how much is known about us, you know. We spread many of the rumors ourselves to muddy the waters a bit. Anyway, I overheard your conversation with Marlowe. You were already of some interest to us, but having discovered your true identity, it would be a great honor to be of service to you, not to mention great fun to deprive Marlowe of you."

Eldon did not know what to make of this strange man. "Sorry, you *overheard* my conversation with him? One doesn't just follow Marlowe around, listening over his shoulder."

"On the contrary," Percival answered. "One does exactly that."

Eldon continued to look at him skeptically until Percival grinned sheepishly. "Okay, not *exactly* that."

More inquiring silence.

"Well it's like this," Percival said. "We... the Maskies that is... discovered some time ago that we aren't subject to the same magic as the rest of our poor fellow citizens. It's probably similar for you, I imagine, being from Arden and all. All the spells and whatnot Marlowe uses to control the populace don't seem to work on us. They can't even detect when we're using imagination. We used to just try to keep it a secret and act like everyone else, but then we realized what a great disservice it was to do *nothing* with our freedom. We formed a little group, and decided to do what we could to overthrow Marlowe's empire. That's what we're always working toward."

Eldon felt a great joy well up in him at these words. For so long he had believed that he and Brogan were the sole dissidents in this dark country. "Go on!" he said breathlessly.

Percival did. "We began experimenting with different kinds of magic ourselves – not dark magic of course, just simple defensive stuff – and discovered that we weren't half bad. Eventually we learned to do some of the really tricky stuff... you know, invisibility and teleporting, walking through walls and doors, that sort of thing.

"Not long ago, we heard a government official had been arrested, which wasn't much news, but worth looking into at least. When we heard Marlowe was going to the prison to see him in person, though... well *that's* really interesting isn't it?"

Percival paused as if waiting for an answer but Eldon merely gestured for him to continue.

"So we thought we'd better see what kind of traitor warranted a visit from the old man himself, and I drew the short straw. It was just by chance that I showed up right before he did. In fact, it was quite a narrow escape. I was just about to lift the invisibility charm when I heard him coming."

"So you were there the whole time," Eldon said, sinking to a sitting position against the wall. Then, suddenly, "You might've stepped in *before* that brute made a punching bag of my face, you know!"

"And give myself away?" Percival said, seriously. "Security first, friend. I knew you wouldn't be killed. Didn't Marlowe say so himself? Anyway, I had to be *quite* sure you could be trusted. The way you laughed the whole time, I must admit, I thought you'd gone quite mad!"

"I thought so too," Eldon admitted.

"Besides, I was feeling a little mad myself. You may have noticed Marlowe has something of a depressing effect on folks."

Eldon laughed humorlessly. "To put it mildly."

Both men's heads suddenly snapped up as they heard the clanging of a plate being shoved through a door some ways away. Within a few moments, they would hear the shuffling of a prisoner's feet, coming to bring the evening meal.

Percival grew serious and began to speak quickly. "I've got to get going. But we must get you out sooner rather than later if you want to avoid another visit from the guard, and especially if you want to find the children. You need to be in traveling shape. Your part will not be easy, I warn you."

In a whispered voice, Percival laid out the escape plan. While Eldon was still trying to process all this new information, the sound of the dinner delivery moved closer and closer. Eldon thought nothing could still surprise him at this point but, as the prisoner reached the cell door, Percival proved him wrong by disappearing. At first Eldon thought he'd simply gone invisible, but a moment's inspection of the cell proved him wrong. The visitor had gone, like it was nothing. Eldon envied him his freedom.

8

PERCIVAL'S PLAN

The dwarves were not happy about losing Molly, and they took their displeasure out on Hatch. He, much to his credit, did not treat Alice any worse for her betrayal. Even in his anger he understood that she could hardly help acting like a little fool. Looking at her smug, gloating face after he let her go made him almost feel sorry for her.

The dwarves, on the evening of Molly's escape, brought three plates of cold dinner for the children, but brought none for Hatch. Dudley, who seemed to be in charge, taunted him mercilessly as he distributed the food.

"Too bad your little girlfriend couldn't save you, eh?" he mocked. "Maybe she'd have made you something to eat. You could have cooked one of your cat friends! Fat lot of good they did you, running off at the first sign of trouble!"

Hatch only smiled. The dwarf's mockery told him that Molly had not been recaptured, for if she had, they would have been quick to hold it over his head.

"I'm quite sure the cats have gone for help, and my friends will be along shortly," he said brightly. "I wouldn't want to be you fellas when they get here either."

The bluff was a brave one, but the dwarf only roared with laughter.

"Friends!" Dudley exclaimed. "You haven't got one left in the world, boy. Better not get too attached to these three either. They'll be sold as slaves before long and you'll be turned in to the capital police." At that, the dwarf left, chuckling to himself as he stomped away.

Ben offered some of his dinner to Hatch, which he gratefully accepted. Alice, seeing this, began to shout again.

"Hey! Guards! Heeey!"

"Shut up Alice," Ben snarled, turning on her. "You've done enough damage with your squawking."

Alice looked startled at this sudden outburst from the normally docile Ben, but she stopped shouting. Folding her arms, she sat in the corner and glared at the two unlikely new friends, while Rob simply watched without interest.

This newfound camaraderie had a positive effect on Ben. He grew more animated as he and Hatch talked, and Hatch wondered how he had failed to recognize the intelligence in the boy's eyes when they met. Hatch thought back to what Eldon had said in the cabin... *All citizens of Druinor are really Ardenians. They just don't remember.* It pleased him to see Ben come alive a bit, as though his small act of rebellion had sparked something in him.

For the next few days, Hatch remained in his cell with the children, talking to Ben as much as he could to pass the time. He paced back and forth often, which annoyed Alice greatly. With nothing else to pass the time, Hatch resumed practicing his imagination exercises. But nothing of any other consequence took place until the seventh morning of his imprisonment.

On that morning, Dudley and another dwarf named Pongo visited the cave again, just after the children had eaten breakfast.

"Up an' at 'em!" Pongo shouted, his nasally voice piercing the quiet cavern unpleasantly. "We're off on a journey today, kids! Off to your bright futures! You've been enough trouble to me, it's time to make a profit off your sorry little hides."

Alice and Rob had no reaction to this, but Ben looked a little dejected. Hatch watched them with curiosity. He wondered if this dull indifference was the effect the Institute had on everyone.

The children stood still while three more dwarves who had just appeared bound their hands with rope, attaching them to each other so that they had to walk in a single file with the rope between them. With two dwarves at the front and three at the back of the line, the children marched out of the cave.

✧

No doubt you've been wondering what became of the cats. Why did they abandon the children in their time of need, you might even ask. Oh you of little faith! What would *you* have had them do? Fight the pack of dwarves and be captured themselves?

Of course Seamus and Melody had no intention whatsoever of leaving the children to their fate. As soon as they were sure the dwarves had given up chasing them (which didn't take long. Cats are very fast you know) they returned quietly, taking care to remain hidden. It was not hard to relocate the party of dwarves, who were brazenly shouting to each other about their quarry, as you remember.

Seamus and Melody followed at a distance and saw

them descend into the cave. The cats, of course, had been government agents, so they knew all about the unsavory dangers lurking in Druinor. Unlike the children, they were very familiar with the slave underground, and knew immediately what the children's fate would be if they weren't rescued. As soon as they saw the location of the cave's entrance, they shot off in the direction of the cabin, knowing that if all went according to plan, Eldon and Brogan would be there preparing to join the children.

They did not find Eldon and Brogan at the cabin, of course, as Eldon was otherwise occupied, and Brogan had already set off in pursuit of the children. The trail left by the travelers from the cabin was clumsy and easy to follow, but Brogan, knowing that great tragedies have been wrought by the impatient, had followed it slowly and carefully.

When the cats reached the cabin and found it unoccupied, they too retraced their own steps, but a bit more quickly, having made the journey once before.

So it was that just as Brogan was reaching the edge of the Wasteland, he was met by the two bedraggled felines, who burst out of the underbrush so suddenly that if Brogan's horse had been of a different disposition than he was, things could have gone very badly indeed. As it was, the horse merely shied out of the way, and the cats halted, breathless and relieved.

"Seamus!" Brogan exclaimed, knowing instantly that something had gone badly awry. "What's happened? Where are the children?"

"Captured," panted the tabby. "By slave traders. We've seen where they're being kept."

"Show me," Brogan said as he reached a hand down to pull the cats up into the saddle with him. Thankful for the rest, they each found a spot, being careful not to claw the horse by accident. Brogan immediately set out at a brisk pace, taking directions from the cats.

It was late in the afternoon when they began to hear the sounds of dwarf songs and marching feet in the distance.

"That has to be them," whispered Melody. "Off to the slave market already. The brutes."

Brogan reigned the horse to a stop and dropped silently to the ground, finding a place where the underbrush was thick to lie in wait.

"I see them," he whispered after a few minutes. "They've got four children with them... three boys and a girl."

"Must be two other prisoners," Seamus commented. "How many dwarves?"

"Only five," answered Brogan. "I'll make quick work of them."

Before very long the dwarves were nearly close enough to touch. Brogan burst out of the woods, startling them in a very satisfying manner. He made good on his word and the ensuing battle was very short. Dwarves are, on the whole, fairly formidable foes, but Brogan was both a policeman and a trained soldier, so he had very little trouble subduing them. In two minutes' time one of them lay dead and three more were disarmed, while the fifth, Dudley, had escaped and scampered off into the woods. The three conquered dwarves stood with their hands up at the point of Brogan's sword.

"Untie the children," he said to the nearest one, who you, reader, will recognize as Pongo. "If you so much as think about running, you'll join your unlucky companion over there in the afterlife."

Pongo obeyed without protest. The instant the children were free, Seamus and Melody leapt into Hatch's arms, who greeted them with joyful shouts. For a few seconds there was confusion as everyone asked questions at the same time:

"Where's Molly?"

"Who's he?"

"Where's Eldon?"

"Who are they?"

Brogan, sword still pointed squarely at the dwarves, asked Hatch to gather up the ropes.

Hatch happily obeyed, and Brogan retrieved the ropes from him and tied all three of the dwarves tightly to a tree, before turning to greet the children.

"Thank you, sir," Hatch said with a polite bow. "I assume, since you come here with my friends," he motioned to the cats, "and as you've kindly rescued me from my captors, that you can be trusted. And as there's only one person in Druinor other than Eldon himself whom I know to be trustworthy, I believe you must be the other soldier from Arden," he said. "I'm very pleased to make your acquaintance."

Brogan grinned widely. "Brogan Borhagen at your service. But where's the other child? And who are these?"

"These are Druinian children who were taken from the Institute," Hatch said. "Molly escaped yesterday. We must find her."

"Ha! You won't have much luck with that!" shouted Pongo gleefully. "She got snatched! Saw it with my own eyes."

Brogan turned on him, lodging his sword tip beneath the fat dwarf's chin. "By whom?" he demanded fiercely.

"By the headmistress herself! She's in the Institute she is. You can kill me if you like, but you won't get her back!"

Hatch turned pale. Brogan lowered his sword and stood thoughtfully for a moment.

"We've got to rescue her!" Hatch said frantically. "We

can rescue her, right Brogan?"

Brogan turned slowly to face him. He looked pained, but he answered honestly.

"I don't know, Hatch," he said. "But of course we'll try." Turning to the other children, Brogan said, "And you three? What would you have us do with you?"

The Druininan children looked dumbfounded. Never in their whole lives had anyone consulted them about anything regarding their own fates.

"We can't return you to the Institute," Brogan said thoughtfully. "I've got an idea, though. You'll have to come with us for now. I know just the place to take you."

Alice looked doubtful. Until now, she had demonstrated little concern for her future, but she had been taught quite well in the Institute about loyalty to the crown. She feared Marlowe's wrath far more than she feared slavery. This fellow clearly was *not* a loyal Druinian, but he hardly seemed to be a barbarian, either, as she had been told Marlowe's enemies undoubtedly were.

"I won't go," she said defiantly. "I won't be caught with a traitor to the crown."

"You won't be caught, but you most certainly *will* go," Brogan answered cheerfully.

Even Rob looked a little frightened as Brogan lifted the children (except for Hatch) onto the back of the horse one at a time. "What's your name?" Brogan asked him, kindly.

"Rob."

"And yours?" This time the question was directed to Alice, who only glared, turned up her nose and looked away.

"She's Alice. Don't mind her, she's always contrary. And I'm Ben," said the third child. Brogan regarded him with mild surprise.

"Ben's been very kind to me," Hatch said.

Brogan shook Ben's hand warmly. "I thank you for it," he said. "And I'll make sure it's not forgotten."

Once he had settled Ben on the horse behind the other two children, Brogan tipped his hat to the dwarf and began to lead the horse away with Hatch and the two cats walking alongside him. Hatch couldn't tell what direction they were headed, but Brogan and the cats seemed confident, so he followed without question. The day had turned out much better than he'd imagined it would, but fear for Molly's fate still weighed heavily on his young heart.

⌒

The plan was a dangerous one, but Eldon rather liked dangerous plans. He was also fond of the sort of plan that resulted in him not spending his life in prison. This plan, therefore, contained not one, but two highly desirable elements.

For it to succeed, he only needed to find a way to get outside his cell, even for a moment. Although Percival could apparently come and go at will, he couldn't take anyone with him. Whatever magic he used didn't extend beyond the person using it. Eldon would have to find a more mundane way out. What the plan lacked in safety, though, it made up for in pure simplicity. As the prison was located in a deep pit, with no way to scale the walls upward and nothing but a plunge into darkness below, there was little fear among the guards of the prisoners escaping. Their chief occupation was to ensure the inmates would have an unpleasant stay.

For this reason, getting out of the cell was not difficult. When the fellow who brought breakfast shuffled by, Eldon called out to him once again.

"Hey! You!" The prisoner reluctantly met his gaze.

"I've got a message for Marlowe. Go and tell the guards."

"For... the emperor?" stuttered the perplexed inmate. No one *ever* initiated contact with the emperor.

"That's right. And for that guard that brought him yesterday too. Tell that great fool he did a poor job. Tell him I've thought it over and I'm willing to give him another go, assuming he's not too much of a coward."

The prisoner stared at him, aghast.

"And tell Marlowe, his ridiculous spells won't work on me. He doesn't know as much as he thinks he does, and if he ever wants to find the children, he'll have to drag it out of me first."

"I feel confident that he can," said the prisoner, who seemed a little concerned for Eldon's sanity.

"Thank you, your opinion means the world to me. Tell him what I said. Those *exact* words."

The inmate shook his head in wonder and shuffled away to continue his deliveries.

Eldon wondered if he would give the message to the guard, or if he would simply ignore the mad prisoner who, not content with waiting for his beatings, wanted to seek them out.

He didn't have to wonder long. Within fifteen minutes he heard the sound of boots marching down the catwalk. There were clearly more than two of them, something Eldon had not bargained for. Beads of sweat began to form on his brow. The cell door swung open and the giant guard ducked into it, followed by two others, as large as himself.

Thinking quickly, Eldon decided to capitalize on the appearance of extra guards. He began to laugh out loud again, and hurl insults the minute the door opened.

"You couldn't do the job yourself, eh? Had to bring two of your friends to help you manage one little prisoner?"

Eldon mocked. "Does Marlowe know he's got weaklings for prison guards?"

It worked even more quickly than he'd hoped. The guard's face turned red, then purple, and he lunged. Eldon saw his chance and ducked under the guard's arm, dashing out of the cell door to the catwalk beyond. As he rushed past the second guard, the man grabbed Eldon roughly and picked him up by the windpipe as the first guard had on the previous day. This was inconvenient, as it prevented Eldon from breathing for a few seconds, but he chose to ignore that. The guard slammed him against the catwalk railing, holding him out over the abyss. As he gasped for breath, Eldon took a moment to appreciate the massive strength that allowed one man to toss another about with such ease. The third guard raised a fist and began to swing, but this was exactly what Eldon had hoped for. Picking up his feet and planting them firmly on the guard's chest, he kicked with all his might, breaking the man's grip on his throat and launching himself out into the middle of the pit. With a glow of satisfaction, Eldon watched their dismayed faces as he fell. Marlowe would not be pleased with them.

It was a sickeningly long plunge. Eldon twisted his body around and reached his arms over his head as if diving into a swimming pool. As he fell, he contemplated just how much trust he had put in Percival, a complete stranger. As likely as not, he was about to meet a bloody end on the rocks below.

After what seemed like hours, during which time his innards liquefied and reformed as a twisted mass of fear within him, he plunged into shockingly cold water. The momentum of his leap drove him impossibly deep into the dark, freezing reservoir. Rather than trying to resurface, he swam deeper still, until finally his fingers touched the rock lake bed. Eldon could just make out a dim blue light a few yards away and swam toward it. As the light neared, it revealed the opening to a small tunnel, into which he proceeded. He felt certain his lungs would burst and began to wonder why this plan had ever sounded like it might work. But for lack of any other viable options, he swam on, until, finally, he emerged into an underwater cavern and, after few eternal seconds, broke the surface of the water.

After gasping and retching for a few minutes, he began trying to examine his surroundings. The cavern was adorned with little glowing lights under the surface of the water that lit the ceiling with shimmery blues and greens. They appeared to be magical in nature and were presumably placed there for his benefit. In their dim light he saw that the ceiling was low, only three or four feet above the water, however there was a small opening in the roof about ten feet away. The instant Eldon reached the opening, several strong hands reached out and grasped his own, pulling him up out of the water. And so it was that he found himself lying in a warm, dry cave occupied by at least ten smiling men. Exhausted, bruised and shivering on the floor, Eldon thought irrationally, *how did they get furniture down here?*

9

THE INSTITUTE

The Institute contained miles of hallways, or so it seemed to Molly, who had never seen a building so big in her whole life. And compared with the provincial onion-farming town in which she had grown up, she had certainly never seen anything so slick and modern. Molly had, of course, seen some rudimentary machinery in her life, but nothing like what occupied some of the classrooms here. She had heard of electronics in school – the glowing achievements of Emperor Marlowe – but never seen them, and the teachers had never described them, for fear of stirring up the children's imaginations. So it was with awe that she had watched the headmistress press a button near the door and saw it open in response.

She had been dragged inside by the angry woman, who you now know was the headmistress herself, and led down endless hallways, all sterile, shining and devoid of life. Their footsteps, especially those of the headmistress, echoed from the high ceilings as they marched.

Molly wondered how anyone ever found their way around this place. As she was prodded along, she looked around with curiosity (something she soon discovered was not encouraged in the Institute) and occasionally glimpsed classrooms full of children through open doors as she passed them. It occurred to Molly that this wasn't so different from the march she had taken a few days before with the dwarves. There it had been dark tunnels, here it was sterile halls, but the children here were just as much captive as those in the cave had been. She found the thought oddly comforting. She had escaped from her first captors, perhaps she would from these new ones as well.

The headmistress, whose name was Professor Agatha Bell, led Molly straight to her own office. Molly half expected it to be outfitted with instruments of corporal punishment, but it was clean and respectable, almost pleasant. Sunlight streamed in from the window, gently illuminating a soft sofa against one wall, an oak shelf full of books, and a cheery looking potted flower on the desk. This last item Molly found the most grotesque.

Professor Bell indicated that Molly should have a seat at the desk. She seemed to have recovered some of her composure by the time they reached her office and spoke now in a tone of clinical indifference. Molly obeyed. The woman seated herself on the other side of the desk and folded her hands on its glossy surface.

"Now," she said, with a mirthless smile. "You will start at the beginning, and you will tell me exactly how you escaped, and why, and where Rob and Ben are now."

Molly, despite her fear and discomfort, had been thinking carefully about this during the journey here. This woman had apparently mistaken her for a child named Alice Green. Molly had wisely decided that it would be best not to correct this misconception. Perhaps, Molly thought, if she raised no suspicion, she may still have a chance to escape. However, Molly was an honest child and had resolved not to lie, if at all possible.

She raised her head bravely and answered, "I was captured by dwarves."

"What?" Professor Bell sounded surprised.

"They caught us unawares and took us to an underground cave. They separated us."

"Go on. Every detail. Rest assured that you will regret anything you leave out." This threat was delivered in a polite tone, as if she was offering Molly a cup of tea.

"Some of the children were in caves with bars on the doors. They left me in one without a door, all alone."

"How is it that we found you in the forest?"

"I walked out," Molly said simply. In her attempt to be truthful without revealing too much, she managed to deliver just the sort of short, unclear answers Professor Bell expected from her pupils.

"How? Why were you not under guard? How did you find your way out?" The awful woman appeared to be genuinely curious.

Molly shrugged. "I don't know. I just... walked out. They almost caught me but I ran away."

Professor Bell stared at her for a moment, as if wondering whether to believe what she heard. Then she laughed derisively.

"You're lying," she said flatly. "*And* you're using quite a bit of imagination to do it. How dare you. How *dare* you use imagination in *my* school? You'll be punished severely." The headmistress seemed to intentionally work herself into an increasingly agitated state as she spoke. She rang a bell and a younger woman in a suit appeared at the door, looking frightened.

"Yes ma'am?" the younger woman said in a mousy voice.

"Take Miss Green to her room. She's to go without supper. And she's to have detention every day for two years. If she tells us where Rob and Ben are, that will be reduced to eight months."

The woman's eyes widened. "Two *years* ma'am?" she asked. "Not… not two months?"

"I meant what I said," Bell answered coldly. "And you would do well to never question me again. Unless you'd like to share her punishment?"

"No ma'am. Of course. Forgive me." The woman said quickly.

"Forgiveness is not offered by this office," Bell said. "This will be a strike on your record."

The woman ushered Molly out of the office as quickly as she could, afraid to say another word.

Molly found herself again traversing the halls, this time following the frightened little faculty member. After a few moments they approached a shiny silver door. The woman pushed a button. Another bell rang, and the door opened to reveal a tiny square room, with no apparent exit. The woman stepped inside. Molly hesitated. She considered making a break for it then and there, but the poor woman had such a frantic look in her eyes – nearly pleading – that Molly could not bear to be the cause of another strike on the woman's record. As she stepped in after the woman, the doors closed and Molly felt the room lurch into motion.

Several seconds passed in silence. The woman pushed another button and the room stopped again, but this time the doors stayed shut. As the woman turned to Molly, her demeanor changed entirely. The serene, dignified woman now standing before her was wholly unlike the little timid one who had been in the headmistress' office. She surveyed Molly for a few seconds, and then spoke quietly.

"You're not Alice," she said.

Molly looked up at her, terrified. She was found out already! She felt as though her heart might beat the breath out of her lungs. The room seemed to grow dimmer. Before the answer she was wildly searching for could reach her lips, the fear, hunger, and exhaustion of the preceding days overcame her and she did what any child would do in such a situation. She fainted.

૭

You remember no doubt, that when Brogan escaped the capital, he had in his pursuit a singularly unpleasant man, nicknamed "the Weasel". Despite rallying a whole posse of soldiers to cut off Brogan's escape route from the capital, the Weasel had failed to apprehend him, and was now furious at himself for having missed the opportunity. Like most men of his caliber, he took great care to ensure that everyone he encountered would pay for his failure.

On the afternoon of Molly's introduction to the Institute, the Weasel was brooding over maps at the police station, determined to find Brogan and bring him to justice. Or, if not justice, to bring him to a great deal of pain.

"Snyder!" came a gravelly shout from down the hall. Cursing under his breath at the interruption, Snyder threw down his pen and marched into Colonel Conway's office.

"You like children, don't you Snyder?" Conway asked without looking up from the memo in his hand.

Snyder, who disliked children with an intensity that could accurately be called a fervor, snorted derisively. "Whaddyou want Conway? I'm busy."

"Well I beg your pardon," Conway answered with a

sarcastic bow. "How thoughtless of me to interrupt your scowling and pacing with my silly police work. On your way now."

Snyder rolled his eyes and took the memo from Conway's hand, perusing it disinterestedly.

"Couple of truants from the Institute," Conway said. "Escaped from detention. The girl's been caught but the two boys are still missing."

"So what do they need us for? Make the girl tell them where her friends are."

"That's *exactly* what they want us for. Apparently Professor Bell had a bit of a hard time getting the truth from her. The girl was going on about being captured by dwarves. They want you to question her."

"Captured by dwarves?"

"You heard me," Conway sounded annoyed.

"Well that's a bit odd, isn't it?"

"She was lying, obviously."

"Obviously. But don't you think it's odd that she'd come up with a story about dwarves at all? How'd the little brat even hear of them, much less think to make up a story?"

"So?"

Snyder shrugged. "Just strange, that's all. I'll take care of it."

Conway gave him a sharp look, suspicious of the sudden change in attitude. He was a mean spirited old miser who could not stand to see anyone get something they wanted. After all, what other sort of man could get himself promoted to chief of police in a place like the capital of Druinor? Conway was starting to suspect that Snyder wanted this case, and therefore could not be allowed to have it.

"I've changed my mind," he said abruptly. "I'll give it to Parker. Leave the memo on the desk."

Snyder was every bit as cruel as Conway, but a good deal smarter, and understood perfectly. He had played this game before and knew he'd overplayed his hand as soon as he'd done it. Hearing the story of the dwarves, had sparked something in his mind, and now he knew that he *must* get this case.

He shrugged dismissively. "Good. I hate children." Synder threw the memo back down on the desk, turned on his heel and walked out.

"Parker!" came Conway's snarl from behind him. "Get in here!"

Snyder went back to his desk and waited to see if his bluff had worked.

He didn't have to wait long. Parker, a bald, paunchy fellow, marched around the corner only two minutes later, brandishing the memo and looking triumphant.

"Conway says you have to take this one," he announced. "Says I'm too important to be saddled with truancy cases."

"Too important my eye," Snyder mumbled, snatching it from him. "Too stupid, more like."

"He also said you're an ass," Parker rejoined, less than cleverly.

Snyder glowered threateningly until Parker decided there was something very important he had to do on the opposite side of the police station.

10

~

DAMASCUS

Eldon was both fascinated and delighted by his new companions. He had worked in Druinor for twelve years and had only encountered people who treated him with suspicion and hostility, albeit to varying degrees. These men, on the other hand, were both kind and brilliant. For years, his only companion had been Brogan and they had been forced to meet rarely and in secret. In all that time Eldon had nearly forgotten what it was like to be happy and free, but the Damascus Guard managed to bring the joy of his homeland right into the heart of the Druinian capital, and with it an ache of homesickness so fierce he sometimes felt he might weep. He loved them at once and they seemed to feel the same. In the course of the first evening spent in their subterranean headquarters, or Damascus as they called it, they revealed themselves to be a noble-hearted company. Eldon and Percival immediately became confidantes.

Despite this, Eldon was anxious to be on his way to rescue the children. Between the beating, the escape, and the prison food, however, he was weaker than he'd realized. Eldon insisted that he was more than equal to rescuing the children, but the Maskies prevailed upon him to lay low for a while longer, and promised to teach him some magic in the meantime to protect himself and the children.

"Marlowe presumes you are dead," Percival pointed out. "And you will be, if you're found popping out of the ground ten feet from Kalgren's front door. Let's use your death to our advantage, shall we?"

Reluctantly Eldon submitted to this advice and spent the next few days regaining strength, making plans, and learning as much as he could from and about his rescuers.

The Guard was made up of eleven men and two women. Originally there had been fourteen, but three had been caught and killed in the early days of their rebellion. Those who remained had become highly skilled in the art of secrecy. All but two – Percival and a burly fellow called Nathaniel – maintained regular jobs in the capital as well as their positions in the Guard.

Wes, a short, muscle-bound man with long whiskers, worked as a blacksmith and had a loud, wholesome, and frequent laugh. A blonde, wiry man named Luke was a librarian who provided a great deal in the way of research. He was quick-witted and sarcastic, always pushing his bent glasses up the bridge of his nose as he cracked jokes. Another, Joel, worked at the county registrar's office monitoring citizen lists and society tasks. Andrew, a factory worker by day, was brilliant with magic. He was studious and rarely spoke but was always listening carefully. It was he who had discovered the invisibility and porting spells. Harmon was a deliveryman, Raymond a palace guard and Tobias a grocer, while Regan kept an inn and Philip was the owner of a stable. Percival and Nathaniel, the Maskies' captains, had become too well-known by Marlowe's agents and had been forced to go underground entirely. The Guard boasted only two female members; Raymond's wife Martha, a gifted healer, and Ava, whose skill at espionage was legendary. This last was the only member of the guard Eldon did not meet, as she was away on business indefinitely.

Damascus itself consisted of a very large common room, six small sleeping quarters and two bathrooms. The common room was brightly lit, warmly furnished and fortified by magic to protect it from natural disasters and enemy detection. It was outfitted with a kitchen and a long dining table, as well as a meeting area with comfortable couches and a fireplace. Work benches were pushed against the walls and covered in odd tools Eldon had never seen, while the walls themselves were lined with maps, photographs and shelves of books. Tucked into various corners, Eldon found a writing area, several standing wardrobes, two bicycles and a wide variety of weapons, both ancient and modern. The sleeping areas were much simpler, featuring two bunks and a desk in each. At first Eldon assumed they all lived here, but he soon discovered that most of the men lived in the city and a few even had wives and families on the outside, so it was rare for all twelve bunks to be filled at once. On the night of Eldon's escape from prison they had all been present, except for Raymond, Tobias, Ava, and Martha, who were otherwise engaged.

"How hard is it to learn magic?" Eldon asked as they lounged near the fire a few nights later. The porting spell that Percival had used to enter his cell was of particular interest to him.

"It takes a while. Andrew has studied it diligently. Most of us are only passable," Nathaniel said. "Some are better than others." This last was said with a wink.

"Some of us literally couldn't cast a spell to save our lives," Luke added, jerking his head not at all discreetly in Raymond's direction.

Raymond leaned back and put his feet up on the coffee table with a good-natured grin. "Not everyone *needs* magic to be useful. Not a one of you could do my job half so well, even with all your spells to keep you sane."

"Raymond's a palace guard," Wes said by way of explanation. "And he's right. We have no idea how he manages to spend so much time around the emperor and keep his wits about him, much less his cheery disposition."

Eldon regarded Raymond with frank admiration. He thought that he would go to great lengths to avoid spending even a few moments in Marlowe's presence after their last interview. He wondered how any man could be in the presence of evil daily and yet stay both good and sane. Perhaps it was his imagination that saw, behind Raymond's breezy exterior, weariness in his eyes. Not wanting to stare, Eldon turned his attention back to Percival.

"The trouble is, Druinians don't use magic much," the Maskie was saying. "They prefer machinery. There are no resources on it, no books. We have to learn it all by trial and error. Lord knows what we would do without Andrew."

"How did you start to learn it at all then?" Eldon asked Andrew.

"Before the wall came up over the Wasteland, I used to trade with folks in the mountains near there, and even a few on the border of Arden itself."

Eldon's eyebrows arched. He hadn't thought there was any commerce between Arden and Druinor. But then again, he reminded himself, he hadn't known Druinians such as these existed.

"The mountain folk are very magical, or at least they were back then, and of course you know all about northern magic. You've used a bit of it yourself, I'm sure?"

"Basic spells," Eldon shrugged. "A little cloaking here and there, a little misdirection. Just things to keep Brogan and me from drawing any attention to ourselves. Nothing so advanced as what you do."

Andrew nodded. "I got a few books and such from Ardenian traders that taught me those sorts of things too," he said. "That's where I started. Luke has managed to find me a few little volumes here and there in his library work, but the capital has been well scrubbed of nearly everything but school books for the Institute. Magic always came naturally to me, though. I practiced the spells I learned until they were second nature. Once I understood the underlying principles, it wasn't much of a leap to apply them to other things."

He said this modestly, as if it were not a monumental accomplishment.

"I'm very grateful that you did," Eldon said sincerely.

"Bravo!" Luke exclaimed. "That's the most consecutive words we've heard from Andrew's mouth all year!"

Andrew smiled sheepishly.

"Don't thank us yet," Nathaniel laughed. "By the time we're done with you, you might wish you'd never been rescued. It gets a bit wild living with these ruffians."

Eldon laughed too. Were it not for his concern for Brogan and the children, he thought he would have joined the Maskies then and there.

༄

When Molly came to, she became aware of two things simultaneously: first, her aching muscles, and second, a small, mean face leaning over her. Its owner, a plain looking girl a few years older than her, had her hand poised over Molly's forehead, thumb and forefinger drawn together. A dull ache in Molly's head indicated that this girl had woken her up by flicking her repeatedly in the face. When the girl saw that Molly's eyes were open, she said "Oooh!" delightedly and flicked her hard one last time.

"Ow!" shouted Molly and sat up, pushing the girl forcefully away. "What'd you do that for?"

"To wake you up of course!" said the girl, sitting down on the bed opposite Molly's. "Miss Perry said you should rest, but what does that silly old bat know?"

Molly stared at her.

"She's the most idiotic person in the whole faculty," the girl prattled on, laying back on the bed with satisfaction. "I heard Professor Sanford say so to Professor Sharp. They can't understand why she's even allowed to work here, and neither can I. Professor Sharp said she ought to be in prison. She's a sympathizer of the *anti-progs*, you know."

"Who's Miss Perry?" Molly asked. She touched her forehead gingerly to see if it was bruised. It was. The girl must have been flicking her for some time without success. *I suppose I should admire her perseverance*, Molly thought ruefully.

"Now you sound like an idiot yourself," said the girl. Molly thought this was very rude. "You know very well who I mean. Where did you go, anyway? Are you an anti-prog too?"

The girl sat up suddenly, as if this thought had just occurred to her and looked at Molly with renewed curiosity. "I heard you're to be punished severely. I'd be surprised if you survived it. Is it true that you got two *years* of detention?"

She said this last part gleefully, almost greedily. Molly

was beginning to hate this girl. In the back of her mind she heard Eldon's voice saying, *It's a rescue mission for the whole population, not just the two of you,* but she pushed the thought away. Throughout these past weeks, when Seamus and Melody had described the wonderful land of Arden, she had pictured herself and Hatch living there happily, doing just as they pleased all the time. She had even pictured them being honored by the King for having set Fairy Tale free from her captivity. But suddenly it came to her like a dash of cold water that if everyone was rescued, everyone would be allowed to live there freely too. Looking at this cruel, spiteful little girl on the opposite bed, Molly began to hope Eldon had been wrong about King Mardius' intention to rescue all of Druinor. She didn't *want* this girl with her ugly, hard eyes and her wicked grin to be included. Molly quickly swallowed the bitter shame that rose up in her at the thought.

The girl began to snap her fingers in front of Molly's eyes, trying to draw her out of her reverie. "Alice! Hello? Ha ha, you really *are* an idiot, aren't you?"

At the name *Alice*, Molly started. Could it be possible that this girl, who had clearly shared a room with the real Alice, really hadn't noticed that Alice had been replaced? The woman in the elevator had known immediately that she was an imposter. And what about that woman? Surely she had gone straight back to the headmistress and given Molly away, and yet here she was, in a tiny room with a girl who obviously thought she was Alice. Molly felt a tiny surge of hope, which inspired her underworked imagination to splutter slowly to life.

"Look here, how did I get here?" she asked sharply, sounding much more like a Druinian child. "Who brought me here?"

This sudden change in tone seemed to have a positive effect on the girl, who was apparently used to Alice being bossy.

"Dunno!" she said cheerfully. "You were unconscious when I came back from class last night. Miss Perry brought in some food this morning and said you were to rest."

At this, Molly, who was ravenously hungry, looked wildly around and saw for the first time a desk, just behind the bed to the left. It was piled with books and papers, and perched precariously atop the pile was a tray of food, which the other girl had clearly helped herself to while Molly slept. Jumping up as if it might disappear, she began to eat what was left of the cold chicken soup, bread and coffee. In ordinary circumstances it would have been pretty unpleasant, but to Molly it seemed like the best thing she'd ever tasted.

"She knows perfectly well there's no food allowed in the rooms too, I don't know what she was thinking," the girl was saying. "You'd better be careful if you've got Miss Perry doing special favors for you. I ought to report you both. Not that it'll matter, they can't do worse to you than two years detention." She laughed, then added as an afterthought, "I should probably report her anyway."

"Don't you dare!" Molly shouted, turning on her. "If you do, I swear I'll tell them you put me up to escaping, and I'll make sure you take detention with me!"

Molly was just as surprised as the other girl was by her outburst, but it worked beautifully.

"Alright, you needn't shout," the girl sulked. "You'd be reporting her yourself if you knew what was good for you. Probably get you a few months off."

The girl folded her arms across her chest and made a show of pouting, but Molly knew that Miss Perry, whom she now assumed to be the woman in the elevator, was out of danger for the time being.

At this moment a siren began to blare, startling Molly so much that she dropped the piece of bread in her hand. It sounded like the whistles that blew in her village to signal the end of the work day, but amplified by a hundred times in the tiled halls. A blue light over the door began to flash.

"What's the matter with you?" the girl asked. "It's only the bell."

"The bell?"

"Yes, the bell!" the girl snapped. "I swear, you're the stupidest girl I've ever met." And with that, she snatched a pile of books off the end of her bed and marched out of the room, slamming the door behind her.

Molly guessed that the bell must be intended to tell the children classes were starting but, she realized with panic, she had no idea where she was supposed to go.

She lifted the tray and looked at the pile of books underneath. The titles were all meaningless to her. *The Theory of Obedience* and *Don't Turn Back the Clock: How to Stomp Out the Anti-Progressive Rebellion* and *Emperor Marlowe's Age of Enlightenment*. Unsure what else to do, she picked up the top one, *The Emperor's Economics,* and a slip of paper fluttered out of it and onto the floor. Picking it up, Molly saw it was a note for her written in tiny letters.

> *Go to class. Class information on the back. Keep your head down and don't cause a scene. Let them all think you're Alice for as long as you can. Trust me, it'll be much worse if they find out you're not her. Not much I can do about detention... I'm so sorry. But stay strong. I'll think of something.*

She flipped the note over and saw a neat schedule of classes in rows, with notes about what books were needed, and room numbers for each class. The first class was *Economics, Room C5, 8:00, Professor Sharp.*

Bless Miss Perry!

Still marveling that her real identity hadn't been discovered, she took the whole stack of books and ran into the hall. It was full of students, some walking with their heads down, others laughing and talking, all looking wholly unpleasant. Most of them seemed to be headed toward a set of elevators, so she fell in with them, hoping it would be easy to find Room C5.

11

THE PROPHECY

Molly's time in the Institute went from bad to worse with astonishing speed. She managed to find C5 with little trouble thanks to Miss Perry's map, but Molly hesitated to go in. Though the girl in her room had somehow mistaken her for Alice, it seemed impossible that others would as well. But the instructor, when he saw her, did not seem at all perturbed.

"Ah, Alice, there you are," he said. "Thought you could get away, did you? Not to worry, I've all the homework you missed right here. Have it on my desk tomorrow morning, or you'll regret it."

Utterly mystified, Molly could only mutter, "Yes sir," as she retrieved the stunningly tall stack of homework presented and found an empty desk.

So it went throughout the whole school. The children and faculty, it seemed, had no interest in questioning little things like the complete physical transformation of one student. The headmistress had said that this was Alice, so of course, this *must* be Alice. Unbeknownst to Molly, Miss Perry, who was passing fair at magic, had done a few spells here and there to support these convictions and keep her concealed. Everyone was thoroughly convinced. Fellow students smirked and whispered when they saw her, but only because they were morbidly delighted by the severity of her punishment. From conversations she overheard, most of the students seemed to think she had actually killed Rob and Ben, but they didn't appear to think less of her for it. Indeed, even the teachers seemed more concerned by the fact that she had tried to escape than the possibility that she had dispatched her two companions in the process.

Despite this mysterious bit of luck, she soon found that the Institute was far worse than she could ever have dreamed. Molly couldn't help but wonder that none of her fellow classmates found their treatment at all shocking. Although they all lacked imagination, Molly was intrigued by the variety of ways this ailment manifested. Some were simply dull and seemed stupid, like Rob had seemed to Hatch. A great many others were cruel and spiteful like Molly's roommate, whose name turned out to be Edith, and who appeared to be wicked through and through.

Molly was intrigued to discover, however, that there were quite a few others who showed signs of intelligence and compassion, though these characteristics were aggressively stamped out wherever the faculty discovered them. Despite this, a surprising number of students possessed a great capacity for goodness, though they did their best to keep this hidden. Molly supposed these must be the ones who would grow up like her parents – honest, and hardworking, but content to keep to themselves. It must be based on these differences that the teachers assigned society roles.

The classes were unlike any she had experienced in the

little rural schoolhouse in which she had spent her childhood. The professors here shared a love for draconian punishments and enforcing absolute, unquestioned authority, though what they taught seemed at times to be entirely incoherent. Nevertheless, they spoke with such unreserved confidence that they were almost believable.

However, the Institute's crimes against intelligence were the least of Molly's worries. She was certain she could easily overcome these by employing the gift of an imagination unhindered by dark magic, which she only now began to fully appreciate. This was risky, however, as the main goal of the Institute was to scour children's brains of any remnant of imagination, and thus the Imagination Council enforcers were frequent visitors. At any moment, students could find themselves dragged off to a testing room to be scanned for any sign of imagination misuse. This fact alone, however, was somewhat stimulating to Molly, who discovered that finding creative ways to disguise her imagination from the enforcers could be turned into a sort of terrifying game.

And it was truly terrifying. The punishments to which the children in the Institute were subjected could only accurately be described as abuse. In extreme cases, torture. Sometimes these punishments were doled out for actual misbehavior, of which there was no shortage, but more often than not, it was simply a show of power, or worse, a way for professors to ease their boredom. Due to the vast number of students, most of them experienced far less punishment than the professors would have liked, but still they lived under the constant fear of it. The exceptions were those students assigned to detention.

Detention was so horrible, in fact, that school policy allowed for no student to receive more than one week of it every three months. That hadn't always been the case, but a few students had actually gone mad, and mad people were of no use to the empire, besides which they had to be disposed of, which was extra paperwork. Molly, as you will remember, had been assigned two solid years of detention by Headmistress Bell. No one had ever heard of such a punishment before.

The professor in charge of detention rather relished this extreme sentence as a rare opportunity to plumb the depths of his own cruelty. This was one of the few characteristics to which imagination could be freely and liberally applied in Druinor. He decided, therefore, on something of a progressive experience for Molly, in which each day's detention would be increasingly difficult, to see just how far he would be allowed to go. The instructor, whose name was Professor Dalton, took great pleasure in deriving new ways to inflict harm on his young charges, with all imagination sanctions lifted.

Sometimes he would keep them in a stifling classroom for hours, forcing them to do advanced mathematics and punishing any slight mistake with boxed ears. On other days he would make them stand at attention for hours on end, memorizing and reciting various mantras of Marlowe's, or reading gruesome accounts from history books and newspapers to them. On one occasion, Professor Dalton tied students to their desks and simply chanted a list of reasons that nobody could ever love them, in a low, infuriating monotone. The next day he made them chant it about themselves instead. Sometimes he forced them to stand barefoot in the cold for hours on end, or locked them outside the grounds overnight, tied to the fence so they could not escape. Once he even released jars full of poisonous looking spiders into the room with the students and commanded them to stand stock still without so much as flinching, or risk a holding cell full of snakes instead. No doubt you can see why some students went mad.

Molly, you will be pleased to know, stood up quite bravely under this inhumane treatment, retreating as often as she could into her imagination and drawing on stories Seamus had told her of life in Arden. She imagined that she and the other students were undergoing some great test of strength and valor before being made into a king's personal army. Standing in the cold, she imagined they were on a ship at sea, preparing to face an oncoming gale. She imagined the spiders as tiny friends, come to comfort the captives with messages one could only hear by listening intently since their voices were so small.

Molly even attempted to guard herself against hating Dalton, as even her young wisdom understood that hating him could only make her like him. Still, it did not take long for the torment to wear on her young psyche. Within a week, some of the childlike exuberance we have come to love in her had faded, and her small spirit was terribly wounded in that wretched place. Dark circles began to form under her eyes and sleep evaded her many nights. Naturally she had no hope of keeping up with the load of homework assigned to her, and so was often subjected to humiliation, corporal punishment, and further detention assignments during her classroom time.

Yet do not despair, faithful reader! For though none of us escapes a dark night of the soul, it is rarely as long, or as destructive as our enemies intend it to be. Very soon, an event would take place which Molly would count as disaster but which would turn out to be her salvation.

In the meantime, she was not entirely abandoned even in those echoing halls. She remembered, from the day of her arrival, that Miss Perry had stopped the elevator to confront her about not being Alice. Since Miss Perry had not given away her identity, she deduced two important things: first, that Miss Perry was a friend, and second, that the elevators were safe places to talk. She therefore made it her singular mission to be caught alone in an elevator with Miss Perry again. Her first few attempts ended discouragingly, including one maddening occasion in which she darted into the elevator behind Miss Perry, only to be followed by Edith, who squeezed through the doors at the very last moment, looking triumphant, as if she was fully aware of what she'd done. Finally, on the fifth day, Molly found herself blessedly alone in one of the school's less frequented elevators. She was thankful just for the space to herself, and sighed in disappointment as the box settled at her destination floor. It opened and, *miracle of miracles*, Miss Perry stepped inside! The woman seemed as pleased as Molly was at this turn of events, and the instant the doors were closed, she struck the button that temporarily disabled the elevator.

Miss Perry knelt and took poor Molly in her arms without a word. Our little heroine let all her pent-up fear and pain escape as gasping sobs on the strange woman's shoulder.

"Now, now," Miss Perry soothed. "It'll be alright dear. I'll find a way to help you."

"But I shouldn't even *be* here," sniffed Molly.

"No one should be here," Miss Perry said sympathetically.

Molly shook her head. "No, you don't understand. I *can't* be here. I'm meant to be on a journey. My friends are waiting for me."

Miss Perry nodded as if this were not surprising. "I thought it might be something like that. You didn't come here through the usual channels. Tell me what happened."

Molly opened her mouth to tell the truth, but then stopped. Could this kind faculty member be putting on an act? To tell a member of the Institute about the mission could jeopardize everything. Her intuition told her Miss Perry was trustworthy, but a small voice inside reminded her that it wouldn't take much to gain a child's trust in a place like this.

Molly shook her head. "There's no time. I need to get out. Can you help me?"

Miss Perry didn't press the issue, realizing that they didn't have long to talk. "I'm here to help all children. Of course I'll help you."

The relief nearly brought a fresh bout of tears, but Miss Perry kept talking. "Listen, it's not easy to get out of this place, even for me. We'll always have to be on the lookout, do you understand? When the opportunity comes, we'll both have to act immediately. I know it's trying, but you must keep your eyes open and your mind sharp. Can you do that?"

Molly nodded, wiping her nose with the back of her hand. Miss Perry stood and reached for the elevator button but Molly stopped her.

"How will I find you?" she asked. "And... who are you? How did *you* come here? Did they capture you as well?"

Miss Perry smiled and shook her head. "I came here of my own accord. I have friends outside the walls as well. All of us have been through the Institute ourselves and we know first-hand the horrors that go on here. I came back as a sort of... spy, I suppose you could say. To find out if there's anything to be done for any of the children here, to stop the Institute from breaking them entirely, if I can."

Molly felt that her heart would stop. *Friends outside the Institute?* Somewhere in Druinor there were people who saw what went on in places such as these and wanted to fight back? You cannot imagine, reader, (or maybe you can, and if so, I'm sorry for you) how it encourages a frightened heart, in a place like that, to hear that somewhere in the world, someone is fighting injustice on your behalf. Molly had already begun to be afraid that she would never leave that wretched school.

"You may call me Ava," Miss Perry told her, gently wiping Molly's tears. "I'm going to get you out of here. I promise."

From that day on, Molly knew she had an ally. This knowledge alone would have been enough to keep her going, but she did not have to satisfy herself with the knowledge alone. Miss Perry took every opportunity to send her little notes dropped into Molly's stack of school books or slid into her pocket. Some were encouraging, some contained helpful advice and some were just friendly. Sometimes she even managed to get Molly alone for a walk on the grounds, though how she managed this Molly never knew. Ava would often wait until Edith was gone and stop by Molly's room for a friendly talk, leaving apples, chocolates and nuts behind. Molly occasionally saw her slip these little treats to other students as well. This was a dangerous game for her, but even Druinian students were unlikely to betray the only person who showed them any kindness. Ava seemed to be quietly making a friend of as many of the children as she could.

Ava was a careful but constant presence, and her friendship strengthened and sustained Molly during her tenure in the barbaric Professor Dalton's detention lab.

෴

Brogan, Hatch, the two cats, and the three Druinian children had been getting along quite well. Like Eldon, Brogan had been waiting a long time to meet Hatch and he was not disappointed. The two of them liked each other immensely and each had a great many questions he wanted to ask the other about the past twelve years. Unfortunately, they could not discuss anything of Fairy Tale in the presence of the Druinian children, but they still managed to find much to talk about. Even Ben joined in the conversation now and then, proving himself brighter than Hatch had at first imagined. The other two children were far less agreeable, especially Alice, who refused to cooperate with Brogan in any way. For all that, Brogan maintained a cordial manner toward all of them.

All in all though, Hatch felt much safer in Brogan's company than he had since leaving the cottage, and would have been entirely at ease had he not been so intensely worried about Molly.

It was nearly midnight when Brogan halted abruptly and, holding his torch high above his head, began to peer into the darkness around him. Hatch could not tell what he was looking for but he seemed to have found it, as he made a sharp turn into what appeared to be nothing but thick underbrush.

Leading the horse that carried Rob and Alice after him, Brogan shouted, "Come on then!"

The cats followed immediately. Hatch and Ben looked at each other hesitantly, before following as well.

They fought their way forward for a minute or two, the thick foliage scratching their arms and faces. Hatch could hardly see anything, but he maintained his course by following Alice's shrieks of protest and absurd threats. After a moment they emerged into a small clearing, with a quaint little house right in the middle of it.

"Here we are! Looks like he's home." Brogan laughed as if this were a joke, though Hatch couldn't understand it. "Wait here, children, I'll go and let him know we're here."

As he said this though, the front door swung open to reveal a large man, silhouetted by the bright light of the kitchen.

"Well?" the man shouted, sounding irritable. "What do you want? Why've you made me come all this way?"

Hatch thought this was an odd thing to say. The other children thought nothing of it whatsoever.

Brogan, appearing blissfully unaware of the man's aggravated tone, called out. "Hello Abner! Good to see you old man! Might we come in?"

The man stepped back inside, which must have signaled his assent, for Brogan (after lifting Alice and Rob off the horse and setting them on the ground) followed him in and beckoned the children to come as well.

They found themselves in a warm, comfortable looking kitchen. The table, Hatch was delighted to see, was set with a large supper that included piping hot soup, beef, sausages, vegetables, bread and butter, and cold milk. The old man seemed to be expecting someone, for there were six place settings at the table and – amazingly – two dishes on the floor containing fish and warm milk for the cats.

"I can't tell you how glad I am to see you!" Brogan said to the old man. "I couldn't be sure we'd find you."

"You didn't, of course. It's I who found you." The man looked as if he had been very formidable in younger days, although these had evidently been an impossibly long time ago. His leathery skin was deeply lined, and he had white hair and a short white beard. His countenance seemed frozen in a scowl but Hatch couldn't help feeling he was more friendly than he appeared. After all, Brogan had greeted him joyfully, as an old friend. Hatch already had a great deal of respect for Brogan's opinion.

"Which one of you is Master Holland?" the old man demanded, glaring at the children as if he suspected them of a crime.

"I am," Hatch admitted, stepping bravely forward and holding out his hand.

"Ah yes," Abner shook the hand, nodding his approval at Hatch's forthright manner. "Glad to hear it. You're not a coward, I can see that quite clearly. If you'd been a coward, all would be lost."

Not knowing quite what to make of this, Hatch simply said, "Thank you sir."

At this moment Alice stepped forward, crossing her arms and screwing up her sour little face in a way that was presumably meant to be very mature.

"Now look here," she announced. "You are all obviously anti-prog criminals. I demand that you take me back to school immediately, and I will report you to the authorities."

Hatch reflected on how odd it was that Alice was animatedly interested in escaping these men, but had been nearly catatonic with apathy about escaping slave traders. *What must the Institute do to a person?* He wondered, with a stab of fear on Molly's behalf.

Abner chuckled and nudged Brogan. "Here's a girl who'll never be in trouble with the Imagination Council, eh?"

Brogan smiled kindly at Alice.

"I think you may find you're wrong about that, Abner," he said.

Alice, of course, did not understand the insult and assumed that it was she who had not been properly understood. She was about to restate her demand, when

Ben shouted, "For the last time, Alice, shut *up*. You don't even *like* school. You were perfectly content to be taken away by criminals when they were slave traders. Listen to yourself! These people have been nothing but kind to us and you don't deserve an ounce of it!"

Everyone (including Ben himself) was astonished by this outburst, but especially the adults, who had never before seen such a display from a native Druinian. It seemed Ben's mind had begun to put up a struggle against the poisonous fog of Marlowe's magic.

Rob, less surprisingly, had ignored this entire exchange and had been staring steadfastly at the table with an expression of dull longing. Seeing this, Abner remembered his own manners and invited them to join him for supper, a request to which even Alice could not object.

It was a delicious meal which they all enjoyed tremendously, though poor Alice had to pretend not to, so as not to give the others the satisfaction of having pleased her. After it was over, Abner showed Rob and Ben to a small, comfortable bedroom, and Alice to another, and told them to get some rest. Alice informed him that she would be escaping immediately, at which Abner laughed heartily, but not unkindly, and closed the door. He then invited Hatch, Brogan, and the cats into his cozy sitting room, where he poured them all coffee as they sat down to talk.

"So you've come at last," Abner began when they had all settled in. "I'm very sorry to hear what's happened to young Miss Morris."

Brogan's expression darkened.

"Pardon me sir," Hatch said, looking bewilderedly from one to the other, "but how *can* you have heard? We've only just arrived."

Abner waved a hand dismissively. "The point, Mr. Holland, is that I *have* heard, isn't it? I'm afraid your friend is in for quite a trial."

"But... we *can* save her. Can't we?"

Abner looked at him for a moment before nodding slowly. "Possibly. Is that your intention?"

"Naturally," Brogan answered, but Hatch was disturbed to see no confidence in his face. He seemed as eager for encouragement from the old man as Hatch himself was.

Abner thought about this for a moment more. "I don't recommend it," he said finally.

"But we *can't* leave her there!" Melody exclaimed, with more fervor than Hatch had yet heard in her gentle voice. "We can't. I *won't*!"

Hatch loved that cat more than ever in that moment. Brogan only leaned forward, resting his elbows on his knees and looking intently at the old man.

"What do you have in mind?" he asked.

Abner sighed. "I can't say. That is, I don't entirely know. I just *feel* it. Will it be enough to ask you to trust me?"

"Respectfully, no." Hatch said firmly. "If Molly's been taken to the Institute, there cannot be a good reason for abandoning her there."

"Hear, hear!" Seamus chimed in, again to Hatch's immense relief. Surely the four of them would prevail over this old man's cryptic advice. But to his dismay, Brogan did not join their protest.

"Of course I trust you, Abner," he said simply.

Hatch gaped. "But... you can't mean..."

Brogan turned to him sympathetically. "Hatch, I know you don't understand, and I don't blame you one bit. In fact, I applaud your bravery. But I've known this man for longer than I can remember. He's wiser than any of us can imagine and I'd trust him with my life. If he says we're not to go after her, it is not for me to question what he has in mind instead."

Hatch's heart sank. He glared angrily back at Abner, but the old man was unperturbed.

"I promise you Master Holland, your young friend will *not* be abandoned." He said. "You have my word."

Hatch, having momentarily forgotten his previously high opinion of Brogan's judgment, didn't care a fig for this old stranger's word. As it seemed he had no choice but to submit to this unpleasant turn of events, however, Hatch retreated into moody silence. Sensing his distress, Melody jumped into his lap and curled up there.

Abner turned back to Brogan. "You've brought the prophecy, I assume?"

"Of course."

"May I?" he held out a withered hand as Brogan retrieved from his satchel the faded piece of parchment he had hastily taken from Eldon's cabin. He handed it to Abner, who took it eagerly and examined it for a long time.

Finally, he turned to Hatch. "Would you like to read it?"

Hatch was interested in spite of himself. He took it from the man's outstretched hand and saw that it was written in verse, with long, spidery letters unlike any he'd ever seen. It took his eyes a moment to adjust before he could make it out:

Ne'er day nor night should close, travelers,
With no grand story to tell,
Here I sit weaving my tale, travelers,
And spinning yours as well.
Come knock, come knock on my door, children,
While there's still light to see.

Before sun departs your eyes, children,
Come rest those lamps on me.
Though you should be betrayed, wanderer,
Love not your own young life,
Though she whose soul you love, wanderer
May hold the traitor's knife
Come see, come kiss my cheek, pilgrims,
I'll whisper a fairy tale,
Death is a fleeting foe, pilgrims,
Her wanton glance so pale,
Heed not the voice of woe, hero
And fearless heroine,
Make haste to bring me aid, heroes,
Before your story's end.

Hatch read it once or twice before handing it back, but could make neither heads nor tails of it. Seamus had sprung onto the arm of his chair and was reading it as well.

"What does it mean?" Hatch asked.

"Well, we can't be sure. It's believed to be an ancient prophecy concerning the ones who will save Fairy Tale. We thought," Abner said, "that it might be about you and your friend."

"Believed by *some*," Brogan interjected. "Others believe it's just a story."

Abner snorted. "So casual! *Just* a story. As if that weren't powerful enough on its own!"

Brogan could not deny this. It was, after all, fiction that Marlowe was most afraid of. Even if the bit of parchment held nothing but literary value, that was enough to make it worth guarding with one's life. Still, Hatch instinctively knew that this was more than a story, though what it could possibly mean was beyond him.

Not long after this, Brogan decided it would be best if Hatch went to bed as well. The tiny cabin was, it seemed, equipped with many rooms, and Hatch was relieved to be given his own instead of joining Rob and Ben in theirs. He drifted off to the sound of the adults and cats talking in low voices as they attempted to wrestle with the cryptic verse again. Every now and then, a phrase would rise above the murmur and hang in the air like an unanswered riddle.

...Make haste, it says...

...No, it's not the same "she" this second time...

...seems clear there's only one traveler...

... the traitor's knife...

12

~

WHAT ABNER KNEW

As the rising sunlight tumbled through Hatch's window the next morning, a line from the prophecy drifted into his mind.

Before the sun departs your eyes, children, come rest those lamps on me...

The prophecy!

Hatch sat up in bed, all the disappointment and frustration of the previous evening washing over him with an icy shock. What was he to do? He couldn't abandon Molly to the Institute.

Right then, he made up his mind. He would go and rescue her by himself. Hatch sat quietly for a moment, but didn't hear any movement in the rest of the house. Perhaps they were all still asleep. Ever so cautiously, he slipped on his shoes and tip-toed to the door. Still not a creak from anywhere. He slowly turned the latch and swung the door open.

For the first time in his life, he was sorely disappointed to smell bacon cooking. It was too late. Abner was evidently up.

Still he made his way down the hall as quietly as he could, nurturing the rapidly fading hope that he might still make his escape. As soon as he emerged from the hall, Hatch encountered Brogan and Abner, who both appeared to have been up for some time and were talking quietly as Abner prepared breakfast. They both greeted him cordially.

Hatch plopped disconsolately into a chair and glared at them. Abner and Brogan graciously pretended not to notice.

"Hatch," Brogan said after a few moments of stony silence. "Do you trust me?"

Hatch thought about it for a moment, then answered honestly. "Why should I? I've only just met you. I don't even know that you are who you say you are, and I have no one to confirm it. I don't even know who Eldon is. I've known him by two different names in as many weeks. He came and took me from my house in the middle of the night, and told me some story about my being kidnapped as a baby... for all I know, *he's* the kidnapper! For all I know, *you're* a slave trader! Why should I trust any of you?"

The more Hatch had talked, the more frantic he had become, and by the time this outburst had spent itself, he was trying bravely to hold tears at bay. He expected Brogan to be angry, but instead he looked pleased, which was disconcerting. In the brief pause that followed, Abner set a plate of food on the table. As Hatch was a twelve-year-old boy, this was probably the best move he could have made.

"You've every right to feel that way," Brogan said calmly. "In fact, I'm glad of it. I'd be concerned if none of those things had occurred to you. But tell me, Hatch... what do you *think* is true? Do you think Eldon or I kidnapped you?"

Suddenly Hatch felt ashamed. Looking down, he shook his head.

"Why not? What evidence do you have in our favor?"

Hatch thought about this. "Well… you both talk to me as if I were an equal. No one in Druinor does that. And even though Alice is so spiteful, you talk to her that way too. You're always kind. And the cats trust you."

"Thank you," Brogan said seriously, as if this description carried much weight with him. "If I had time, I would do what it took to win your confidence. But as I haven't, I'm going to have to ask you to give it to me anyway, though you've nothing more than what you've just said on which to base it. Will you?"

Hatch nodded. If Brogan wasn't all he seemed to be, he was still the best option in Druinor.

"Thank you again. Now, I know this is difficult, but I assure you that I want to see Molly free as much as you do. I am half inclined to go after her myself, but my friend Abner promises me that it will not end well if I do, and furthermore that there are forces currently at work toward the same end. That being the case, I have decided that you and I will proceed toward Arden."

"I thought we were headed to the Western Mountains."

"We were," Brogan said, "but Abner assures me that it is vital we go to Arden first."

"It is," Abner interjected, "or you won't have what you need when you get to the Western Mountains."

"I don't understand," Hatch said. "I thought it was impossible to travel between here and Arden."

They were interrupted at this moment by Seamus, who hopped over the low kitchen window sill from outside.

"So did I," he said.

"Where's Melody?" Hatch asked.

"Hunting."

Hatch grimaced. He had never quite gotten used to his

sweet house cat killing her food.

"So how are we getting to Arden?" Seamus pressed.

"Through the Wasteland," Abner answered. The room erupted in protestations, but Abner motioned for quiet. "Yes, yes, I know, the wall is impassable. Only that's not entirely true these days. Cracks have begun to appear in it."

Brogan was thunderstruck.

"You mean..."

"There are a few small passages through it. No one but I could ever have seen them, and even I am at a loss as to what has caused them."

"How could you see them?" Seamus asked.

"They can only be seen from above. I can fly over the Wasteland, though it takes a terrible toll. I noticed them a few months ago. Like tiny fractures spreading out across a looking glass."

"What's everyone looking so stunned for?" Melody asked with a yawn as she appeared in Seamus' recently vacated perch on the window sill.

By the time they had repeated this latest piece of astonishing news, the other children had begun to stir. They quickly agreed that Brogan, Hatch and Seamus would leave that night, while Alice, Rob and Ben were to stay with Abner until another arrangement could be made for them. Ben and Rob, when they were informed of this, had no objection. Even Alice only put up a perfunctory resistance. Perhaps the wholesome food and soft bed had begun to temper her contrariness.

That evening, when the air had begun to cool but darkness was still a long way off, Brogan, Hatch and Seamus set off for the Wasteland. Brogan would have preferred for Abner to accompany them and show them where to find the breach in the wall, but the Druinian children had to be cared for. Hatch had assumed that they would be returned to their parents, but Brogan pointed out that, after a few years in the Institute, they weren't supposed to remember they *had* parents. Besides, Brogan reminded him, they'd only be returned to the school immediately.

Melody, in the meantime, had agreed to return to the capital to search for Eldon, and help him stage Molly's rescue.

Before the company parted she fretted over each of them, reminding Hatch to stay close to Brogan, admonishing Brogan not to push the child too hard, and fussing particularly over Seamus.

"Watch out for dogs," she told him, "and wizards, and whatever you do, don't get stuck in the wall. If you allow anything to happen to yourself or Hatch, you'll have me to answer to."

"What about me?" Brogan asked, feigning woundedness.

Seamus, who seemed ambivalent to admonition from anyone else, answered meekly, "Don't fret, mother cat. We will all be together again soon."

Hatch bid her an almost tearful farewell, then shook hands with Ben and Rob. Even Alice's departing glare seemed a little less unfriendly than usual. Perhaps because she was glad he was leaving.

Abner and Brogan had pored over Abner's hand-drawn maps of the various cracks in the wall to determine the nearest one. Hatch thought they were putting an awful lot of stock in the memory of an old man who had only seen these fractures while supposedly flying about in his house. Had Brogan not taken the hermit's word so seriously, he might have laughed at the whole thing. But he had promised Brogan his confidence, and a promise was a promise.

So the three of them set out on foot, in as good spirits as

could be expected. Hatch was still dreadfully concerned about Molly, but Brogan and Seamus did their best to keep the mood light. Hatch found their conversations fascinating, though they talked of things he had never heard of and could not picture.

So far in his journey, so many calamities had befallen them that Hatch had found no time to contemplate the country of his birth. Yet now that they were really headed toward Arden, his thoughts began to turn toward that country in earnest. What would the people be like? What would they think of him? He felt a sickening fear that his childhood in Druinor had caused him to be so much stupider than the people of Arden that they would all laugh at him, as the Druinian children in his village had laughed at him on account of his imagination.

I don't belong either place. Not really, he thought. And for a few moments, it is my duty to report, he felt exceedingly sorry for himself. He did not, however, carry on in this state for long. He had far more sense than he realized, and quickly saw that indulging self-pity was only making him feel worse. Hatch did what many an adult would be well-advised to do; he laughed at himself, and it worked wonders on his spirits.

The current location of Abner's house was not far from the Wasteland, and the travelers reached its edge within two hours. They paused for a moment as they emerged from the wood, all feeling the same hesitation, perhaps. To cross the vast expanse of desert that stretched out before them would have been a daunting undertaking even if there were no magic wall. The intense daytime heat would be taxing enough on its own, but magnified by the glass-like substance that made up the wall, it became downright deadly. This was not a wall such as you or I might understand it, which might border a garden and be relatively thin. No, dear reader, this wall was miles thick, and there was no guarantee that a crevice on one side would stretch all the way through to the other. Now that the wall was within their grasp, the travelers considered the very real possibility that they would find themselves trapped halfway across. For this leg of the journey, Brogan and Seamus were no longer guides, but companions. For what lay ahead of them was wholly unknown to them all – indeed to any man in the world.

Suddenly, a new thought occurred to Hatch. *Brogan has been here before.* For the first time he realized how great a sacrifice Eldon and Brogan had made by coming to rescue him and Molly that night so many years ago. The staggering weight of his sudden understanding took his breath away. Brogan's face – usually so composed and cheerful – was for a moment unguarded and Hatch saw all the man's pain and weariness laid bare as he gazed toward his homeland.

"Brogan?" Hatch said quietly.

"Yes?"

"Did you have a wife in Arden?" Brogan looked startled. Looking at that boyish face, upturned in childlike concern, he saw immediately what Hatch had been thinking, and it moved his heart.

"Aye. I did. And I'll be honest, even if you think I'm a fool… I hope I still do."

"I don't think you're a fool. I think you're the kindest man I ever knew."

Feeling tears threaten to well up in his own eyes, Brogan laughed instead.

"Well enough loitering!" Brogan said quickly. "We had better find this breach in the wall before it's too dark and we lose the whole night's progress."

"I haven't found anything yet," said Seamus, who had begun investigating the wall by nuzzling it methodically.

Hatch and Brogan approached it and, not knowing what else to do, began to run their hands along it. Though he'd felt it once before, Hatch was again startled at the soft texture of the surface. It seemed almost alive, quivering with some unknown energy. Leaning his face close to it, Hatch even thought he could hear it humming – not a mechanical hum, but a mysterious and enchanting thrum, like the distant chant of monks in some island monastery. As he walked along the wall, the hum became so distinctive that Hatch wondered how he had missed it on his first visit.

"Hey! I think I've found something!" he shouted, turning back to Brogan and Seamus, who had been walking in the opposite direction.

"What is it?" Seamus asked, bounding toward him. "Did you find the breach?"

"No, not yet. But listen. Do you hear that?"

"Yes…" Seamus was hesitant. "The wall has a bit of a hum, it seems. But that's to be expected, isn't it? The whole wall is sort of… trembling, I suppose."

"Yes, but I didn't hear it before, and it seems to be quieter farther down," Hatch said.

"Nor I," rejoined Brogan, who had joined them. "It seems to grow louder the farther east we get. Bravo Hatch!"

At that, they all three quickened their pace, man boy and cat holding hands and tails against an invisible wall, and making quite a spectacle out of themselves, should anyone have been there to see it. Sure enough, the low murmur of the Wasteland Wall soon became loud enough that they could hear it clearly without leaning close to the wall.

Before long, the resistance against Brogan's palm yielded suddenly, and he nearly fell into the gap in the wall.

"Got it!" he exclaimed unnecessarily.

They all stopped and stared in fascination at the wall, straining their eyes for the slightest sign of variation in the air before them, but to no avail. The breach was as invisible as the wall, detectable only by the chanting song that radiated out from the wound.

At its opening, the crevice was not much taller than a man, and about six feet wide. A few feet in, it grew slightly wider. Brogan was tall enough to touch the low ceiling with his fingers as he entered, but measuring it gave him an odd feeling of confused claustrophobia. He could stare out into clear sky, seeing every ripple in the sand for a mile, even feel the breeze that blew from one side of the Wasteland to the other. He found the illusion of freedom maddening. They would spend their journey constrained to a small, sealed in space, unable able to guess its changes in width or direction ahead of time.

Hatch was feeling the same unease. "Brogan?" he asked timidly for the second time that evening. "The night you... you know... came after me. You got across the Wasteland in one night, didn't you?"

"I did. One long night on horseback."

"I see. And we're on foot."

"On foot and in an invisible tunnel. Thank Ealdor for Seamus. He'll be of great use to you and me in keeping us from jamming our feet against the walls every two minutes. Keeping our heads safe will be up to us."

Hatch smiled weakly. Brogan put a hand on Hatch's shoulder.

"You know, we don't know where that tunnel leads." Brogan said seriously. "We don't know if it narrows til it's completely sealed halfway through. Or becomes too low to travel in anymore. We could end up turning around and starting over. Or getting trapped inside. Are you prepared for that?"

Hatch drew himself up bravely and said in the solemn voice of a child doing his best to behave like a man, "It must be done."

"Well then!" said Brogan, forcing a cheerful air. "Off we go then boys! No time like the present, I always say." For Brogan knew (as I hope you do too, reader) that an unpleasant task should never be postponed.

13

~

THE INTERROGATION

Eldon and his new friends were just settling down to supper when Percival burst into Damascus looking uncharacteristically distressed and clutching a letter in his fist.

"Eldon! It's the children!"

Eldon had been with the Maskies about a week, and had allowed himself to hope the children had made it out of Druinor by now. He had heard nothing from Brogan, but their intelligence suggested that Marlowe had found nothing as well, and he was certain that the children must now be in his friend's care. His initial fear that Brogan had given away their secrets had subsided the instant Marlowe had departed his cell, and he now reproached himself for it. Eldon knew his friend well enough to know that his actions were always cautious and measured, and the chances of him being caught were minimal. At the urgency in Percival's voice, however, Eldon sprang to his feet.

"What? What is it? Did he find them?"

"Not yet. But he's likely to soon." Percival held up the letter. "I've just taken this from the mail coach. Thank the gods we intercepted it before it got to him." From force of habit, Percival touched his right hand to his left collarbone as he said this, in a gesture of respectful thanks to Heaven. "Do you know how difficult it is to steal a letter when you're invisible? The letter doesn't become invisible too, it turns out."

Eldon snatched it from his hand and began to read.

Steven Snyder, Captain, Royal Police Force

To His Eminence, the Honorable Emperor Marlowe,

Your Highness, I beg a brief audience with you on a matter of some importance. It has come to my attention that your Grace has set his eye on two children, namely Molly Morris, of the Town Just West of the River, and Hatch Holland, of The Village Just East of the Bridge. I understand that these individuals have been found guilty of treason to the crown, and further that they are known to be in the company of the proven traitor, Lieutenant Spencer, a former member of this very force. You cannot imagine, my Lord, our deep shame at the Police Station at having served our emperor in the company of this rogue, though I myself never found him the least trustworthy and am glad to have my discernment in this matter confirmed.

I am certain that the matter at hand requires the urgent and personal attention of your devoted servant, and as such have taken it upon myself to discover the whereabouts of these villains. After a meticulous investigation, I believe I have uncovered the possible whereabouts of the girl, who seems to have been interred in the Institute, although the school officials do not yet seem to be aware of her identity.

Of course, I will waste no time in retrieving her and bringing her to justice, after I have verified her identity by means of thorough interrogation. I flatter myself that I do not need to beg your Grace's permission to pursue such a worthy task. I only trouble you to request that, having done so, I may also be allowed to lead the investigation until I have Lt. Spencer and the boy in my custody. I mean no disrespect to Colonel Conway, of course, who is as competent a policeman as could be expected of a man his great age. However, in a matter of such importance, I humbly suggest that I, having no other distractions such as misconduct hearings, will be able to bring these blackguards to justice more swiftly than my counterpart might.

With great deference,

Your humble servant, Capt. Snyder

Eldon finished reading and threw the letter down, groaning. "Molly in the Institute! It can't be! He must be mistaken."

"I doubt he is," Nathaniel said glumly. "I know this Snyder fellow better than I would like. He's a villain, but he's no fool. He'd never have written directly to the emperor if he were unsure."

"The letter really didn't become invisible?" Luke asked, pushing his glasses up on his nose. "That's curious."

Percival shrugged and Eldon shot him a fierce look.

"I don't understand," Tobias interjected. "If Molly's in the Institute, surely we'd have gotten word by now." He looked worried.

"I'm sure our contact will send it at the very first opportunity. You know how hard it is to get messages back and forth," Percival said with a reassuring hand on his shoulder.

"We must get her out," Eldon said firmly. "We have to

find Hatch. And Brogan!"

"That's Lt. Spencer, I presume?" the ever-serene Raymond asked.

"The same."

"It's good news that they've found neither," remarked Percival. "It's likely that means they're together, wherever they are. But either way, we have to find Molly and get her out before we do anything else."

A chorus of voices rose, saying, "Agreed!" "Hear hear!" and "When do we begin?"

"But how?" Eldon asked. "That place is locked down tighter than the palace."

"We've got an inside contact," Tobias said.

So it was that the next night, Nathaniel and Tobias found themselves on the roof of the giant schoolhouse, holding Percival by the ankles as he peered through a top story window, attempting to get the attention of Ava Perry, administrative assistant to Headmistress Bell.

Eldon, much to his frustration, had not been allowed to come. Percival insisted that he was not well-versed in magic enough to penetrate the school's security system. Eldon had blustered and raged at this, but Percival told him the entire operation would be canceled unless Eldon agreed to stay in Damascus. Seeing that he meant it, Eldon conceded, but upon Percival's departure, he commenced pacing so furiously that the rest of the Maskies wished he had been allowed to go after all.

The three who went had a difficult time getting past the barbed wire fences, trained dogs, and roving guards that kept the school's perimeter secure, but once they reached the grounds themselves, it was simply a matter of finding the right window. This was especially crucial since Miss Perry, as Headmistress Bell's assistant, slept in the room adjacent to that frightful woman.

Percival was the smallest of them, which was why he had been chosen to be lowered to the window, though Tobias would have much preferred that office. He tapped lightly on the window and waited, while the two men on the roof strained to keep their hold on his ankles.

After a moment the white face of Miss Perry appeared, framed in the dark window, and the glass raised.

"Percival!" she said joyously.

"Hello darling!" Percival said with a wide grin.

"Don't flirt, Percival, it's not proper," Ava rejoined, and a vicious jerk on his left ankle told him Tobias agreed.

"Why didn't you send word?" Ava asked. "It isn't safe for you to be here. You ought to have sent a message instead."

"Ah, but then Tobias up there wouldn't have got to hear your lovely voice, my dear." Percival joked.

Even in the dark he saw her eyes light up. She leaned out of the window and peered up into the moonlight, hoping to catch a glimpse of the aforementioned fellow on the roof, but of course could not call out to him.

"Besides," Percival was saying. "Sending a message by the usual channels takes too long. We're here on a rather urgent errand."

"Well I'm glad," she said. "I've some very important news as well. What's yours?"

"We need you to find a girl who was think was recently sent to this school. She wouldn't have been admitted through the normal channels, we don't think."

"That's just the child I was going to talk to you about," Ava whispered excitedly. "I'm afraid she's in terrible danger here. They're treating her so poorly, I'm not sure she'll survive."

All this was said very fast, for which Percival was grateful, as his head had begun to throb from carrying on this conversation upside down.

"She's extremely important, and in much more danger than you realize. Marlowe himself is looking for her. When he finds out she's here, she'll wish she could stay."

Ava's eyes widened. To her compassionate heart, this was the worst news.

"Can you help us get to her?" Percival asked.

"As if you have to ask."

"It'll be dangerous," he warned, though he knew it wasn't necessary.

"It always is," Ava said with a wry smile.

They both heard a noise from inside the school and froze. After a few seconds, when no further sounds followed, Ava relaxed.

"I'd better go," she whispered. "Can you come back tomorrow night?"

"I don't think we've got anything else on the schedule," Percival said.

As he spoke, his comrades began lifting him up so that he was no longer aligned with the window frame. He caught her hand as he departed and gave it a friendly squeeze before disappearing from view.

When the Maskies returned to Damascus that night, Eldon was relieved to find that Molly had a friend inside the school, but his heart broke at the news of her treatment, which Percival had relayed to him kindly but honestly. He dearly hoped that when the Maskies returned the next night, Ava would have secreted Molly up to her room and they could escape with her then and there. But alas, it was not to be.

It took the men longer to break onto the grounds that second night. Perhaps evidence of their previous trespass had been noticed by someone on the faculty. Whatever the reason, security had been heightened. A guard patrol seemed to appear every two minutes and the whole lawn was lit by giant floodlights.

When they finally succeeded in breaching the perimeter and scaling the walls of the school, they were met with disappointment. Percival's repeated tap on Ava's window went unanswered. They waited as long as they could, but she never returned.

The three of them dejectedly made their way home to regroup.

~

What happened inside the school was this.

The very morning after Percival appeared, much to Ava's joy, at her bedroom window, Captain Snyder also appeared much to her dismay at the school's front door.

Ava nervously showed him into Professor Bell's office and hovered outside the door, straining to hear what was said.

"Madam, I hope you'll do me the honor of indulging me for a moment," Snyder said.

"Of course, Captain," Professor Bell answered, in an uncharacteristically smarmy tone she reserved for people she deemed important. "You've come about the truants, I presume? I must say the speed of your response to my request does you credit."

"While your inability to keep track of your students no doubt requires the swift attention of the emperor's police force, I have come on a far more urgent errand."

Bell's voice went cold. "I beg your pardon?"

"I have reason to suspect that the student you believe to be the recovered truant girl is in fact not a student at all, but rather a fugitive from the emperor," Snyder said.

Ava's breath caught in her lungs.

There was a long pause, wherein Bell wrestled within herself. She was torn between her desire to maintain the school's pristine reputation and the desire to see a treacherous child punished by the emperor himself. She hated her students with an intensity that could only be matched by Marlowe himself.

"I see," she said at last. "May I ask what has led you to this conclusion?"

"You may not."

After another pause, Bell finally sighed.

"Very well, Captain," she said stiffly. "But if you are correct, I find myself once again faced with the problem of three missing students. I hope the police force will be so kind as to…"

Snyder cut her off. "Your incompetence is none of my concern. I am here to question the girl. Bring her at once."

Bell glared furiously at the pompous policeman, but nonetheless picked up the telephone on her desk. Within minutes, Molly appeared, in the grasp of a brutish professor who had evidently missed his true calling as a giant block of wood. Snyder was granted permission to interrogate Molly alone, and he lost no time in whisking her away to do just that.

Bell commanded Ava to follow them to the detention room Snyder would use and wait for him to finish, so that afterward Molly could be escorted to the student confinement cells. Ava and Molly were both exceedingly pleased at this command, though neither could think how it would be helpful under the circumstances. Ava only knew that she would not leave without knowing Molly was safe.

So it was that she found herself praying fervently outside

a locked detention room until well after midnight, wondering what was happening to Molly inside. While she waited, Ava took advantage of this rare access to the cell block floor by visiting the cells, and doing her best to aid the poor souls found within. Nearly all of the cells were occupied by Professor Dalton's hapless victims but, foolish man that he was, he had left the keys to each cell on hooks outside the doors.

The first cell she came to was filled with poisonous snakes and the unfortunate student within was suspended above them by some sort of harness hanging from the ceiling. After a little investigation, Ava located a button that opened up grates in the floor and sent the serpents plunging satisfyingly into the dark below. She lowered the student slowly, set him free from his restraints, and quietly sent him off to bed with a motherly kiss on the top of his head. He happened to be one of the more brutish and cruel students on campus, but his look of relief and gratitude was so profound that Ava felt confident she could count on his silence.

In the second cell, a student was writing on every wall and surface. After a quick scan of the room, Ava realized that the young girl was copying a long list of insults and imprecations of her own character, and from the look of her, had been doing so for several days.

"That's enough, dear," Ava said quietly as she stood in the doorway behind her. The girl looked at her pitifully, too exhausted to be startled. Ava reached into her pocket, where she always kept figs and dates and nuts to drop into student satchels, and spent them all on the poor child. She made a mental note that in the future she ought to make an effort to correct the lies the girl had been forced to write. But for now she needed food and water and rest, so Ava sent the girl likewise to bed, with careful advice about how to reach her room unmolested by school guards and other security measures.

When Ava had cleared all the cells, and returned to the classroom, she found the door still infuriatingly closed.

As the night wore on, Ava reminded herself several times that if Snyder were getting whatever information he had come for, the interview would not be lasting so long. This, at least, comforted her.

~

Miss Perry was right that the interrogation was not going as Snyder had envisioned it. He had been quite certain he would have it all out of her in a matter of moments, but then, Snyder had never met a girl like Molly. Had Molly had the remotest idea how badly she was frustrating his plans, she might have reveled in it. But from her perspective, it did not feel like much of a victory – at least not by the end.

Snyder, once he had locked them in, turned to Molly and made his best attempt at sounding sincere.

"Now. You look like a smart child. I think we can agree, it's best if you just tell me what's going on, don't you?" Sincerity did not suit Snyder, and he only managed to sound even more weaselly than usual.

Molly stared at him silently.

"Come now," he prodded, winking at her like a co-conspirator. "It's just you and me in here. You're safe. None of those rotten professors can hear you. Go on, little girl. You can tell me."

Good grief, thought Molly. *I'm twelve, not five.* But still she said nothing.

A better interrogator would have put a little more effort into identifying with her and gaining her trust. There was, however, no better interrogator in the vicinity and Snyder was a man of little patience, so he abruptly switched tactics. Drawing himself up and crossing his arms, he now adopted a straightforward tone as if speaking to an adult criminal.

"Look here," he said. "I can make your life miserable, and don't think that I won't. You'd better spill it all now, or I promise you'll regret it."

Molly, at this moment, seeing that her opponent did not understand the first thing about children, decided to have a bit of fun with this interview. It was a decision we must not blame her for, but one which cost her dearly.

Molly conjured up a look of fear, proving herself a much better actor than he.

"Oh please sir," she whimpered pathetically. "I don't know what you want to know. But I'll tell you anything, so long as I don't have to go to detention!"

Foolish Captain Snyder felt that he was getting somewhere now. He congratulated himself on finding her weak spot so quickly.

"I can't promise you there won't be *any* detention. But if you're *very* good and answer every question, I'll see to it that you don't get more than a week."

To his surprise, Molly barked a laugh.

"I've already got two years of detention," Molly retorted. "I doubt you can do much worse to me than that."

Making him feel foolish only felt good for about half a second, before Molly realized that she ought to have played her hand more carefully. In that careless bit of taunting, she failed to take two things into account: first, that her little trick had betrayed a clever mind, which only served to cement Snyder's conviction that she was a fugitive. Second, and perhaps more importantly for poor Molly, that nobody likes being made to look like a fool. Therefore embarrassing a man whose kindest moments included deciding not to kill people because he might still make money off them, was a dangerous trick at best.

Slamming his fist down on the nearest desk, Snyder leaned close to her, his florid face twisted with rage.

"Just as I thought," the Weasel said, his voice low and seething with hatred. "Miss Molly Morris. Clever little girl from Town West. Look here, you worthless child, I'm not here to play games. I know who you are. I know what you've done. And you had better tell me everything I need to know."

Molly found herself inadvertently leaning away from his foul breath and snarling face. The desk behind her dug into her back painfully.

"I... I don't know what you're talking about," she stammered.

"*Where's the boy?*" Snyder screamed suddenly, grabbing her by her shoulders and shaking her. "*Where is he? Where is that treacherous lowlife, Spencer?*"

Molly stared wide-eyed for a half second, before inexplicably beginning to laugh. Who was this raging lunatic? Who was Spencer? Clearly this man knew who she was, which was very bad news indeed, yet he seemed to be entirely insane. For a moment she entertained the idea that, if he did reveal her identity, no one would take him seriously. However, the laughing only infuriated the deranged captain more and, letting go of her shoulders, he slapped her hard across the face.

Stunned, Molly held one hand to her cheek.

Snyder thought he had surely won at this point, but Molly was just as stubborn as he. He had caught her by surprise, no doubt, but the abuse only served to strengthen her resolve.

No matter what happens, I will not tell this brute anything at all, she said to herself.

The interrogation continued in much the same way for a very long time. Snyder blustered and raged, but to Molly's great relief, he did not strike her again. Perhaps the last tiny shred of decency left in his dried-up bones had awakened to reign him in. Snyder threatened and cursed and shouted, but Molly only stared at him obstinately, or offered wholly accurate but unhelpful answers.

"Where's the boy?"

"There are lots of boys here."

"Where's Spencer?"

"Haven't met that one yet."

"How did you get here?"

"You brought me from upstairs."

"How did you get to the Institute?"

"Extremely bad luck."

He waited in silence for a while after that, hoping to wear her down by hunger and weariness. Whenever she began to nod off, he clapped his hands loudly just next to her face.

It was very late when he had a breakthrough of sorts, though he did not realize it at the time.

"You know," he said casually, as if chatting with a friend, "a little girl in the company of two grown men and a strapping young boy ought to be safe, don't you think?"

She watched him with mild curiosity, wondering where he was going with this.

"I mean, here you are, little Molly Morris, *alone* in the Institute. And where are they? Where are Hatch and Spencer and Holcombe? Running free in the woods, that's where."

As he spoke, Molly felt a tiny knot form in her stomach.

He had somehow hit a raw spot she didn't even know she had.

"And the cats, where are they?" Snyder considered, examining his fingernails as he spoke. "Oh, they're probably having a grand old time. And to think, you grew up thinking Seamus was *your* cat. Ha ha!"

Molly did her best to maintain a disinterested expression, but she could not help but look slightly crestfallen. Snyder saw that her shields were lowered and continued to hammer away.

"Goodness me, did you think he *loved* you?" He laughed heartily at this. "Treacherous spies, all of them. They only ever wanted to use you. They're anti-progs, you know. All they care about is overthrowing our gracious emperor and stopping all the progress in Druinor. They'd rather we all lived in mud huts again."

Perhaps Snyder didn't realize that outside the capital, many people *did* live in mud huts.

"So what was it?" he went on, gaining momentum, driven by the natural intuition of a mean-spirited man. "What great task did they ask you to perform? Oh they probably made it sound very noble, didn't they? Poor, exploited child. Can't believe they'd use a little girl to accomplish their political agenda, and then abandon her to the Institute when she couldn't get it done.

"The thing that really gets me though," Snyder continued, "is the boy. I bet you two were just the best of friends. But when you came to the school you told the headmistress you'd been captured by dwarves right? And then you escaped?"

Molly was beginning to feel sick.

"*You* escaped from a pack of dwarves? But the boy you were with couldn't? You know what I think?" A wicked grin was beginning to spread itself across Snyder's face. "I think he didn't even try. He probably saw you get nabbed by the truant officers, eh? Didn't want any part of that, so he just let you go."

"No!" Molly shouted. "You're wrong! He would *never* do that, you're a liar!"

Of course, the Weasel's words *were* lies as you know, but they stirred something in the back of Molly's mind. She remembered how she'd tried to save Hatch, how she'd been sure he'd find a way to get out himself, and how she had waited all night outside the mouth of the cave for him. Waited, in fact, until she'd been caught and put in this wretched school. And she began to wonder...

Snyder saw at once that he'd found a foothold.

"You see Molly?" he said. "You're all alone. You might as well stop protecting the rest of that lot. They're not your friends. You have no friends."

Molly didn't tell him anything. In fact, she spoke not one more word that night, and Snyder eventually gave up in frustration.

He demanded that Miss Perry leave Molly in the holding cell. He had found her weakness and was certain he could wear her resistance down with a few more days of that treatment. Perhaps she just needed a few nights in solitary confinement to convince her that she was really alone.

So Molly was, in a sense, victorious. She had gone up against a full-grown man, one trained in methods of interrogation at that, and had bested him. Still, more damage had been done to her poor soul than she was willing to admit.

Be warned, dear reader. Never give ear to what your enemy has to say about your friends.

14

~

A TRAGIC TURN OF EVENTS

Traveling in the Wasteland was an experience Hatch would not soon forget. He had wondered if the tunnels would become visible once the travelers were inside them, but the illusion of expansive skies and mirrored sands was not the least degraded by their new perspective. They could see for miles, could feel the breeze and the heat of the sun, but were restrained in their movements to a path no wider than the length of Brogan's body.

Travel was slow. They walked by night and by day they slept in the shade of a canvas shelter Brogan put up each morning. To avoid sunstroke or worse, the travelers had to change its orientation several times throughout the day, and between this and the suffocating heat, the days were far from restful. They were all extremely grateful each evening when the sands began to cool and the breeze picked up.

The group made halting progress, as they were forced to hold their arms up to feel the height of the ceiling, and gingerly feel their way forward. Like any crack in a sheet of glass, this crevice was jagged, often turning sharply, sometimes narrowing drastically so that they had to walk single file. Brogan became very nervous when this happened. Hatch, too, often felt his throat constrict and his breathing become shallow. Only Seamus seemed relatively unfazed.

To pass the time, Brogan told Seamus and Hatch about Arden. He described the courts of King Mardius, its lords and its ladies, the traditional harvest festivals of the villages, and the tribe of fierce but beautiful maiden warriors who passed from town to town, dancing and singing as they went. Eventually the conversation turned to Abner, whom Hatch had wondered about more than once since meeting him. "How is he able to fly around?" Hatch asked. "And why doesn't he just fly back to Arden and carry messages back and forth?"

"Well, Abner is a unique sort of fellow," Brogan replied. "I suppose you would call him a prophet. Even back when he lived in Arden, he always liked to travel from place to place. He said the feel of a new place helped him clear his head and made his second sight keener. He has to move his house with him, but to do so takes a great amount of focus, and ages him significantly each time."

"He's much younger than he looks," Seamus said.

"Yes," agreed Brogan, a little sadly. "He tends to stay in one place for long periods of times these days. That's why he seemed a bit disgruntled when we met him the other day. It was no small sacrifice to come and find us."

"But why doesn't Abner just stay in Arden?" Hatch pressed.

"Unfortunately, our dear friend was on the wrong side of the wall when it appeared. Theoretically he *could* get back, but the intensity of focus required to pass over the Wasteland would likely kill him. The cost in years would be too great to chance it." Brogan explained.

"Then why not just travel on foot and move into a new house?"

Brogan shrugged. "I asked him that once too. He just said, 'This is my house' and left it at that."

"Don't worry about Abner," Seamus said gently. "Traveling is hard on him, but he wouldn't have come if he didn't know it was worth the cost."

"It's not *him* I'm worried about so much as his advice," Hatch said grimly.

Seamus saw at once what he meant. "His prophecies are never precise – he sees as if looking through a glass, dimly – but they are always accurate. Never once has his advice been bad," the cat said.

This eased Hatch's mind, but only a very little.

On their third night in the Wasteland, they encountered a narrow spot that seemed to go on much longer than the others. They talked very little that night, as Hatch focused all his attention on not hyperventilating, and Brogan attempted to stave off his increasing fear that the tunnel might soon narrow to a dead end. They shuffled and waited and hoped for the path to expand before them again, but it did not. The travelers were forced to walk until late into the morning, as there was no feasible way to set up the shelter in the slender stretch of the fracture they traversed.

Finally, though, at about ten o'clock, Hatch was trudging dejectedly along, feeling the walls brush lightly against each shoulder, when quite suddenly they fell away on both sides. Startled, he stopped and slowly lifted both arms (one learned to be cautious with one's limbs in the presence of invisible walls) until they were fully stretched out on both sides. His fingers made no contact with the magical surface, by which he had been so fascinated a few short days before, but had since learned to hate. This newfound liberty was so dizzyingly wonderful that he thought for a moment he might burst into tears. Looking up at Brogan he was relieved to see he wasn't alone. The man's eyes were shining too as he began to set up the tent.

"We're not out yet," Seamus said, having walked the width of the path to determine that the walls were, in fact, still present if a bit farther away. "But I daresay this stretch of path will be a bit more comfortable for you two."

"We ought to have been there by now," Brogan fretted. "It did only take me the one night all those years ago, you know."

"You would've crossed in a different part of the Wasteland entirely," Seamus reminded him. "It's not the exact same distance from every spot, you know."

"I suppose you're right," Brogan said as he drove in the tent stakes. But he still looked concerned, and that made Hatch concerned too.

⸎

Having once been a student of the Institute himself, Snyder had no desire to stay on school property any longer than necessary. Nevertheless, he chose to leave Molly confined there for the time being, and out of range of any nosy colleagues on the capital police force. As he made his exit, he thought only of his pounding headache and the location of the nearest pub. The school was quiet at that hour. Most likely, Ava and Molly were the only two occupants still stirring except for the night guards, who tipped their hats to him as he made his way out of the imposing doors into the warm quiet of the night and across the grounds to the stables to retrieve his horse. The sound of the animal's hooves proceeding down the long driveway was the only interruption of that night's tranquility.

෴

One reason cats make such excellent spies is their ability to move quickly, silently, and in very small places. They actually enjoy tight fits, which is why Seamus was not perturbed by the constricting walls of the Wasteland tunnel. Nor was Melody nearly so uncomfortable as you and I would have been, squashed behind a potted plant on the steps of the great schoolhouse.

When the Weasel stepped outside those imposing doors into the warm quiet of the night, Melody dashed through the opening he left.

She found herself in the same massive hallway that Molly had marveled at a few weeks earlier, but was herself unimpressed. As a defected government agent, she had learned to appreciate the difference between things that are truly large and those that make themselves look large to hide their abominable smallness. It was not unusual for government officials of different sorts, including quite a few cats, to visit the Institute, so she knew that had she been wandering the halls during the day, she would have aroused little suspicion. In the middle of the night, however, she would need to be very cautious.

Melody, as you will remember, had been sent forth from Abner's house to find Eldon and only *then* to come in search of Molly. As we have seen, however, cats have extremely sharp intuition which, when employed in the service of good rather than evil, can be extremely useful. On her way back to the capital she had to pass the Institute and that impulse which drives good cats to do great things led her to the school's front door. We must attribute at least part of her very good luck inside the school to that same instinct. She knew not where she was going, nor was she led by magic or anything mystical, but as she navigated the hallways, she rarely faltered or questioned any of her decisions, and within a quarter of an hour, Melody had found both the holding cells, and Ava and Molly weeping together outside them.

Neither heard Melody approach, and both gave a terrible start when the cat's voice interrupted them, but to their credit, neither of them screamed.

"Molly. It's me, dear. I've come to find you."

For the next moment or so, everything was embraces and purring and tears, both human and feline. But Ava knew they had better not be out in the hallway for long, so she opened one of the holding cells and ushered them inside it, closing the door behind them but being careful not to lock it.

"How did you find me?" Molly exclaimed, drying her face. At once she felt foolish for listening to that awful man and doubting her friends. "Where's Hatch? Is he here too?"

"He's gone on to Arden. You're to meet him there. He sent me to come get you."

Molly's face fell. "Gone on... without me?"

"He had very little choice. Molly, you've got to trust me," Melody said softly, recognizing a dangerous twinge in Molly's voice. "We have to get you out of here right away."

Turning to Ava, she asked, "The policeman who just left the school... who was he?"

Ava shuddered. "Captain Snyder. He knows who Molly is. He's trying to find the boy... Hatch is his name?" She said this last bit to Molly, who nodded.

"Did you tell him anything?" Melody asked kindly.

"No. But he'll be back. And I'm afraid…" Molly bravely swallowed a few sobs before continuing. "I don't know how much longer I can stand this."

Melody looked back and forth between them. "We need to get you out immediately. Before he comes back. But how? They're watching everything and the grounds are heavily guarded."

"I know a way," Ava said. "Do you know how to get to Kalgren prison?"

༄

So it was that before the sun rose that morning, a bedraggled white cat, having made her way through miles of underground tunnels, scratched at the door of Damascus. She was greeted (not unexpectedly) by the tips of two swords and the barrel of one gun, while three shocked faces stared down at her from the doorway.

"I was sent by Ava Perry," she said. This helped the situation greatly. The men were still highly cautious but they allowed her in and agreed not to kill her while she explained herself.

She allowed Harmon to serve her some water, but refused his offer of food, saying "We have no time to waste. I need to talk to Percival and Tobias immediately. And Eldon, of course, if he's here."

The three of them were roused from sleep at once. Eldon was surprised and delighted to see Melody in the common room. She quickly explained everything that had happened since they had last seen each other while the Maskies listened with keen interest, frequently interrupting to ask questions.

"How did she escape from the dwarves?"

"Why didn't Hatch get out too?"

"Where is the Alice girl now? I'll give her a piece of my mind!"

It was Joel who said this last, and for several minutes he would not be persuaded that finding Alice and giving her a good scolding was not high on the list of priorities. Joel was a generally mild man, but his sense of injustice, once stirred, was not easily subdued. Eldon had come to feel that Joel, by far the most hot headed and impetuous of the Maskies, was a kindred spirit.

The rest of the Maskies were particularly interested in Melody's encounter with Abner and the discoveries made thereby.

"There are *cracks* in the Wasteland Wall? What do you mean?" Percival asked, astonished.

Finally, after many more interruptions of this kind, they allowed Melody to finish her speech. Once Molly's current plight was made known, the urgency of the situation commanded their full attention.

The Maskies decided that it would be impossible to contact Ava by traditional methods, and certainly not by those they had employed the last few nights. If they did not make their move this very morning it would be too late. The plan they hatched was bold and fraught with danger, both of which were fairly common traits of Damascus Guard plans. Tobias, Nathaniel and Percival, having made the trek to the school the previous two nights, now felt themselves too invested in Molly's fate to stay home and insisted on being members of the extraction team. Eldon, of course, would not hear of being left behind, and was deaf to his comrades' objections that his face was too well-known to participate in such a high-profile operation.

"I'll wear a disguise," he said dismissively. "Besides, they all think I'm dead. They won't be looking for me."

Seeing that he would not be dissuaded, Percival consented and the plot was formed. They would march openly up to the school that very morning dressed as a police squad, under the pretense of arresting Molly. In the wake of Snyder's visit, this would not be alarming to the faculty. Of course, the Damascus Guard had acquired several police uniforms and accoutrements over their years as renegades. Having thus attired themselves, and once they'd convincing Nathaniel to stop admiring his costume in the mirror, they set out at once to retrieve our little heroine.

⌒

Professor Bell was annoyed. Miss Perry had not arrived at her desk that morning, and there were several errands she wanted the woman to run immediately. None of them were urgent, but Professor Bell was in the habit of having her desires catered to instantaneously. It never crossed her mind that Miss Perry might still be with Molly, as her concern about the girl's situation was not enough even to warrant remembering it the next morning.

The headmistress was scowling out the window of her office, looking not unlike a spoiled child who has been denied candy and planning all the cruel punishments she would soon inflict upon her tardy secretary, when four men on horseback appeared in the gated entrance of the school grounds. Bell could see by their demeanors that whatever brought them to her door was of some importance, and by their uniforms, guessed what it was.

Will that wretched Alice never cease disturbing my days? She thought. The Weasel had informed her, of course, that it was not Alice whom she had captured in the wood, but this detail did not seem significant enough to merit calling the child by her real name. One brat was much the same as another. The only real difference to Bell was that she now had the opportunity to find and punish the real Alice (as well as Rob and Ben), something she greatly looked forward to.

Sighing at her misfortune in having to deal with the other Alice, who was proving to be quite a nuisance, Bell waited patiently in her office until she heard the boots of the four men approaching. The men were quickly ushered in by a timid house maid who had undertaken the task in Miss Perry's increasingly irksome absence. The headmistress rose to greet them with none of the condescending charm with which she had welcomed Snyder the previous day.

"Shall I expect the police to disrupt my students' education on a daily basis?" she snapped. "Perhaps we can spare an office for you, to save you the trouble of coming all this way."

"That won't be necessary, professor," said the one who seemed to be their leader. "We've come to arrest Molly Morris. Take us to her at once."

"Good heavens, then be quick about it. Good riddance if you ask me. I hope you've a stiff punishment in store for her. The stocks perhaps, or Kalgren, or both!"

Bell did not notice one of the policemen clenching his fists and glaring at her. The first officer did, however, and quickly stepped in front of him.

"We do apologize for disrupting classes, Madam. Show us where she is and we'll be gone in no time."

"Bertha, take these men..." Bell began, but she paused, realizing that Bertha had slunk away the moment the officers had been delivered to the headmistress' door. She sighed again as one greatly wronged, and threw up her hands. "Oh very well, I'll take you myself. Follow me please."

She briskly stepped into the hallway. The group walked down several halls and squeezed into an elevator together, plunging into the bowels of the school. They emerged several floors below ground, and found the holding cells, all but one of which was empty (much to the headmistress' consternation). In the last one they found Molly and Ava curled on the floor together, peacefully asleep.

"What on *earth*..." Bell screeched. At the sound of her shrill voice both the cell's occupants started awake and leapt to their feet in bleary-eyed confusion.

"What is the meaning of this, Miss Perry?" the headmistress asked, shaking with rage. "Why you ungrateful, traitorous woman! When I finish with you..."

She gathered Miss Perry's hair in her fist and began to drag her from the room.

"That is *enough* Madam!" Percival bellowed. "You will unhand that young lady at once."

Professor Bell looked mightily affronted, but did loosen her grip on Ava's hair.

"This woman will be coming with us as well," spoke up another officer, who was careful not to make eye contact with the girl in question. "Clearly, she has knowledge of this investigation and will need to be interrogated."

"You do not have the right to take my staff out of this building," Bell bristled. "She is *mine* to deal with as I please."

The officer who had spoken stepped forward so that his face was very close to Bell's. She was accustomed to being the intimidating one, and involuntarily took a step back.

"Professor Bell," the man said quietly. "We are here on behalf of the emperor himself. If you kept abreast of current events, as I would have expected the headmistress of a prestigious school to do, you would have realized who

Molly Morris was when she arrived and turned her in yourself. Whether your failure to do so was incompetence or treason remains to be seen. I assure you that it will be thoroughly investigated. In the meantime, if you have any desire to remain headmistress of this school, you will hand over *both* of these fugitives and impede our business no more."

Bell was cowed as she had never been before. Her face had paled and her grip slackened enough during this speech that Ava was able to regain ownership of her hair. Nathaniel, who stood off to the side, grasped her elbow and pulled her out of the headmistress' reach.

"Very well then," Bell said, attempting to maintain whatever composure she had left. Turning to Ava she added spitefully, "If anyone here is guilty of treason it's *you*, and I assure you, I will do everything in my power to expedite your prosecution."

With that she turned on her heel and marched out, leaving the policemen to find their own way.

Ava and the Maskies were all brimming with joy to see one another. Molly hadn't yet realized who her rescuers were, but they wasted no time on greetings, except that Tobias kissed Ava's cheek tenderly and whispered something in her ear that the others couldn't hear, while Eldon tearfully embraced Molly.

After a hurried explanation, the men handcuffed Molly and Ava and made their way back to the entrance hall, where servants waited with their horses. Hardly daring to believe that their plan had worked, Eldon lifted Molly onto his own horse, and was preparing to swing up behind her, when a man's voice stopped them all in their tracks.

"What's going on here?" Captain Snyder asked, looking from one of them to the next. "What treason is this?"

Eldon, Nathaniel, and Tobias quickly drew revolvers from under their coats and aimed them at Snyder, while Percival, who been about to help a handcuffed Ava onto his horse, drew his sword. Snyder had, likewise, drawn his firearm, but seeing that he was outgunned, he pointed it at Molly instead of the men.

"That girl goes with me," he said boldly. "You can kill me if you like, but she'll die too."

During the silence followed this ultimatum, the Maskies weighed their options. Unless they could disarm Snyder, Ava realized, they stood no chance of escaping with all their lives, especially with her and Molly still bound at the wrists. Without wasting time to think about the prudence of her actions, she hurled herself at the Weasel, hitting him square in the chest with such force that both tumbled to the ground.

Eldon and the Maskies instantly sprang into action. Tobias rushed forward to pull Ava off Snyder, while Nathaniel and Percival wrestled him back to the turf. In the confusion two guns were fired, one Snyder's and the other Eldon's, but only one found its mark. Molly dove sideways off the horse at the sound of gunfire, and felt the sickening crack of her still restrained arm as she landed on it.

Just as suddenly as the melee had begun, it was over. Ava looked on in horror as Tobias knelt next to where Eldon lay motionless, blood seeping through the folds of his tunic and covering Tobias' hands. They had no time to mourn, however. The servants were, no doubt, calling the *real* capital police even now.

Nathaniel used the butt of his pistol to render Snyder unconscious, then bound him tightly before loosing Ava's wrists. Molly screamed in pain as Percival lifted her back onto the horse and swung up behind her. Ava mounted

Eldon's horse, and they thundered out of the gates of the school. Tobias rode expertly with Eldon's body draped over his horse in front of him, while Snyder occupied the same place on Nathaniel's mount.

The Maskies rode deeper into the woods for quite some time to be sure they were not pursued, before stopping just long enough to rid themselves of Snyder. They were not the type to kill an unconscious man in cold blood, but neither did they intend to lead him to Damascus. They left him alive, but still bound. Deciding that they would draw too much attention if they re-entered the city in their current state, the group headed instead toward the cabin Eldon had fondly described as the last place he had seen Molly.

15

MOLLY WITH THE MASKIES

The only things that saved Molly from inconsolable grief were Ava's calming presence, and the throbbing pain of her broken arm. Other than Hatch and the cats, Eldon and Ava had been her only friends. The former had rescued her from the oppression of Druinor and given her purpose, while the other had borne her up through weeks of misery in the Institute.

The Maskies were grief-stricken as well. They, too, had only known Eldon for a brief period of time, but he was the kind of man that inspired affection and camaraderie among all who knew him.

It was a bittersweet party that occupied the cabin that night. They gathered around the fire, all grateful to have snatched Molly from the grip of Marlowe, but grieving the loss of their brave comrade. But they were of the company of the faithful, as some of you may also be – they did not sorrow as those who have no hope, for they were certain to see him again.

Tobias bound Molly's arm in a makeshift sling, and they talked and laughed about their memories of Eldon, his incorrigible impulsiveness and his kindness, his best traits and his worst, for they did not believe that it honors the dead to lie about them. Molly listened eagerly to the tale of Eldon's escape from prison, of his furious concern for her and Hatch, and his restlessness as he waited for news of them. These insights into the soul of her beloved friend made her feel as if she was coming to know him better than she ever had before. The Maskies were just as eager to hear of her brief acquaintance with Eldon, and when Molly spoke of how he had spent twelve years watching over her while cut off from his homeland, Ava's eyes filled with warm tears.

It was summarily decided that the best thing for Molly would be a good night's sleep, and she was allowed a little wine to this end. The Maskies stayed up and talked with her until she fell into a fitful sleep by the fire, then crept into another room and fell to more serious discussion.

In the morning, they held a brief funeral for Eldon. Molly had woken in a cold sweat and her arm felt as though it was in a molten vice, but still she stayed devotedly at her friend's side until he was gently laid to rest by Tobias and Nathaniel. They dug Eldon's grave by hand, but they adorned it by magic, causing all manner of lovely wildflowers to spring up around it in vibrant hues of orange and purple and a bright, cheerful blue. Percival recited the Entreaty for Divine Mercy, and the entire company wept beside the newly grown flower bed. Molly stood holding Ava's hand on one side and Tobias' on the other. They each plucked a flower in their favorite color – Molly chose a vivid, fiery orange that faded to pink – and all those assembled put it in a breast pocket, except Molly, who put hers in her hair.

Though she was immensely grateful for the presence of the Maskies, Molly felt herself unmoored as she watched the one tie that bound her to Arden and to Druinor, to Hatch, the cats, and her supposed destiny, disappear between the fresh earth and flowers, and found herself injured and alone in the company of strangers. She clung tightly to Ava throughout the journey that followed.

When the ceremony was complete, the Maskies and their new companion cautiously made their way to the outskirts of the city, where one of their many tunnel entrances lay and headed back to Damascus.

The fever Molly had awakened with worsened on the way. Her broken arm quickly became swollen and burning to the touch, and by the time the little party reached their fortress, she had become too weak to walk. The men soon had to take turns carrying her.

Damascus was a somber place that night, as the small group relayed the news of Eldon's death to the rest of the Maskies. Harmon, with a patient gentleness that his rough hands belied, set her arm and bound it tightly to give it the best chance of healing. Molly bravely endured this, only whimpering a little, but when it was done, the normally stoic Luke had concerned tears in his eyes. On seeing Molly's condition, Raymond immediately went and fetched his wife, to come and care for her.

Martha was a plump, matronly woman with kind eyes. She was both a skilled healer and exceedingly practical, so she fell to making soup and tonics at once, brightening the gloomy room with her humming as she did. The hearty soup brought some color back to Molly's cheeks. Wholesome homemade meals often do make a world of difference to a youth deprived of sustenance both spiritual and physical. Molly slept peacefully after this, and the

Maskies began to reassure themselves that she would be well on the way to recovery by morning.

But when morning broke, the fever had heightened once again, and her complexion, so briefly improved by Martha's ministrations, had returned to the waxy pallor of the previous evening. Ava sat devotedly by Molly's bedside, monitoring her for any sign of change as she tossed and turned, and muttered incoherently.

"She shouldn't be here," Martha told Percival as he consulted her over coffee. "This is no place for a sick child. It's alright for you men, but she hasn't the constitution for it."

"We can't exactly parade her around in the sunlight, you know," said Wes, who was standing nearby. Wes was the quickest of them to turn everything into a joke, but he got a bit out of sorts when things needed to be taken seriously. "Though I don't deny some sunlight would do the poor girl a world of good."

"Not *this* sunlight, though," Regan noted with a shudder. "Marlowe must be in a mood. The sun's as sick as she is."

It was true that the weather had been particularly ill these past weeks, though it wasn't due to storms or rain. Marlowe's arcane influence was so great, especially inside the capital, that the climate often adopted some of his temperament. On this particular day there were no clouds, but the very air was tainted with Marlowe's ire, so that the sun's harsh rays, far from bringing comfort and health, left many a laborer with a pounding head and seared skin.

"A mood indeed. A *rage* more like," said Joel, who had been in something of a mood himself since learning of Molly's internment at the school. An action-oriented man, he did not like to feel helpless, as all of them had of late. "His lordship is not accustomed to being thwarted, it seems. Least of all by children."

"It'll do him a great deal of good!" Martha said cheerfully.

Raymond looked at her affectionately. "I doubt very much whether there's any good left to be done to him, my dear."

"I am sure you're right, love. But there's still breath in his lungs you know."

Raymond kissed the top of her head and poured more coffee.

Nathaniel had been listening to this exchange thoughtfully.

"I suppose there's only one thing to do, then," he said decisively. Everyone looked at him. "We must get her to Arden immediately."

Percival, who had been absent-mindedly stroking Melody's head as he listened, looked up with a laugh. "And how, pray tell, are we to do that? You know she could never make the journey through the Wasteland, even if we *could* find the cracks Melody spoke of."

"I am well aware of that, Percival," said Nathaniel. "But we can't leave her here in this cave, you've said so yourselves. The sun won't do her any good, and it isn't safe to be in it anyhow. Besides which, if Marlowe's in the state you say he's in, nowhere in Druinor is safe for the girl. Arden is our only option."

"These are all fine points, but they still fail to address the tiny little detail of *how* in the name of sanity such a feat could be accomplished," Percival answered.

"I know how," Melody said quietly. "We must get her to Abner at once."

⌒

Molly was dreaming again, but not like she had in the past. These dreams were borne on the back of a raging fever, poisoned by the treacherous winds of Druinor. They had none of the charming whimsy those fancies of her recent childhood had boasted.

While the grown-ups discussed their plans in the common room, Molly found monsters round every corner. Each shadow hid a malevolent spirit, and looming over the horizon, his otherworldly eyes locked on her in a baleful stare, was Marlowe himself. Molly had never seen the emperor, but she had no doubt it was he. His cloaked silhouette towered over her, eclipsing the sun and blocking every path to escape. She tried to cry out but, as is so often the case in nightmares, no sound escaped her lips. The spidery fingers of Marlowe's giant hand were curled around an object that she couldn't quite make out, which hung limply from his fist like the carcass of a wild animal. His ghastly eyes, which watered but never blinked, narrowed as he raised his free hand and extended his finger toward her.

Suddenly the dream changed and Molly found herself standing on the edge of a steep precipice. Behind her, there was nothing but wind and sand. The air was orange as sunset, but there was no sun, only a cloudless sky. The earth fell away sharply just past where she stood. Compelled by some nameless impulse, Molly leaned out to peer into the canyon below but she could see no floor, only endless miles of smooth rock, as though someone had sliced that part of the earth off with a knife.

Just then, something caught her eye. Just below where she stood, something glinted on the cliff face, like a gem struck by sunlight. Knowing it was foolish, she leaned out farther still, straining her eyes to see what treasure was embedded there. She lost her footing and would have toppled over and plunged to her death, had not Eldon caught her round the waist and hurled her away from the edge, slipping on the loose gravel as he did so and falling backward. He tried to catch himself, but it was too late. Molly saw his terrified eyes pleading for help as he disappeared into the abyss below.

~

When it had been universally agreed that Molly must be taken to Abner straightaway, a plan was quickly formed. Wes suggested taking the tunnels to one of their spots well outside the city and going the rest of the way on foot, but Percival and Ava agreed that the journey was too long to be made on foot, especially with Molly in her current state. She had awakened screaming throughout the night and Ava felt an increasing sense of urgency to remove her from the capital city. The only alternative was to go straight through the city in broad daylight and hope they could make it to Philip's stables, where their horses were kept, before leaving the city on horseback.

"Of course, there will be guards at the borders," Joel pointed out, "but it shouldn't be too hard to get past them with a little sleight of hand and a bit of magic."

It had to be a small group that went, but every one of those mighty men felt a tender sense of responsibility for their young charge and it took quite a bit of discussion to determine who would go. Finally, the Maskies settled on Ava, Percival, and Tobias. Despite their protestations, Martha insisted on going too, as Molly's attending physician, and would not hear a word of dissent on the subject. Raymond put up a bit of a fight, but he was secretly very proud of his wife's bravery and knew perfectly well that she could hold her own in any situation, so he was quickly persuaded.

They dressed as well-to-do, if heavily armed, businessmen

from the upper quarter of the city, banking on the appearance of status to ward off any prying eyes, and set out. Tobias carried Molly in his arms till they emerged in the weary sunlight.

"Do you think you can walk, dear?" He asked gently. "Only for a little while."

Molly nodded weakly and he carefully set her down. Percival swung a frilled cloak over her to hide her face. As they made their way to the stables, the group encountered only disinterested workers carrying out their mundane tasks. Druinians were rarely enthusiastic, but they appeared to be even more dreary than usual today. It seemed a heavy pall had fallen on the city which everyone could sense, though not, in most cases, consciously.

They made it to the stables with no trouble and Ava was relieved to set Molly on horseback and clamber up behind her. The girl leaned against her chest as they rode toward the edge of the city.

It was here that they encountered the first obstacle on their journey. A small roaming patrol caught sight of them as they neared the commerce region and called for them to halt and be examined. Percival produced the necessary paperwork, skillfully forged by the studious and careful hand of Luke, to grant them access to the area.

The patrolman nodded lethargically and was on the verge of waving them on when another policeman interjected, "What's wrong with the girl?"

"She's sick, obviously," said Ava. "We're taking her to the hospital."

"Shouldn't the school faculty be doing that?" the policeman asked suspiciously. It was well known that the Institute faculty had the final say in any decisions related to child welfare. Parents were strictly forbidden from interfering, not that any of them would have tried.

"Naturally," Martha piped up, in the crass tone of a Druinian businesswoman. "But as the whole school's caught up in some important progress exercise, they sent for us to fetch her instead. Normally we wouldn't have bothered, but since we were headed this way anyway, we thought we might as well make a penny or two for the road."

The cop laughed at this, though it wasn't particularly funny. "A progress exercise, eh? Wonder what they'll come up with this time."

Everyone in the city remembered the last school-wide progress exercise, which had resulted in a whole new set of laws prohibiting all manner of things, from drinking orange juice on Fridays, to questioning the existence of anti-progs.

"It'll be just as brilliant as the last time, I've no doubt" Ava smiled sweetly and nudged her horse into motion. Tobias, taking her cue, tipped his hat and moved on. The rest of the Maskies quickly followed suit.

They were careful not to quicken their pace until they were well out of sight of the cops. The moment they were past the city's border, however, they broke into a full-on sprint, hoping they were headed in the right direction. As you know, reader, it was Abner who determined when and where he would be found once a person had set out to find him.

16

ABNER PERFORMS A SERVICE

Fortunately for our heroes, Abner was keenly interested in Molly's fate, and had kept his second sight trained on the situation. He found the little party with hardly any trouble.

"I know what we're asking of you," Percival said as they sat around Abner's supper table that night, "and that you don't know us from a tankernut tree and we've no right to ask it." Martha had brought Molly's supper to the quiet room where she was resting. This was just as well, since she would not have been pleased to find herself in the company of the treacherous Alice at the dinner table. The Maskies had made Abner's acquaintance only an hour previously, but as Eldon's friend, Melody's recommendation carried great weight with the old seer.

Abner shrugged good naturedly. "I'm an old man, if not in years, certainly in body. It is the duty of the old to protect the young. Besides," he said, "all the best services done to mankind cost the doer something, you know."

Percival nodded. "For this service, we will be forever in your debt."

"What are we to do with the children, though?" Martha asked. "If we return them to their parents, they'll just be sent right back to the Institute."

Rob, Ben, and Alice, who were accustomed by now to having no say in their fate, listened to this conversation placidly. They had not yet been with Abner long enough to have gained the full benefits of his influence, but their manners had certainly improved. Alice even shook hands with the new adults and said "pleased to meet you," in a tone that bore only the slightest sullen twinge. Ben, for his part, was looking less like a Druinian child every day, though of course only Melody and Abner could testify to the difference. It seemed that Marlowe's magic was losing some of its grip.

"Well," Percival said at length, "as they've been privy to more than a few of our plans, I'm afraid they will have to be prisoners of war for now."

"Prisoners of war!" spluttered Martha, who could see nothing but three small, frightened children.

"*Which means…*" Percival continued determinedly, "that they are under our protection for the time being, until they can safely be returned to their families without jeopardizing the mission. I had hoped, Martha, that you would be willing to act as their warden, seeing as you are by far the most suited to the job."

"Oh I see," said Martha, duly mollified. "Yes, that's a very wise plan of course."

Percival smiled and bowed slightly before speaking again. "Now then! About the business at hand. Ava, I know that you have commitments here, and it's a lot to ask, but I wonder if you'd be willing to travel with Molly. She seems to have come to depend on you."

Before she could answer, Abner interjected. "I wish it were possible, but I am afraid I can only take one. I fear I may find even that too taxing."

"I see." Percival said. He seemed to be genuinely grieved by this news, but Tobias wore an expression of guilty relief.

Nathaniel, in a moment of uncharacteristic thoughtfulness, turned to Abner and said, "Will you make sure they know in Arden? About Eldon? About how bravely and faithfully he served?"

Abner looked as if he didn't trust himself to speak, but he nodded silently. He and Eldon had been old friends.

When it was at last time to go, Ava went to the room where Molly lay, feverish and half-coherent, and bid her goodbye. She kissed her forehead with tears in her eyes, feeling as if her own daughter was leaving her.

On her way back downstairs, Ava stopped in the kitchen to kiss Abner on the cheek as well, before ushering everyone else out of the house. Once the Maskies and their new young charges were all outside, they turned back to the house and waited expectantly to see what would happen.

Abner strode upstairs to Molly's room and, kneeling beside her, took both her small hands in his wrinkled ones.

"Now my dear," he said kindly. "You must try not to be afraid. This part is a bit tricky."

As he said it, the house began to shake violently, sending dishes and books flying off the shelves. It seemed as if the walls might cave in and the roof be torn off at any moment. Abner himself focused intently on Molly, a pained but steady look on his face.

The spectators outside didn't see the contortions of the house. In fact, they didn't see anything at all, not even the house's disappearance. Though they watched it raptly, none could tell at which point it vanished. They only realized, after a while, that they were staring at an empty clearing, at which point they all shook their heads as though they had woken from a dream.

౿

Hatch dreamed of dwarves that mutated into grotesque gremlins, meeting him at every turn of the Wasteland wall. He could see Molly behind them, and strained to reach her but the monsters blocked his way and laughed as they did. He called to her, but one of the goblins put his hands over her ears, whispering something between his own misshapen fingers. Hatch awoke in a pool of sweat that formed salty coastlines on his bedroll as the air cooled. Brogan and Seamus had also slept fitfully and were in poor spirits as they packed up their gear, ate a quick supper and set out for the evening's travels. They talked very little.

Brogan's face bore the marks of worry and exhaustion. They were out of water and food, and he knew that if they didn't reach Arden soon, they wouldn't reach it at all. He did his best not to let on to Hatch and Seamus, realizing that those he traveled with were enduring just as great a trial as he.

It is not uncommon, though, for children to be a great comfort to the adults who are trying to be strong for their sake, and this was the case for Hatch and Brogan. Hatch walked close to him for most of the night, appreciating, even in his dark mood, the space that allowed them to walk side by side. He was becoming more of a man every day. He was now nearly as tall as Brogan and his face was that odd combination of brave and boyish that is common in young men who have had to grow up quickly. Brogan had begun to think of him more as a comrade than a child in his care, and his mere presence uplifted that soldier's soul as they inched forward.

Just as the light began to break over the horizon, Seamus stopped so suddenly that Hatch tripped over him, catching himself just in time to keep from dashing his head against the wall (though, of course, he didn't know that). He had no time to be irritated, however, for he saw at once what had caused Seamus' abrupt halt. Ahead of them, as they would have seen much sooner had they not been traveling under cover of darkness, the sand they had thought would never end, did, and in a very distinct fashion.

A vast expense of trees formed a solid border not 100 yards away, and what trees! Far removed from the weary handful of drooping saplings that made up a Druinian wood, this one seemed to be bursting with life and color. Ash, pine and sequoia rose proudly to stunning heights, while cherry, plum and magnolia wove their flowers between their noble trunks. The canopy shone a resplendent yellow gold brushed by sunlight, that sank to a deep, rich emerald in the lower regions of their branches. Hatch knew at once that a world all its own, full of mystery and drama dwelt between those mighty trunks, from which depths harkened the sound of a thousand woodland creatures, navigating busy lives to which a human could never be privy. What wonders such a wood must hide! And what kind of country must lie beyond it!

This would have been enough to give them all pause, but what now drew their attention was the two men standing between them and the tree line. Their swords were drawn and they stared at the travelers with unabashed disbelief. They, too, were distinctly different from any men Hatch had seen before, though he could see the resemblance in Brogan and Eldon. They carried themselves like warriors, wearing nobility like a badge, and yet seemed to do so without effort, affectation, or even consciousness of it.

Brogan, realizing that they had found Arden at last, and that he was face to face with his own countrymen, could barely hold back tears as he called out to them joyfully.

"Brothers! Men of Arden! We come in peace."

He began to walk cautiously toward them, Hatch and Seamus following closely. This was, understandably, difficult for the Ardenian men to wrap their minds around, having just seen a man, a boy and a cat emerge from what they knew to be an impenetrable barrier. They were guards of the border, instructed to alert the palace at once should there be any sign of the Wasteland Wall lifting. Having patrolled this area for years with no sign of change, however, they were unprepared to cope with the actual event. Their swords remained drawn.

"Who are you?" demanded the taller of the two, directing his question to Brogan but keeping a wary eye on Seamus.

"I'm Brogan Borhagen, formerly Captain of the very guard I presume you serve, separated from my homeland these many years by this accursed wall."

Hatch noticed that Brogan's speech and dialect, always kind and a bit formal, took on a quality he had not yet heard.

The man's eyes widened. "Brogan Borhagen? How can that be? He died twelve years ago."

"Not dead, friend. Simply exiled. It's a long story, which I'll gladly tell. But my companions and I have travelled long and are weary. May we impose on your hospitality for some water, and perhaps food?"

"Of course," said the second man with a solemn bow. "But as soon as you've eaten, I must beg your patience for the discourtesy I'm about to do you. As you know if you once served this guard yourself, we have certain protocols. And, until we can be sure of your identity, I'm afraid I must place you under arrest."

"Naturally," Brogan said good humoredly.

"You must be brought to the King straightaway," the second man added.

"That would be greatly appreciated," Brogan answered.

Hatch had never been arrested before, but he thought that as arrests go, this was probably as cordial as they came.

PART II

"The baby has known the dragon intimately ever since he had an imagination. What the fairy tale provides for him is a St. George to kill the dragon."

G. K. Chesterton

INTERLUDE

C aptain Snyder was rethinking some of his recent life choices.

The Weasel was accustomed to making others come to terms with their helplessness in the face of his unmerited power, but now, waiting outside the imposing doors that separated the emperor from himself, he found himself wholly at the mercy of another. Unfortunately for Snyder, Marlowe was not someone in whom mercy was likely to be found. I wish I could report that this role reversal produced in him some empathy for his own victims, but alas, it had quite the opposite effect. Given the option between being the oppressor or being the oppressed, Snyder decided that he preferred the former.

Of course you have probably found, or will find in the future, that many things we fear the most are not nearly so scary as they were in our imaginations. Very often, in fact, the anticipation is much worse than the reality. Unfortunately for poor Snyder, this was not to be one of those cases.

He stood waiting anxiously for about ten minutes under the unfriendly gaze of the guards stationed on each side of the black double doors. He did his best not to look at them, or at the vaguely threatening carvings on the doors, or at the ground, for fear of appearing weak. For ten endless minutes, therefore, Snyder determinedly maintained an emotionless mask as he watched a single shaft of pale sunlight from a narrow window behind him make slow progress up the wall.

Finally, the doors groaned inward on their ancient hinges to reveal a gaping darkness, from which a putrid fog spilled forth.

For a moment, Snyder considered turning on his heel and running. The only thing that tempered his terror at the prospect of entering the blackness before him was the certainty, settled stone-like in his bowels, that to refuse would be worse. In fact, it might be impossible. Snyder felt, as Eldon had, that his body was no longer his to command, and he soon found that it had stepped inside without his permission.

Snyder felt the emperor before he saw him. A cold terror gripped his insides, while the stench of decay choked his lungs. For a few seconds the blackness was so complete that Snyder was possessed of an irrational certainty that he had been struck suddenly blind. But even magical darkness allows the eyes a chance to adjust, and after a moment, the emperor's shape formed out of the inky blackness directly ahead of him. Again as if obeying an external impulse, Snyder knelt. The emperor did not bid him rise, but instead continued to toy with the small obsidian looking glass in his hand.

"Do you know what this is?" the emperor asked disinterestedly.

Snyder was taken aback. This was not what he had expected. He looked at the dark object. Instead of the room's reflection in the glass, Snyder could just make out a dark, poisonous looking mist swirling below the surface, as if in a deep pool.

"No, my lord," Snyder said.

It is a link between me and my loyal servants. Those servants fortunate enough to be trusted with this talisman, can reach me directly by speaking just a few simple words," Marlowe mused. Suddenly his eyes snapped back to Snyder and his voice cooled. "But then you're *not* my loyal servant, are you?"

The Weasel's stomach tightened. He felt tears of sickening fear well up behind his eyes.

"Do you understand," Marlowe asked quietly, "what you have done?"

"Yes, my lord." Snyder's voice trembled as he spoke.

"I'm not sure you do," the emperor replied after a moment. He remained disconcertingly motionless. "You stumbled across the whereabouts of a traitor to the crown, and without so much as asking leave from our royal person, proceeded to take her capture and interrogation into your own hands."

Snyder of course did not know that his letter had been intercepted before reaching the emperor. "Your lordship," he began.

"Silence." The word was just above a whisper but it pierced with cold clarity. "You then proceeded to let this small *child* slip through your fingers. Not content with this failure, you came face to face with the Damascus Guard themselves and *let them go*."

Marlowe did not raise his voice, nor did his face betray rage, yet every soft word conveyed the threat of a thousand tortures, each one more sadistic than the last. During the long silence that followed, Snyder could not have spoken if he had wanted to. He kept his eyes on the floor and marinated in Marlowe's wrath. His insides seemed to have begun boiling within him. Certain that he was not long for this world, (or rather that world, if we're being accurate), he was wholly unprepared for Marlowe's next words.

"I trust," the emperor said quietly, "that you will not make the same mistake twice."

"Never, my lord," he hurriedly croaked. "Never, never!" In his overwhelming relief, Snyder found that he was unable to stop babbling until Marlowe gestured for silence.

"Should I choose to extend you mercy today, I trust that you understand how much worse it will be for you, should you fail me again." The emperor's tone belied any hope of future mercy.

"Thank you my..." Snyder began, but was again silenced.

"Do not misunderstand me, this is not an act of benevolence. It is simply a matter of *incentive*," Marlowe said, his tone now almost light-hearted. "Another man might think himself a loyal servant, but *you*, who have failed me, you who have disappointed your *emperor*..." a wicked smile broke across Marlowe's face. "I trust that you will be torn apart in pursuit of your mission rather than face my... displeasure."

Snyder understood completely.

"I am sure that I need not say it, Captain, but as I have so few pleasures in life... Allow me the indulgence. If you fail me again, you will die slowly by my hand. You will watch as I twist your insides around my fingers. You will beg for death. And it will be my great pleasure to deny your request. Do you understand?"

In that moment Snyder knew beyond doubt that this was no hyperbole.

"I will not fail you, my lord," he answered, surprised at the certainty in his own voice.

"Good. Then find the children and kill them."

17

⌒

ARDEN

T he soldiers brought Brogan, Seamus and Hatch to King Mardius' palace, a magnificent edifice whose flag-tipped towers pierced the horizon like sentries, and which, like everything else in Arden, was vibrant with light and color and life.

The travelers were asked to wait in the courtyard while the king was notified of their presence. They were, much to Hatch's surprise, not guarded while they waited, as the soldiers did not wish to insult them. Hatch looked around in wonder at the open air vestibule in which they found themselves. The palace was, quite simply, beautiful. There were no ostentatious displays of gold and gemstones, but everything was carved with delicate precision to create graceful, sweeping lines. A sheer pearl-colored drape hung from an archway to one side, fluttering back and forth in the warm breeze to reveal the palace gardens beyond. Hatch saw ambling walkways lined with white paving stones and flower beds that were simultaneously carefully kept and a little wild looking.

In the center of the courtyard stood a marble fountain with a statue of a woman in its center. She was tall and slender, cradling a baby in one arm, its mouth pressed to her breast. The other hand reached up to steady a basket, overflowing with fruit and other bounty, that she carried on her head. At her feet, two other children played between her skirts, which seemed to be blown by an invisible wind. A long, graceful sword peeked out from behind her back, where it was secured by a strap that ran from her left shoulder to her right hip. Water cascaded from the basket and flowed over the windblown hair, the nursing babe, and the laughing little ones. Hatch found himself smiling at the joyful little family, and wondering how something could simultaneously be so elegant, warlike, and domestic.

Just then, King Mardius rushed out to the courtyard. As soon as he had been told that Brogan had returned, the king had dropped everything in his eagerness to greet his prodigal soldier, and, seeing his face, at once embraced him with tears.

"My friend!" he cried. "My dear friend, I never thought to see your face again. You are most welcome here. But tell me! How came you here at all? And who is this lad? And this noble cat?"

"This is Seamus, a cat of great courage who has been more help to me than he can ever know." Seamus, who would have blushed furiously if he were human, bowed his head humbly at this.

"And this," Brogan beamed proudly, "is Hatch. One of the babes the pursuit of which found my comrades and I on the wrong side of the Wasteland so many years ago."

Mardius stared in wonder at Hatch, who stared back, equally awe-struck. The boy had never seen a man like this before. Though he was old, he was full of strength and vitality. Above his silver beard, his deep brown eyes sparkled with joy and wisdom. Hatch wondered if he'd ever seen anyone really truly alive before now.

Then, much to his surprise, the king caught him up in a warm embrace that nearly took the breath out of his lungs. *What kind of king is this?* Hatch wondered. The king released him and let out a long, loud laugh that seemed to ring out from his very soul.

"This is a merry day indeed!" the man laughed. "Come in, come in, there is much to say and much to hear. Tonight we feast!"

"Your Majesty..." Brogan interjected.

Mardius, who had turned to lead them into the palace turned back, and seeing Brogan's face, slapped his hand to his forehead enthusiastically. It seemed that this King made no gesture to which he did not devote his entire self. "Of course. What was I thinking? You'll be wanting to know about your wife!"

At these words, Brogan's eyes lit up with a hope he had not yet allowed himself to indulge. "Is she still...?"

Mardius' merry eyes crinkled as he smiled. "Why don't you go ask her yourself? You remember where you lived, I should hope?"

But before he finished the sentence, Brogan was off like a shot. Some conversations ought to be conducted away from prying eyes, so we will leave Brogan to reunite with his wife in private.

Hatch, though delighted, didn't know quite what to do now that his friend and bodyguard had abandoned him in a strange country with a strange king. He needn't have worried, however, for when Mardius had composed himself, he turned to Hatch with a look as though a wonderful new thought had occurred to him.

"You'll be wanting to reunite with your family as well, no doubt."

Hatch was thunderstruck. The king was talking about his *real parents*. Although he had dreamed of them from time to time, the eventuality of meeting his parents face to face had never felt real to him. Hatch's palms began to sweat and he suddenly seemed to lose the capacity to speak. After a few moments, he regained his composure.

"If you please, your Majesty… I don't know where *I* live."

Mardius laughed again. "You're a brave man, I can see that son. I have an idea." The king put his arm around Hatch and began to lead him inside. He whispered to Hatch conspiratorially as they walked, and stopped only briefly to say, "Join us Master Seamus, your counsel will be a great addition to our company!"

༄

Molly could not remember ever having felt as nice as she did when she woke up two days after her great journey with Abner. The nausea, cold sweats and pounding head had departed entirely, while the pain in her arm, though still present, had significantly diminished. Opening her eyes, she was surprised to find herself lying in a soft bed, nestled in a pile of warm, silky furs. A pleasant breeze carried the scent of wildflowers in through an open window.

The sunlight poured into the room through various windows in colors Molly had never seen before, and for a moment she felt as though the light itself was teeming with merriment. When her eyes adjusted to the unfamiliar hues, she noticed a far more welcome sight than even these wonders: Hatch's face. He was beaming down at her from a chair by her bedside where he had been keeping a devoted vigil since her arrival.

"Hatch!" she screamed delightedly, struggling to free herself from the bedclothes before throwing herself on him. She wrapped her good arm around his neck, and happy tears sprung from her eyes.

"Oh Hatch! I thought I'd never see you again! Oh it's been so dreadful."

Hatch returned the embrace gingerly, so as not to further harm the broken limb.

"But it's alright now!" he laughed. "It's wonderful here. Oh Molly, I've never been *anywhere* so wonderful. I can't wait to show you... you must meet everyone... and Molly, our *parents* are here!"

All this was said in one breath and for a few minutes the children chattered excitedly without listening at all to what the other was saying. Eventually they fell to talking in earnest, sharing the details of their respective adventures.

Hatch was deeply grieved to hear the horrors Molly had endured in the Institute, though she did not dwell on the details. Her account of Eldon's death was particularly hard for him to bear. He had heard the news from Abner already, of course, but the wound was still fresh enough to draw salty tears.

"After the funeral, I don't remember much," she finished. "I must have been terribly ill. The whole thing is like a dream. I don't even know how I came here."

"Abner brought you," Hatch told her, glad to be able to fill in some of the story. "I met him just before I came here too, only I hardly recognized him when he carried you in. He seems ever so much older, though I saw him less than a fortnight ago. I don't understand that part, really. Brogan says it was coming here over the Wasteland that aged him. The king doesn't think he'll be able to travel anymore."

Molly interjected here. "The king? You don't mean you've met King Mardius! And who's Brogan?"

"I have! And Molly they're both so wonderful, and there's so much to tell you!" Hatch exclaimed, and he began to recount his own tale. He told of his good fortune in meeting Brogan and then Abner, of their harrowing trip through the Wasteland, and his first encounter with the king. He spoke with glowing admiration for that man, and soon Molly could hardly wait for her own meeting with him.

"And Molly," Hatch finally said with wide, reverent eyes. "I've met my parents. My *real* parents."

He told her how Mardius had thrown the feast he'd threatened upon first meeting them, and summoned his parents on the pretext of urgent business that needed attending to in their neighborhood. Hatch recalled how anxiously he had waited as he watched them approach – a strong, vibrant looking man with a yellow beard, and a slender, beautiful woman with fiery red hair – wondering what they would say to him. Would they still want him? Would they be disappointed with how he had turned out? After all, he'd been raised by people who seemed like mere shadows compared to these Ardenians.

The couple had approached the king and greeted him with gracious bows. Hatch could see the kindness and strength in both their faces from where he stood. Mardius and the couple spoke cordially to each other for a few minutes while Hatch stood by, having been taken for a servant. After a moment his mother caught sight of him and gave a start. Her eyes grew wide and her face paled as she examined him for a few seconds, and then remembered herself and laughed – a sad, wistful laugh that seemed at odds with the joyful gathering.

"I pray your pardon, young sir," she said with a shallow bow. "You look very like someone I used to know. The resemblance is downright uncanny. I almost wondered for a moment... but never mind that. Please forgive me for staring." And she laughed again, awkwardly.

Hatch's father, Aodhan, had now turned to look at him as well, and Hatch blushed under his gaze.

"By my soul, Grace, I see what you mean!" he said. "He's so very like him, I'd swear it was the boy himself if I didn't know better!"

Mardius could barely contain his mirth as he watched this exchange. As Hatch's father turned to face him again, he said, "Then you don't know the boy? I felt sure you might. Perhaps you should take a closer look?"

Aodhan's expression grew somber. "Surely your majesty knows whose resemblance he bears? And that the child is either dead or lost forever? It would not credit your grace to toy with his subjects, sire."

"Ah, yes," returned the king. "That's right. The Wasteland is entirely impassable, as everyone knows. Only... someone forgot to tell Brogan, it seems. For he stumbled out of it this very day, and with this remarkable boy in tow."

"Brogan?" Grace breathed in an awed voice, not daring to tear her eyes from Hatch lest he disappear. "Do you mean..." Before she could finish the sentence, tears pooled beneath her eyes and threatened to spill.

"Aye, madam," Mardius said softly. "'Tis your son, returned from the grave."

Grace cried out and embraced Hatch with more joy than he had ever thought could be attributed to his own existence. Looking over her shoulder he saw that Aodhan's face was wet with tears and wide-eyed with wonder.

Molly had listened to Hatch's tale with rapt attention,

awestruck by the possibility of finding a home here in Arden.

"They call me Sam," Hatch went on. "That's my real name, apparently. But... I'm not sure I like it yet. That is... you could still call me Hatch. If you don't mind."

"Not in the least!" Molly laughed. It felt wonderful to laugh and really mean it after all the wretched days she had endured of late. She had been fascinated and delighted by Hatch's story, but as he told it the same fearful wonderings rose in her own soul. She knew her father to have died in the Wasteland on the night of the kidnapping, but what of her mother? Was she still alive? Would she recognize Molly as Hatch's parents had? What would Molly do if she didn't?

Just at that moment, the door opened and a sweet looking woman walked in carrying a tray. Seeing that Molly was sitting up and talking, she gave a start.

"You're awake, miss!" she said happily. "Everyone's been awfully worried about you!"

Hatch, realizing he had kept Molly to himself all this time, suddenly looked guilt-stricken.

"I'll tell them now!" he said, having sprung to his feet.

The woman set the tray down on a table in the middle of the room and the delicious aromas emanating from it reminded Molly how long it had been since she'd had anything wholesome to eat.

"Nonsense, sit down and keep her company for dinner. I'll tell them." She smiled and winked at Molly. "Your mother will be beside herself. She's been here day and night, you know. She only left an hour ago to get some rest because his majesty insisted. I'll go and fetch her right away."

Molly's heart nearly stopped. She felt a combination of joy, dread, and a pang of guilt when she remembered her adopted parents in Druinor, who had been kind and loving to her.

A few minutes later, the king himself rushed in to greet her joyously with the queen, a woman unlike any the children had ever seen, hard on his heels. She kissed Molly on the forehead and asked her tender questions about her health.

All fell silent though when, after a few more minutes, another woman entered the room. Rowena had deep brown hair streaked with silver and a face that brimmed over with both youth and wisdom. As her striking green eyes fell on Molly, she rushed to her side and grasped both her hands with a cry of joy.

"You're so beautiful!" Rowena exclaimed, and Molly, who was feeling very shy, squirmed a little. She had never thought of herself as beautiful to begin with, but to be described as such in this place and among these people made her blush. Rowena looked as though she would like nothing more than to sweep Molly up in her arms, but seeing her discomfort she laughed instead to put her at ease. "I know this must be so much for you to take in, but I've waited so long... and I thought you'd left me forever." Her voice cracked as she said these words, and her face twitched with emotion.

Molly couldn't think of anything to say, so she simply said, "It's very nice to finally meet you,"

After a pause, Molly pulled her mother to her and embraced her with a childlike laugh. The reverent silence the others had maintained during this initial meeting soon dissolved and the room erupted into exclamations, questions and laughter. It was at least half an hour before Molly got to eat the wonderful things on the tray, but she didn't mind at all.

༄

The next few days were the best of the children's lives.

Brogan had returned to the palace with his wife, Lydia, who would not leave his side, and soon regaled the king and queen with the details of his twelve years in their service in Druinor. The king, though he would have expected nothing less, was moved to tears to hear of Brogan and Eldon's faithful service in that dark country, and grieved by the news of Eldon's death. Brogan, likewise, was equal parts grief and joy, having lost his best friend but regained his wife.

For the time being, Mardius had decreed that the children's most pressing task was to enjoy their families and become acquainted with the ways of their homeland, which they both took to enthusiastically. Many feasts were held and many nights the three reunited families sat up talking and laughing and learning to know each other. Molly and Hatch felt there could never be a happier time in their lives, though Molly (who, it turned out, had originally been called Sarah) was still plagued by nightmares that left her trembling and sweating. Each one was a variation of the nightmare she'd had in Damascus. Every time, Marlowe's eyes promised to find her. Every time, the object he clutched in his left hand seemed more curious, more dreadful to her. When she woke from these dreams it took her several hours to shake the pall they cast over the morning.

Nonetheless, her waking hours were full of joy and wonder. She found Rowena easy to love and the two of them talked late into many nights. During some of these talks, however, Molly could not help but feel a stab of regret for her Druinian parents, seeing now the richness that their lives lacked. She even found herself thinking about Edith one night, the wicked girl with whom she had shared a room at the Institute. At the memory of her wish that

Edith should never come to Arden, her conscience reproached her.

These thoughts were fleeting though, as life in Arden consumed her thoughts. She was fascinated by the women of the court – especially Queen Meara, who swept gracefully from room to room as a spirit might, always adorned with gowns and jewelry so exotic they took Molly's breath away. All the women were so beautifully arrayed that she was often intimidated by them, and when they spoke to her, she always felt as though some goddess or fairy had condescended to acknowledge her presence. She had never encountered beauty for its own sake before now and found herself enamored with it. Rowena, however, though beautiful, was not a member of the royal court and preferred a plainer (though still quite fetching) ensemble.

Hatch, though he rarely wanted to be separated from his parents, spent all his spare time in the king's company. He had found no man on earth so full of wisdom and goodness, and he soaked it in as if he were the Wasteland itself and Mardius the rain. Many nights he, Brogan, Seamus, and Aodhan sat conversing with the king about every topic from politics to farming, Hatch hanging on his every word. Sometimes he even found himself alone with the king, who talked to him as an equal, just as Brogan had. Unfortunately, after a few weeks spent like this, Hatch began to think himself quite the authority on a variety of kingly subjects, and in an attempts to impress Molly with his vast stores of knowledge, ended up making a bit of a fool of himself.

Overall, though, Hatch did benefit from his time with the king, particularly on one occasion. On the night in question, he was standing alone on a balcony, drinking in the fresh air of his homeland, with which he had fallen deeply in love, when Mardius joined him. The king stood beside him in silence, also looking out on the countryside with satisfaction.

"Sire," Hatch said, respectfully. "I was wondering..."

"What is it, my boy?" the king gave him his full attention, which made Hatch feel simultaneously nervous and honored.

"What will happen now? Molly and I, we were supposed to free Fairy Tale and bring down the wall, but we didn't. Whatever it meant, the prophecy wasn't fulfilled."

"Well," the king mused, "I suppose we must wait a little longer until the time is right. Or perhaps it was not a prophecy after all, just a lovely bit of fiction. To tell the truth, I am a little relieved. It was too much to ask of children as young as yourselves, to break a curse that has thwarted the wisest among us." Mardius suddenly smiled at Hatch. "The important thing is that you are finally safe. You've spent your whole life in exile. No one would dream of sending you away again."

Hatch returned the smile, but he did not find the answer entirely satisfactory. Eldon's talk of the prophecy and the curse had stirred something in him. To dismiss it as a mistake now felt somehow wrong. Hatch quickly shook this thought out of his head and voiced the other thing that had been occupying his mind.

"When Eldon told us about everything that had happened – about Emperor Marlowe and the wicked Druinians and the Wasteland – he said that the Wasteland Wall was protecting Druinor from *you*. We thought we were supposed to lift the wall so you could sweep in with your armies and destroy Druinor, but Eldon said it was so that you could save them."

"That's right," the king answered. "The people of Druinor

are greatly oppressed. It's my dearest desire to see them freed from Marlowe's rule."

"That's what I don't understand sire," said Hatch. "They don't seem to mind it. Most of them are just like him. Respectfully, Your Majesty, I don't think they could live here very well. I'm afraid they'd spoil everything."

"They only do what they've been taught. They don't know any other way. We could show them how free people ought to live."

"But sire, they hate you!" Hatch said. "If it's true that they were once Ardenians themselves, they chose to rebel against you. They *chose* Marlowe. They're traitors to Arden. Do you think they could really become citizens here?"

"They don't hate me, lad. They don't even know I exist," Mardius said.

When Hatch turned to look at him, he found the king looking back and was surprised to see his eyes shining.

"I don't know what it will look like," Mardius said. "I only know that I look at them and see miserable wretches, under a powerful spell from which there is no escape. A good king cannot turn a blind eye to the miserable, and *especially* must not disdain them for their misery. They may have come to be in such a state through their own foolishness, but who among us has not been foolish in some way or another? Should we not be shown compassion in spite of it?"

"I think I understand," Hatch said after a pause, but he didn't really. Not yet.

18

AN INTRODUCTION TO FAIRY TALES

Conditions had become much more difficult for the Damascus Guard after the children had left Druinor. The sky was fairly boiling with Marlowe's malevolence over the following weeks. All of Druinor could sense his displeasure and reacted to it as people under poisonous spells are wont to do: by turning on one another. Crime became more common, work days became longer and more laborious, employers more demanding, arguments more violent, insults pettier and the heat more oppressive. It seemed there was no aspect of life outside the reach of the emperor's foul mood.

When Snyder's sentries, who had gone deeper and deeper into the hills in search of the children, continually returned empty-handed, the emperor began to fear that the children had escaped his grasp. Having grown accustomed to always having his way, Marlowe flailed for any target on which to unleash his fury. He quickly settled on the Maskies. The emperor had always hated them, but never so fiercely as he did now. Before, he had simply seen them as an irritation, a gnat to be swatted. Sometimes he even saw them as a tool to be exploited in the press. Marlowe had quickly found that rebels and fanatics could be quite useful in keeping citizens loyal, so long as he could paint an adequately dangerous picture of them.

But now, all that had changed. For the first time in a hundred years, Marlowe found himself facing the possibility of being thwarted in a really meaningful sense. Worse, by children! In the absence of the culprits themselves, the Maskies had come to represent that humiliating defeat, and became the sole objects of his wrath. Having correctly guessed that the Maskies had played a hand in spiriting them away, he now fully focused his energy on capturing the traitorous members of the Damascus Guard themselves and through them discovering the trail that would lead him to Molly and Hatch.

The Maskies immediately began to feel the precarious nature of their position. They had been accustomed to being allowed to do as they pleased for the most part, being both more creative than the local police and better acquainted with magic. Now that Marlowe's eye had turned toward them in earnest, however, it seemed that the typically dull and brutish policemen were having uncanny luck in foiling their schemes. Their usual sources of intelligence, normally easily persuaded by the glint of a coin or two, became tight-lipped. Planned raids on government offices, stage coaches and weapons storehouses turned out to be traps. These were easy to avoid at first, but the police refined their techniques with uncharacteristic speed and efficiency.

One night Wes, Regan, and Harmon, who had made a routine stop to restock one of their many safe houses around the city, were caught unawares by a roaming patrol and barely escaped with their lives. At least one of their safe houses, it seemed, was compromised. On another occasion, Philip was so sure he was being followed that he spent the entire night in pubs and the alleys behind them, not returning to Damascus until he was sure he could do so unobserved. They began to see policemen and soldiers in every crowd and around every corner. The emperor's noose was tightening. After that night, the Maskies ceased nearly all activity. Those who had jobs attended them, but did nothing that would draw attention. The rest of them stayed underground.

Had it not been for Percival, the mood in Damascus would have become dangerously gloomy. Realizing that they were all feeling the effects of the wizard's influence on Druinor – that spiritual pall to which their countrymen had long ago succumbed – he made every effort to resist it. Percival did his best to maintain a jovial air at all times and used his spare time playing music or pranks on his fellow cave dwellers.

Ava was surprisingly helpful to him in this regard. She, too, saw the danger of letting their spirits decline, but having so recently escaped from her duties in the Institute, she was in far less danger of doing so than any of them. Even the oppressive heat could not rob her of her joy at regaining the company of her friends, so Ava went out of her way to encourage and serve her comrades in every way possible. Melody, meanwhile, did her part by telling stories every evening. She and Seamus, having spent much time with Brogan and Eldon over the years, had learned many of the stories of Arden. Every night after supper, the Maskies gathered around the fire while Melody enchanted them all with a new tale, and Luke scribbled along furiously, recording every detail for his expanding library. The Druinian children rescued from the dwarves listened to these stories with rapt faces and sparkling eyes.

In this manner, Percival and company were able to markedly improve the environment of their hideout-turned-prison. Still, they knew the time was coming when they must be ready to take action. They were not the sort who could sit still for long.

༄

On the opposite side of the Wasteland, things were a good deal more pleasant. Molly, Hatch and their respective parents were learning each other's characters and they were each delighted with what they found. Molly's mother, especially, having lost both her daughter and her husband that fateful night, wrung each moment for all it was worth.

The king made a great effort to know the children better as well, and as a result, Hatch, Molly and Brogan's families spent a good deal of time in each other's company, and that of the royal family. Mardius took great pleasure in introducing the children to their homeland, teaching them to love it as he did. He took them on tours through the countryside and they spent many a cool night gathered around campfires, warmly lit dining room tables, and tavern fireplaces in the surrounding towns and villages.

It was on one of these evenings, in a little village called Anodos, that the children's real baptism into the world of fairy tales occurred. All of the villagers had gathered in the open square to celebrate their arrival, and together they danced and sang until late into the night. Eventually the villagers began to settle around the fire to ask the children questions about their adventures. The children had become accustomed to this and related their tale with pleasure. As their story began to wind down, Molly went to sit on the ground next to her mother while Hatch finished the tale.

Her head lay across her Rowena's lap, and she stared fondly at Queen Meara, whose bejeweled fingers sparkled in the firelight. Hatch, who was sitting between the king and Aodhan, his father, concluded their adventures to rapturous applause from the nearby villagers.

One of them, a sturdy woman named Cora, called to the man opposite her, "Why don't you tell them one of *our* stories, Dantes?"

Dantes was a comical-looking fellow with features rather too large for his face, disheveled hair, and an unapologetically carefree air. He seemed to be always laughing and he did so now.

"Surely not!" he answered, despite having every intention of complying with her request. "We've heard the best of all stories from our honored guests already."

"Ah, but our guests have never heard a story from a true master of that craft," rejoined the woman. "A sad day when a visitor can leave Anodos without having known that rare pleasure."

Dantes blushed but appeared genuinely pleased. "Well…"

"Ah! A story!" roared the king, slapping his knee delightedly. "Why didn't I think of that myself? Our new friends were raised in the dark southern lands you know. I'd wager they've never heard a fairy tale at all! You haven't, have you?" he said, turning to Hatch.

"We've heard stories!" he protested. "Seamus told us all the stories of the constellations, and Eldon told us the history of Arden."

"But you've never heard a *fairy tale* told the way a tale *ought* to be told, no offense to Master Seamus of course," Mardius said with a slight bow toward the cat. "Not by a storyteller like Dantes."

"Isn't Fairy Tale a person though?" Molly asked.

Everyone laughed good naturedly, but Molly looked embarrassed.

"Aye, lass," Aodhan said kindly. "She is a person, and the loveliest kind you'll ever meet. It's her habit to pen stories for the retelling – legends and fables and all sorts of stories – to entertain and teach. She's written hundreds of them."

Hatch and Molly both looked mystified.

"How old can she be?" Molly asked, "to have so many stories to tell?"

"Very old indeed," Aodhan said. "But I see that you don't understand. The stories are not all things that have happened to her... nor to anybody, really. She makes them up."

"Makes them up?" Molly looked horrified. "You mean she *lies*?"

Mardius laughed. "Lies? Never. She doesn't pretend they're true stories."

"But then, why tell them?"

"They're told to the benefit of the hearer," the king said. "There are many different types of stories - but each one contains a gem which, if the hearer be of sound mind and soft heart, he is certain to retain. Hearing one is like seeing yourself in a mirror. It's a reflection of what's true. I think Dantes had better tell us one. Then maybe you'll see what I mean."

Molly found this doubtful, but she wanted to hear the story all the same. Dantes cleared his throat and began to weave his tale:

It is one of the great mysteries of the world that practically any time a child is born to a good king and queen, there is in the vicinity a wicked fairy with whom those two sovereigns have some quarrel or other.

The story of little Lilith and Brutus is no exception. These two wee babes were twins – a dimpled brother of fair complexion and golden hair like his noble father, and his cherub-faced sister whose darker coloring was like her mother's.

The royal twins were well-beloved by their father, a good but foolish king, and his kind but simple bride.

As has been the custom for years without number, the king and queen held a great banquet to welcome the newest royals and invited all the nobles and royal families of the surrounding kingdoms, as well as the common folk of the land.

The king's wise men strongly advised him against this, as it is well-known that wicked fairies often use such occasions to exact vengeance fortheir grievances – but custom is custom, said the king.

The day of the feast arrived, and with it hundreds of guests, all of bright countenance and splendidly appareled, bearing extravagant gifts for the prince and princess.

Just as the wise men had predicted, the wicked fairy who lived in that region was among the palace's many guests. Her name was Greichelwald, but that's really no excuse for how she behaved.

Now wicked fairies have a wide range of complaints that they level against humans, from grievous offenses committed generations past to unintentional slights. It was a crime of the latter nature that Greichelwald had suffered – so minor, in fact, that the king and queen were blissfully unaware of having committed it. Among the common people, some held that she had even invented the offense, so as to find grounds for her treachery.

Nevertheless, the old hag honored the tradition of those who had gone before her. She made herself known at the very height of the festivities, and dampened the mood at the palace considerably by announcing that her gift to the two babes would not be a blessing, but a curse.

A dreadful silence fell over the courtiers and nobles and all remained frozen by fear until her work was done. Greichelwald peered first into the bassinet of Brutus, the fair-haired prince.

Cackling, she placed her knotted thumb on Brutus' tiny forehead and declared, "Thou shalt be blind always to what is to thy benefit, and love best that which serves thee least."

At this the good but foolish king breathed a small sigh of relief. After all, was not this an affliction common to all mankind? So Brutus, he told himself, would be no worse off than the rest of us, and would need only to be taught self-discipline.

Moving on to Lilith, Greichelwald placed her thumb on the princess' small, olive-colored brow and cackled again.

"Thou wilt always know and love what is good and right, and furthermore always know the best course of action to be taken, but shalt never be heeded by any, not a whit."

Again, the king smiled to himself, thinking, "Ah, well, that one lies not on her but on us to alleviate. We ought always to remember to take her suggestions quite seriously, and there will be no danger there."

As common as is the appearance of a wicked fairy at a christening, so also is the presence of a great many good and generous fairies, whose role it is to show up just a bit too late and do what is in their power to ameliorate the effects of any curses that may be leveled against the royal progeny. Again, the case of the royal twins was faithful to tradition.

The moment the curse was finished, the queen of the good fairies and five of her handmaidens arrived at the celebration to pay their own respects. Seeing what had happened, they berated Greichelwald severely before offering their services to the king and queen.

"I'm sure something can be done," the fairy queen said benevolently.

The king, though, only laughed and said, "Waste not your generosity on us, your majesty. The curses were hardly damaging at all! Only those things most likely to be suffered by a young boy and a young girl in the course of their lives. No, don't trouble yourselves. Their highnesses will be no worse for it, after all."

The fairy queen looked doubtful, but she was both too well-bred to argue with a king and too dignified to offer again a service once refused, and so she bowed graciously before she and her handmaidens retreated.

As the children grew, it was not immediately apparent that the curses would have any effect on their upbringing, so the king congratulated himself on not having overreacted.

As the years progressed, however, the children began to have more and more trouble. Brutus, contrary to his father's predictions, would not be taught self-discipline, since self-discipline was one of the many things that would benefit him. Instead he indulged his every desire, scorned the good counsel of his parents and sister, and became the most selfish and brutish fellow the country had ever seen.He insisted upon being allowed to do and eat whatever he fancied, drank only wine, and became extremely fat and indolent. Brutus refused to do any work or go out in the sun and, as he became accustomed to getting his own way, he began to exact merciless revenge on any servant who crossed his will.

Lilith, for her part, had a tender heart and loved her brother dearly, and loved his poor subjects as well. She was desperately grieved to see what kind of man he was becoming and sought to better him by all means at her disposal, and to protect the kingdom from him. But of course, the compounded curses of both the children prevented him from everhearing a word she said.

Even the king and queen, who talked often of what must be

done to subdue their son, and who had promised themselves they would take every precaution against the curse placed on their daughter, heard only the silliest of nonsense when she spoke to them about it. Despite the little nagging voice that told them they ought to listen to her advice, they could not bring themselves to take it the least bit seriously.

On one occasion, Lilith came upon her parents talking together about the latest cruel and despotic scheme of the lazy prince. He had just that morning determined that he would enslave half his subjects and force them to build him a chocolate farm. Naturally the king and queen forbade any such thing, and had paid dearly as they always did when their will was crosswise to their son's. He was, even now, storming about his rooms, breaking furniture in a fit of petulant rage.

The queen cried and the king paced worriedly in his sitting room as they discussed this.

"Father," said Lilith, who had grown beautiful and wise beyond measure. "Father, something must be done about my brother. His foolishness and cruelty are without restraint. I have been thinking. Oughtn't we consult with the fairy queen and see if there is anything that can be done?"

Now Lilith did not know about the curses she and Brutus had received in the cradle, nor of the fairy queen's spurned offer of aid. It was, therefore, a source of great frustration to her that her thoughts on any subject were regarded as folly. However, she loved her brother and her kingdom too well to remain silent as she saw him both suffer and cause suffering to others.

Her father turned to her with great surprise. Only a minute before he had been thinking himself that Brutus was a lunatic who must be restrained. As soon as he heard that thought given voice by his daughter's lips, however, nothing seemed more ridiculous to him and he laughed heartily. The queen, who had only just been weeping for her prodigal son, forgot her sorrow and laughed with him. What had they done, each wondered privately, to deserve such a dimwitted daughter, always babbling on and on about who knows what?

They laughed so hard and so long that Lilith, cheeks burning with shame and anger, retreated to her room and would not eat supper.

It happened, though, that the queen of the fairies, had seen this encounter. She had, understandably, been highly affronted by the king's refusal of her offer to help, and so could not resist watching Greichelwald's curses play out. As they grew, she had laughed sometimes, thinking how silly the king must feel for having rejected her. She felt quite justified in letting the events of the royal lives unfold. After all, had she not made a reasonable attempt to intervene? In this way, she amused herself from time to time by observing the royal family's woes.

So it was that she sat on Lilith's bedroom window that night and was witness to the princess' distress. As the maiden wept, the fairy queen's heart smote her. Had not the royal family been punished enough for their foolishness? Furthermore, the fairy queen thought with growing unease, if she continued to withhold aid, was she not every bit as bad as the bitter old fairy who had cursed them to begin with?

It was this second thought that spurred her to action, and she flew straight into Lilith's window and began to speak to her on the subject at once.

Lilith was greatly disturbed to hear the fairy queen's story and learn of Greichelwald's curse. Her eyes grew wide with horror as she realized that all her advice over the years had only served to make her brother worse and diminish the enormity of the problem in her parents' eyes.

"What shall I do?" Lilith cried despairingly. "I see what is good, but he cannot see it himself! And worse, I cannot tell anyone, for fear they too shall lose sight of it!"

"It seems obvious," said the fairy queen. "You must lie to him about what is good for him. Trick him into wanting that which he has always hated."

Lilith looked at her reproachfully. "Far be it from me to do evil that good may come. No, I shan't lie. Not even for his good. For then I would be doing that which doesn't serve me well."

It is a great blessing that fairies are immune to most of the curses of other fairies, for had Lilith said this to anyone else, they would have laughed boisterously at her. The fairy queen, however, was not subject to Greichelwald's curse and saw at once that this was very good counsel.

"I see that you are wise beyond your years," the fairy queen said with a smile, "and that you love what is good and right. We must think of another way."

And they sat together and thought for some time. Suddenly the fairy queen had an idea.

"I know just the thing!" she declared. At that, she flew out the window, much to the surprise and dismay of fair Lilith.

After a short while she reappeared carrying a ring with a sparkling red gem set in it. It was the most beautiful thing that Lilith had ever seen.

"No fairy can undo the curse of another fairy," the queen said. "I can, however, determine the means by which it can be broken. I was unable to give you a gift at your birth, and so I give it to you now."

Placing her tiny thumb on Lilith's furrowed brow, the fairy queen spoke once more. "You shall be freed from your curse of unheeded wisdom, carried since the cradle, if you can but once convince another soul to act with no interest for self."

"What good is that?" wailed Lilith. "The curse itself prevents any such thing!"

"Not so!" declared the fairy queen. "The curse only ordains that your good advice go unheeded. There are other means to *persuade people than by counsel, your highness."*

Lilith saw that this was true and thanked her humbly for the blessing. "But what is the ring you bore with you here, your Majesty?" she asked, looking at the sparkling gem.

"I cannot bless your brother directly," the fairy queen answered. "For he'll never allow it. Instead I've blessed this ring. If he can be convinced to wear it, his own curse shall at once be broken, and he shall never again love what is evil and hate what is good."

"That ought to be easy," Lilith said with delight. "For he loves expensive jewelry and all that sparkles in the light."

"Ah, I wish it were so," declared the fairy. "But this ring is what will serve him best, and so he will find it most repulsive. You will have to use your wit to persuade him to put it on, for it cannot be forced. He must choose to wear it, or it shall come to naught."

This was a problem not easily solved. The fairy queen had very little advice on the subject, so Lilith put the ring on a chain and wore it around her neck at all times, in case the opportunity to convince Brutus to wear it should arise.

It happened, at that time, that a prince called Elpis was traveling through that region. He came from a kingdom far away, and as such he made his way to the palace and enquired if he might stay for a few days and rest. Elpis was a brave young man who, being young and inexperienced, had gone out in search of glory and adventure. The king and queen, who were both very hospitable by nature, warmly welcomed the visitor into their halls.

When Elpis laid eyes on Lilith, his heart beat faster within his chest, for he had never in all his travels seen a lovelier woman than she. He vowed to himself that before he departed, he would have attempted to know her better. With this in mind, he approached her one evening after supper. Seeing that she looked thoughtful and had a wise countenance, and said to her, "Your highness, I must ask your good counsel."

"Pray, do," said Lilith, though she dreaded any question he might ask, knowing that she could not but answer truthfully, and knowing furthermore that her answer would seem like foolishness to him.

"What, pray tell, would a man have to do to win the hand of a woman like yourself?" said Elpis, who was accustomed to saying things very straightforwardly.

"Why, very little indeed," Lilith said. "Only to show kindness to her and to her kinsmen and to all mankind. For a handsome face will fade, but a kind soul is of immeasurable value."

Elpis' eyes widened in surprise. Though this was the very thing he had hoped she would say, when she did so the words sounded as nonsensical to him as if she had suggested he boil his stockings for stew.

Little knowing what to say, he thanked her and went away confused.

Lilith was not surprised by this, but she was saddened, for she had hoped to find in him a kindred spirit.

During the rest of his stay, Elpis made many other attempts to know her mind, but each time her answer only baffled him. Eventually, he concluded that the princess must be trying to diplomatically spurn his advances. Thus, with wounded pride, he determined to let her be free of him and continue his adventures elsewhere.

Lilith, though she understood what was happening, could see no way to remedy the misunderstanding. She saw as well that the prince's declarations of affection could not be further than skin-deep, since he knew only her face and not her soul. So, sighing within herself, she turned her attention fully to the task at hand: protecting her subjects from the wicked prince, even while ministering to him with tender compassion.

This only made her more beautiful in Elpis' esteem. He watched how selflessly and patiently she served her thankless parents and sought the good of all around her. His own heart began to be moved with charitable thoughts he had never before had occasion to entertain.

The day that Elpis planned to take his leave was an especially difficult day for Lilith. She had gone to her brother's apartments, and finding him abusing his servants, had sent them home. While Brutus reclined on his couch shouting all manner of curses and insults at her, she had tried to convince him to try on the fairy queen's ring. Brutus had thrown it across the room, breaking a looking glass in the process. Lilith wept silently as she swept up the shards, not for herself but for her brother and all who were subject to him.

As Elpis observed her from the doorway, his heart reproached him. He had told himself, a bit sulkily, that he loved the princess. But now, as he watched her, he began to wonder if it was she herself he had loved, or merely the idea of returning to his own kingdom with a beautiful lady on his arm. Putting aside his bruised feelings for a moment, he resolved to expose his dignity to further injury, this time not to achieve his own ends, but for the sake of the one whom he claimed to love.

He approached her, speaking gently though his pride cried out against him, and, knelt before her.

"Your highness," he said humbly. "As you know, I have for some weeks pursued your affection to no avail. I know you have no love for me, and I little blame you in that regard, for you no doubt see how selfish my intentions have been. I won't ask you now to stir up affection where you have none, or to betray your own heart. Still, I cannot bear to see you suffer here alone like this. We both know that according to the law of your land, you must marry if you wish to leave this place. If you will not have my hand for love's sake, will you take it for the sake of your

liberty, and with it the promise that you will owe me nothing but the opportunity to serve you by the offer? The moment you are free from here, you shall be free of me as well. Your will shall be your own, and you will belong to no one."

Lilith realized at once that his clumsy attempt at rescue had been made at some cost to his future reputation, if he really intended to offer her freedom from any obligation, and she loved him for it. Still, she could not in good conscience leave her own kingdom in the hands of such a future king as her brother. She was resolved to stay and save her land, so she opened her mouth to refuse the offer.

Brutus, however, seeing the look of admiration on his sister's face, assumed she meant to accept and sprang to his feet at once.

"I won't allow it!" he bellowed. "You cannot have her! I won't have it!" He began to curse and kick Elpis, though the prince had little trouble dodging the blows.

Lilith saw instantly what must be done. "It's alright, brother, I won't marry him!" she shouted. Both the men stopped squabbling and looked at her.

"On one condition, I will turn him down. You must accept the ring I gave you as a gift, and you must wear it. If you refuse, I shall run away with this man today and become his wife."

Now Brutus had hated the ring the moment he saw it (not knowing, of course, that this was because it was the thing that would benefit him most in all the world), but he hated the thought of losing his sister's devoted service even more.

Elpis watched with dismay as that blubbery, pallid prince made his way across the room, picked up the ring from where he had cast it aside, and jammed it spitefully onto his finger.

At that moment, a great change came over his face. Brutus looked around upon the room in which he had lived in opulent self-indulgence for years, and realized the great disservice he had done to himself and all who loved him. He saw that he had set *his heart on worthless things and treated what was lovely as refuse. He fell to his knees before Lilith's feet, weeping bitterly and uttering such words of love as she had never heard from him before. He begged her forgiveness and was granted it immediately.*

Both the curses were broken that day. The moment Elpis had been moved by Lilith's selflessness to perform his own act of selfless love, it was as if a fog around his mind had cleared. At last he found he could understand her, and that her words were, and always had been, wise.

It took some time to convince the servants that all was well, but Brutus made it his mission to make amends to all whom he had wronged, from the least to the greatest. After a few years, he had himself become strong and healthy from working in the sun and the cruel tyrant he had been was remembered no more. The country never saw a kinder, gentler, nor humbler king than the one Brutus became, and he always maintained a very good relationship with the kingdom where Elpis and Lilith reigned as king and queen.

19

THE MASKIES' MISSION

The children listened to Dantes' story in breathless silence. They felt as though they were under a powerful enchantment from which they had no desire to be freed. You probably know, reader, the feeling of restless sadness when you finish a beautiful story that you hoped would never end. Molly and Hatch had never read a novel by the fire or by flashlight long after they were meant to be asleep, and they had never fallen in love with fictional worlds as we have. This brief fairy tale was their first foray into the enchanted lands with which you have become so warmly familiar.

"That was the loveliest thing I've ever heard," said Molly softly, and Aodhan was pleased and surprised to see tears in his young son's eyes.

"What do you think was the gem in the story?" Mardius asked.

"The ring!" cried Molly.

The adults who heard her chuckled softly and again she

blushed furiously.

"It's alright, love," said Meara with a wink. "I would have said the same thing at your age."

"Did you mean," said Hatch, "that part of the story itself is valuable? As a gem might be in real life?"

"Precisely, my boy!" said the king. "Something you can carry with you, in the same way the princess wore the ring round her neck, and use at the proper time. Did you find any such thing in the tale?"

Hatch thought about it for a moment.

"Well," he said slowly. "It seems to me that the king wasn't quite so foolish as he was made out to be."

"Oh?" said Mardius. "Then he's certainly been done a great injustice by the storyteller. What makes you say so?"

"Well it's true that he ought not to have spurned the fairy queen. That was foolish," said Hatch. "And it's true that poor Brutus was made ever so much worse by the curse. But the king said that the prince's problem – that is, loving the things that serve us least and hating those that serve us best – was common to all mankind and I think he was right. Everyone in Druinor does that, you know, and they're not under any curse."

Mardius looked thoughtful. "You speak well, Hatch. The danger is present within all of us. Although I would argue that our Druinian neighbors are most definitely under a curse, it's not quite the same sort, is it? But now you see better, perhaps, why I feel we must make every effort to reverse it."

"Then it *can* be reversed?" Hatch asked earnestly. "Like it was reversed in the story?"

"Perhaps," Meara said. "At any rate, we can only find out by trying, can't we?"

"But how?" asked the boy, to whom the prospect of

piercing such a poisonous fog as that which covered Druinor seemed unsurmountable.

Yet the adults, whose minds from birth had been fed on the hope of conquered dragons, did not see the task in such a hopeless light. They discussed how it might be accomplished for some hours. Molly, bless her young heart, had succumbed to weariness long before the talking finished and missed most of this debate, sound asleep on her mother's lap.

⁓

Alice, Rob and Ben seemed to be improving. As they were now privy to many of the Damascus Guard's secrets, they had been allowed access to Damascus itself and spent much time there under Martha's careful supervision. Initially the Maskies had feared that they would betray their guardians to the police, but as life for the children had been considerably easier since meeting the rebels, all three had expressed their contentment and willingness to stay with their new guardians as long as necessary.

Their young minds had shown a marked improvement in the company of free citizens, and they had even begun to demonstrate an interest in and aptitude for various skills. Even Alice had lost nearly all of her surly demeanor. It seemed Marlowe's magic was weakening the longer she spent in the little underground hideout. She seemed especially interested in studying magic, and Martha recruited Andrew as a tutor for her, though it took some time to teach her how to learn. All she'd known up till that point was how to recite whatever the professor wanted to hear. There were many tears and trials before she understood that considering the lesson and drawing her own conclusions from it was expected of her, and more still before she learned to practice that art. However, Andrew was a patient teacher and his pupil was as much removed from the bitter little traitor in Abner's cottage as the east is from the west.

Ben, meanwhile, was learning archery, hunting, how to read maps and all manner of other skills from Tobias. Rob's progress was perhaps the most surprising. He was a far cry from the near catatonic boy that Hatch had first encountered in the dwarf prison. He watched Andrew and Alice's lessons with curiosity and after a while even began to ask questions himself, but spent most of his time with Luke, poring over every book in the little library. Relations between the children themselves were also much improved. They had begun not only to acknowledge one another as fellow human beings, but even showed each other a hesitant courtesy. Alice had discovered slowly that these strange adults did not view constant tattling in a favorable light, and that refraining from it elevated her greatly in the esteem of her companions. It would be some time before she behaved honorably for the sake of honor itself, but we must be patient with the poor child, having been raised as cruelly as she was.

Percival watched the children closely and noted their development with keen interest. He had always believed, without being conscious of it, that most Druinian children were simply born dull and witless, and that it was their lot in life to be so. But now as he saw these three boorish specimens flourish under the Maskies' guardianship, new thoughts began to stir in his breast, which he mentioned to some of the others one evening as they sat around the fire after supper.

"I wonder," he began. "Whether we haven't been going about everything all wrong."

Naturally, this drew several curious inquiries, but Percival quickly motioned for quiet.

"Let me explain. All the time that the Damascus Guard has been together, we've always focused on petty raids and meddling with government affairs. All in all we have had very little impact. Most people don't even believe we're real."

"The fellows down at the palace might disagree," Luke said. "I daresay we caused them a great many headaches."

"Certainly we have," Percival allowed. "But to what end? Do none of you feel that we lack a real purpose, other than to be a thorn in the emperor's side?"

"Seems like purpose enough to me," Regan muttered.

"Well there's only so much eleven men can do, you know," Raymond said.

"And two women," said Ava.

"That's exactly my point," said Percival. "We've done alright, I don't deny it. But you speak truly that there *is* only so much we can do, so long as we're the only ones doing it."

"Do you have any other candidates in mind?" Raymond asked curiously.

"I do," said Percival, leaning back and putting his feet up on the table so as to enjoy the full impact of his next statement. "The citizens of Druinor."

The others laughed heartily at this.

"Of course!" Wes smirked. "A revolt by the Druinians! They're just the lot to do that sort of thing. Such a useful lot."

"Perhaps they are," Ava said seriously. Her work inside the school had given her an opportunity to observe the complexities of character that hid under the surface of the students. "After all, Alice and Ben and Rob are well on their way to turning out alright."

"Precisely!" Percival said. "*Pre*cisely. It never occurred to me till now that these foolhardy citizens could be changed into real people, but I begin to think they might be!"

"Percival!" Martha roared suddenly. "You should be ashamed of yourself."

"What?" Percival looked startled. Martha's wrath was rare, but universally avoided among the Maskies.

"Anyone would think you'd granted *yourself* the gift of immunity to the emperor's curse!" she exclaimed. "Or earned it by your sparkling achievements. But it's the other way around and don't you forget it. The only reason you've any achievements to boast of at all is *because* you're not subject to the imagination restrictions. The fact that you're blessed by the gods with freedom that your countrymen don't enjoy is not something to be proud of, it's something to be tremblingly grateful for. 'Real people' indeed! I'd be thankful to see *you* turned into a real person."

"I only meant—" Percival started, but Martha wasn't finished. She turned on the rest of them, who had been sitting quietly hoping to avoid the eye of the storm.

"You're all just as bad as each other. Talking about how much more you could accomplish if you could make the Druinians useful. *Useful!* Percival may very well be onto something here. It may be possible to help these poor folks as we've been able to help these children. But not so they can help *us* annoy the emperor. The only reason to help them is for *them*, so they can enjoy the same liberty you all are congratulating yourselves on having."

Percival looked entirely ashamed by the time this outburst came to its abrupt end, but Raymond regarded his wife with frank admiration. The others were looking down at their boots, except for Ava, who looked like she wanted to cheer, and Andrew, who was merely observing with cool interest as if she had presented a dry academic argument. This was Andrew's reaction to most things.

"She's right, you know," Melody spoke up from where she was perched on Luke's lap. "It's not their fault they're like that."

"I know, I know" Percival said. "It's just... you see the little fools day in and day out and it just doesn't feel like there's any hope for them."

"Because they have no hope themselves." Ava rejoined passionately. "Any they have is beaten out of them in the Institute. Which is exactly why that's where we have to start."

"Of course!" said Joel enthusiastically. "We should've thought of it before."

"I don't follow," said Harmon.

"Think about it!" Ava said. "Every child is required to attend the Institute. That six years is designed to break their spirits and scrub their imaginations. They're isolated, subjected to all manner of cruel punishments, and taught all manner of nonsense, until they graduate as good, obedient citizens. If Marlowe could be sure of their undivided loyalty without it, why go to all the trouble?"

"I'm beginning to follow," said Harmon.

"It's as if the magic is a poisonous mist," Andrew interjected in his usual dispassionate tone. "It envelopes the whole mind, but it doesn't sink in deep. It seems that very little is required to make it dissipate."

"So then," Raymond said, growing excited, "there's something still alive in them when they go in."

"Of course! And when they come out, as well, only it's buried a little deeper. Marlowe must have known that all along. If they can be turned toward him, they could be perhaps be turned the other direction as well," Percival said.

"So what do you suggest?" asked Regan. "Kidnap the kids from the Institute?"

"Or we take over the school," Ava said quietly.

"Ha! Well that'll be easy enough, won't it?" said Philip. "Just getting the one out didn't cost enough?"

Ava turned toward him earnestly. "What is the point of having an imagination if we don't use it to help those in need? I'm not suggesting we raid the place and carry them all off. It'll have to be done strategically of course."

"But I thought we'd agreed against kidnapping?" Tobias ventured, not unreasonably.

Percival shook his head. "I don't think it *is* kidnapping. It's the school that's done the kidnapping. It's not as if the children are ever returned to their parents."

"But they do it with the parents' consent," Tobias said.

"Bah. If it's compulsory, it's hardly consent. The whole system is so wretchedly twisted. Anyway, we won't actually *take* them anywhere. We just need to get to where they are and teach them to think for themselves."

"That's what you're really after, isn't it?" Wes, who had been quietly observing the conversation, spoke up for the first time. "You're not just talking about rescuing kids here and there. You want to break the whole system, don't you?"

Percival's eyes lit up. He'd been dreaming of this for some time and it had sparked something in his heart.

"If I could do that," he said. "If I could strike one great blow at the head of the monster that is Druinor... I'd consider that a life well lived."

Martha rolled her eyes and Ava smiled. "You mean if you could see a number of Druinians become free citizens," she said gently.

It didn't take long for Percival's enthusiasm to catch on. Once the plan had been explained to the rest of the Guard, they all agreed that nothing could be more noble, nor more detrimental to Marlowe's reign, than to destroy the Institute, though the task was more daunting than any they'd undertaken thus far. They talked late into that and many other nights about how to go about it.

20

THE RUNAWAYS

Molly had only seen Abner once before their trip together in his flying house, and she had been very ill at the time. Still she remembered the hermit's features clearly; his blunt nose, leathery skin, and eyes that belonged in a younger man's face.

If not for those eyes, Molly would not have believed that she now beheld the same man. She had come to Abner's house to thank him, and although Mardius had warned her, she found herself wholly unprepared for the dramatic transformation that had taken place in the old prophet.

The man, who had looked to be in his sixties when they last met, now appeared to be at least eighty, a mere two weeks later. She had been told that traveling as he did would age him, but it was only now, as she sat across from him that those words began to take on meaning. His shoulders were stooped, his fingers knobby, and his skin spotted with age. His once stubbly gray beard was now snow white and long enough to tuck into his belt. Still, the same sharp, clear eyes gazed out from beneath his milky eyebrows.

Looking into those eyes, Molly felt tears spring up in her own and looked hastily away.

"What is it, dear?" he inquired in a gentle voice that bore little resemblance to the gruff man Hatch had encountered in the woods. As he spoke, Abner reached across the table and took Molly's small hand in his own. "Don't cry, child. There's no need."

Molly composed herself before speaking. "But…" she hesitantly met his eyes and found no resentment there. "I came to thank you sir. I didn't… I never realized how much it cost you to do what you did."

"No more than was reasonable," Abner answered with a smile.

"I'd say a good deal more! Why you're…" Molly flushed. "I mean…"

Abner patted her hand absently. "On the contrary dear. I did no more than is required of every man, woman, and child."

"I'm afraid I don't understand sir," Molly said. "You gave years of your life in an instant. Surely that's not required of everyone, how could it be?"

"Oh it looks different for everyone, to be sure. It may take some people much longer and require a great deal more endurance. And some may rebel. But in the end, we each have the same duty."

"And what is that, sir?"

"To do what's needed and pay no regard to the cost. To pour oneself out in love for our fellow man."

Molly contemplated this. In Druinor people didn't do things out of love for their fellow man. They certainly never did things at a cost to themselves. This philosophy was wholly foreign to her. Yet here she sat with a man whom she'd met only once before, who seemed cheerfully oblivious to the price he had paid for her transportation.

After a moment of silence, Abner spoke again. "What's troubling you?"

Molly felt tears sting her eyes again. "It's just… I don't deserve it, that's all."

"Is that all? Don't trouble yourself over that. No one does! Besides which, my dear, you are a child. The suffering of children should always be borne by grown-ups, no matter what."

"Still," Molly asked tentatively, "don't you regret it even a little? Meaning no disrespect of course, but think of all you'll miss out on!"

"Not for a moment," Abner said firmly. "I'd far rather spend all my years at once in an act of love than live them out slowly in cold selfishness."

Molly had no idea what to make of this. "Well, I'm afraid I don't have much, but if there is anything I do have that I can repay you with… I'm sure my mother would gladly…"

"Don't be silly," Abner cut her off. "There is no debt to be repaid. Only remember what I've said when the time comes for you to do the same."

Molly saw a hint of sadness in his eyes when he said this, but before she could ask what he meant, Abner changed the subject with a smile.

"Now then. How would you like to learn to play Chess? I have a beautiful set somewhere. In Druinor the pieces are all plain granite, but here they're made of crystal and obsidian. I haven't had the pleasure of using them in Arden for years."

This made even less sense to Molly, but she was glad for

the diversion. So, accompanied by cake and a spiced tea, they spent the rest of the afternoon laughing and talking over a very unique Chessboard.

᠁

Brogan had brought the prophecy to Arden, and it had been the topic of much discussion. It was passed around among the adults and examined line by line for clues. Mardius echoed Eldon's frustration at the lack of precision among the prophets. They presented and dismissed theories about the travellers, the timing, and the possibility that it was only meant to be a metaphor. Each of them held conflicting positions about the prophecy, but they universally agreed that it could not, as some of them had once believed, be a reference to Molly and Hatch.

"Much more likely, the curse must be broken by something other than human," Mardius said at one of these meetings.

"The dual citizenship seemed hopeful to Eldon and me," Brogan said. "But at the time we thought the only path to Arden was through the mountains, and I think we read too much into that."

It was Lydia who said plainly what they had all been carefully avoiding. "It wouldn't matter if it *were* about them. They're safe for the first time in their lives, and they are children. If anyone is going to waste their time on a likely pointless but certainly dangerous journey to break an unbreakable curse, it ought to be us, not them."

They all agreed with this and the matter was laid to rest until one night, when all the families had stayed at the palace to avoid having to saddle horses for a late trip to their homes, Hatch was startled awake by the sound of his door creaking open. Sitting up quickly, he saw Molly tip toeing across his room, a tawny cat at her feet. She was fully dressed and carrying a bag over her shoulder. Her arm had mostly healed, but she still cradled it gingerly.

"Molly? What's happened?" he asked as Seamus leapt up onto the bed.

"Hatch," she whispered. "We've got to go."

"Go where? What's happened?" but he knew.

"To the mountains. We need to go now."

"You've been dreaming, Molly," Hatch said irritably. "The prophecy isn't about us after all. We've all been over it a hundred times."

"I know," Molly persisted. "But it doesn't matter. You know it doesn't. What about our parents?"

"What about them? They agree."

"Not *those* parents. Our parents in Druinor. And… you know… everyone else." Molly was thinking again of Edith, against whom she had borne so much ill will.

Hatch had been feeling the same thing himself, but he disliked being awakened from a deep sleep. "What are we supposed to do about it? We aren't wizards." He laid back down and rolled over but Molly was having none of it.

"Hatch!" she whispered loudly as she shook him by the shoulder. "We have to go *now!*"

"Alright, *alright!* But let go of me!" Hatch made no attempt to keep quiet.

"Shhhhh!" Seamus hissed. "You'll wake them all up and then we'll never get out."

"Good," Hatch said, though he did lower his voice. "This is madness."

"You know it's not," Molly said. "They have the best of intentions, but they don't know what it's like over there, and they have no real plan. Something has to be done. Now."

She was right of course, but Hatch hated to admit it.

Instead, he stalked to where his clothes were strewn about the floor, and began to throw them into his duffel. Molly and Seamus waited, casting anxious glances at the door.

Finally, he was ready. "Well, let's get it over with then," he whispered brusquely.

They crept out of his room and through the palace halls, being careful not to attract the attention of guards and servants. Molly remembered the enormous halls of the Institute, also marble and spotless and echoing, but somehow so much colder and more impersonal. With a pang, she realized how little she wanted to leave Mardius' palace, with its tapestries and fur rugs and warm fireplaces and ringing laughter.

They managed to creep out of the palace unseen and set off on foot, with no map, no horses, scarce provisions, and only one cat, heading west.

༄

Brogan had set off in search of the children immediately after news of their flight reached his ears. Neither he nor his wife would consider being separated again after so long, so Lydia accompanied without question. This was good thing too, as Lydia was both a more experienced tracker and more capable cook than her husband.

Brogan knew he should feel angry at the children for sneaking off in the middle of the night, but he understood instantly why they had done so, and reproached himself instead. Other than the children, he was the only person who understood what it was like in Druinor, and knew he ought to have pressed for more urgent action. Instead, he'd allowed two children to bear the burden that ought to have been his.

He felt no fear on their behalf for the journey, for they

had both proven themselves to be brave and capable, but Brogan could not bear the thought of their facing the challenges that awaited them alone, except for a faithful Druinian cat.

He was expressing these thoughts to Lydia as they set out, when he heard the sound of riders approaching from behind. They turned to meet their pursuers and were not surprised to find Aodhan, Grace, and Rowena.

"Not so fast, Brogan," Aodhan called. "You two won't be going in search of our children alone while we wait in comfort at home. You and your wife lost twelve years serving our families. No more. Go home and rest."

"And not see those years of loss bear fruit? I think not," Lydia retorted.

Before Aodhan could object again, Rowena interjected. "Perhaps we should thank fate that we've found you here on the same task," she said, recognizing the resolve behind Lydia's smiling eyes. "More of us can cover more ground. Let us travel west together for now, for there's no doubt about the direction they went. If we don't find them before we reach the mountain range, we can each take a separate route into the hills. You and Brogan take one, Aodhan and Grace another, and I'll take a third."

Brogan shook his head. "I don't like you traveling alone, madam."

"Aodhan can take the third route alone. I'll go with you," Grace agreed.

Rowena only laughed. "I've been traveling alone since the mist, old friend."

Aodhan said nothing, but his grin suggested that it would be more trouble to dissuade Grace of her plan than it was worth.

"Alright," Rowena conceded with a wry smile. "I'll be

glad of your company."

Having settled the matter, they set out at a brusque pace, all feeling confident they would find the children long before splitting up became necessary.

~

The first few days of travel were almost enjoyable. The children did not feel any more prepared for their task than they had the first time they had set out to accomplish it, but they were much more accustomed to adventure by now, and better equipped to meet the difficulties of travel. They had spent precious little time in each other's company during their stay in Arden, and were glad to have their initial camaraderie restored. Progress was slow on foot, but on this side of the wall at least there were no slave traders, invisible tunnels or threat of capture by cruel schoolmarms. Instead, they encountered only sunlit days and warm firelit nights, waving grass, rolling hills and crystal clear fresh water. Laughter and stories flowed freely between them. The children did their best to avoid towns and roads too near the capital, and Seamus, being both a cat and a spy, was incredibly adept at finding just the right routes to remain unseen. As the towns grew sparse, however, they occasionally ventured into them to buy food. Molly had, on Seamus' advice, borrowed some money from her mother, leaving an apologetic note with a promise to pay it back in full. The children often begged to be told more fairy tales, and while Seamus was no Dantes, he was no bad storyteller himself.

Before two weeks were out, they arrived at the foot of the Western Mountains. The terrain had been growing steadily less welcoming for a day or two, and the breeze was just turning cold enough to be uncomfortable. The pleasant foliage of the Ardenian countryside had grown sparse, until they found themselves slowly ascending rocky slopes. Like the gentle shift in the landscape, the first signs of trouble within the little group appeared slowly and initially went unnoticed.

As they neared the outer edges of Arden, Molly's nightmares, which had become rarer during her stay in Arden though they hadn't ceased entirely, resumed their frequency. The dream was always the same: Marlowe, on the horizon. Marlowe eclipsing the light. Marlowe's malevolent eyes finding her, gripping some poor creature in his left hand and pointing at her with his right. As the distance from Arden grew, so did the intensity of the nightmares, until, one dreadful night, Molly caught a glimpse of the old wizard's prey: the figure that hung limply from his bony fist was Hatch.

The real Hatch, on hearing her distressed whimpers, shook her out of the dream's icy grip whenever he could. As this went on, her restless nights and long days of travel began to make her cross, even irrational at times. Hatch, being exhausted himself, had little sympathy for her temperament changes, and the two of them would have fought more often were it not for Seamus' stabilizing influence. Yet though his gentle admonitions frequently quelled their quarrels, they did nothing to stem the increasing frustration Molly felt as the trauma of the previous months took its toll.

Bitterness began to creep quietly into her soul. Almost without realizing it she had begun to resent both of her companions. They seemed to share such an easy camaraderie from which she was excluded. This was largely her own doing, of course. They often tried to include her in their jokes and conversation, but to no avail.

Whenever one of her companions made some passing reference to their shared adventure in the Wasteland, she rolled her eyes, and thought bitterly, *so glad you all had such a wonderful time while I was locked away in that dreadful prison of a school.* And after a few days, these thoughts began to take on an even more alarming slant. *Yes, yes, it's a grand time you had, after you abandoned me to be tortured by the Institute teachers, of course.*

You and I know that she had in no wise been abandoned, and that Hatch had worried himself sick about her. Yet the path of resentment, once embarked upon, becomes difficult to escape. It was as though Snyder's insidious words had stuck in her like a poisoned dart, its venom slowly working its way through her and siphoning all joy as it went.

Hatch, for his part, did very little to smooth things over. The more irritable Molly became, the more he coldly ignored her and spoke to Seamus instead. Seamus' own peppery disposition seemed to have been tamed by his stay in Arden and he turned out to be a great conversationalist. Between stories, he talked to the children about the political workings and culture of their two governments at great length, which Hatch found mildly interesting and Molly highly irksome.

Meanwhile the terrain became increasingly difficult. The rolling foothills lasted only a day before the climb became more treacherous. Seamus was certain Marlowe would not have chosen the location of his mountain prison on the Ardenian side of the mountain range, so they did not slow themselves down by extensively searching during the first part of the journey. This was for the best, since they found the steep climbs and narrow passes taxing enough by themselves. The air grew first crisp, then cold as they ascended, and the children (who'd spent all their lives in the Druinian flat lands) found themselves often short of breath.

Despite all this, the journey still held some of the magic and adventure of those first few days after the children had left home. The snowcapped peaks, forests, and valleys were beautiful in a sharp, proud way, and in unguarded moments, Molly found herself marveling that they had found a place more majestic than even Mardius' palace had been.

⁓

If you had met Alice in the dwarves' cave, and then by some combination of unlikely circumstances made her acquaintance again in Damascus a month or two later, you very likely would not have known she was the same girl. The steady and vibrant love of Martha, the patient firmness of Ava and the freedom of mind and heart she enjoyed among the other residents of Damascus had worked a most marvelous change in little Alice. Her once spiteful eyes now shone with light and curiosity. Though her demeanor still bore some marks of the unruly manners and petulance we witnessed in her at first, these were quickly fading.

Martha and Melody, who had become fast friends, were especially pleased with this transformation, and Martha could often be heard remarking to the cat, "I dare say, that child is almost becoming kind!"

Alice was herself a bit taken aback by how quickly her own heart had softened. When once she had yielded to a bit of kindness, her heart had quite run away with her and before long she found herself actually enjoying people's company and thinking nice things about them. It was a bit dizzying, but she decided she liked it much better than the old way, and gave herself over to it entirely.

Her days in Damascus were the happiest she'd yet

experienced. Only Eldon could have understood the healing balm such a place could be to a soul that had wandered long in Druinor. Alice had grown to genuinely love Martha, and was beginning to quite like Rob and Ben as well. Even Ava, whom she had despised in school, had finally won her over. So it was perhaps a sign of how thoroughly the change had worked its way into her soul when she announced, to everyone's surprise, that she wanted to go back to the Institute.

She and the boys, along with a small group of the Maskies, were eating supper when she said, with a very serious expression, "I think I ought to go back to school."

Rob and Ben gaped at her in horror.

"Sorry, what was that?" Percival asked with polite incredulity.

"You needn't look at me like that," she said quickly to Ben. "I don't mean all of us. Just me."

"But... *why?*" demanded a dumbfounded Ben.

"As a spy!" she declared, relishing the wondering looks on the faces of her supper companions. Alice had been learning about espionage in her lessons with Andrew, and had been quite taken with the idea. "You've been talking about taking down the Institute, haven't you? Well it seems to me you'd better have an inside man, and Ava can hardly go back."

This last was true enough and had caused Ava no end of distress. She had felt entirely useless while she worked at the school, but now that she was gone, she could not bear to think of the children she'd left there without a soul to show them any kindness.

Alice's speech heralded a wide variety of responses, from shock to excitement to utter confusion, and these were just from Percival. They were all quite bowled over by the nobility of this proposition, especially coming from a child who'd experienced the horrors of the school firsthand. Martha barely held back affectionate tears, but nonetheless she shook her head.

"You can't do that, dear," she said warmly. "It isn't safe."

"Certainly not," said Tobias with a darker look than any had seen on his face for some weeks. "After what Molly and Ava went through in just a few weeks? After Eldon? I won't stand for it."

Percival, who for one wild moment had entertained the thought, tossed his head as if just coming to his senses. "Of course not. You'd be risking your life, and you're in our care. But still, it's pretty much the bravest thing I've ever heard anyone say," he said, and the respect in his tone made Alice suddenly feel embarrassed.

"It is a good idea, though," said Raymond thoughtfully. Tobias turned on him with a fierce look but he waved dismissively. "I don't mean the child, of course, I agree with you there. But we ought to get *someone* back inside as a first step. In fact, we really need quite a few someones. A whole team."

"Oh, a whole *team*," Nathaniel laughed. "Why didn't we think of that before? What do you say we all go down in the morning, and apply for faculty positions? We'll just say, 'Hello! We're the Damascus Guard! Have you any openings for professors? Some of us are pretty good at math.'"

Everyone laughed at this. Raymond, seeming wholly unruffled, only winked at him before looking at Martha and saying, "Well, dear, I'm off to bed. These ruffians are far too witty for me. See you in a bit?"

Martha kissed him and put the kettle on to make tea for the rest of them.

"Say, Alice," Ben said quietly. "That was really something."

Alice blushed again.

༄

Captain Snyder knew that any measure of grace extended to him by the emperor was quickly dissipating. Rather than search the hills at random, he had chosen to start his search in the capital by rooting out the Damascus Guard and learning from them the route the children had taken. Once discovered, he felt confident he could overtake them with ease, so long as he didn't wait too long to start.

Of course, dozens of patrols had set out into the mountains in the meantime with instructions to send Snyder word the instant they picked up a trail. But there were many miles of wooded lands to cover and any number of possible routes and hiding places for two small children and two even smaller cats. Luckily for our heroes, traveling first through the Wasteland and then approaching the mountains from the north, rather than the south, was not one of the possibilities their pursuers had considered. Therefore, the many patrolling search parties continued to turn up nothing at all, much to Snyder's (and more importantly, Marlowe's) displeasure.

It was with increasingly panicked fervor that Snyder focused his efforts on ferreting out the members of the Damascus Guard. Once he had almost caught them too, but after that near miss, the rebels had gone completely silent. This infuriated Snyder, whose defeat on the steps of the school was forever branded into his memory. The faces of the three Maskies by whom he'd been so humiliated taunted his every waking moment and he fancied he glimpsed them under every passing hat.

However, for all his many faults, our luckless villain was not a complete fool. Once it became apparent that his search for the rebels inside the capital was likely to remain fruitless, he abandoned the case of the disappearing renegades and instead turned his focus to direct pursuit of the children. He tripled the number of patrols combing the countryside, though he had to conscript ordinary citizens to do so. Once satisfied that there was no corner of the country in which the children could safely hide, he enlisted the aid of four particularly brutal policemen to accompany him, visited a local stable to procure the use of travel-worthy horses, and set out directly to the Western Mountains. If the children could not be apprehended before they reached Fairy Tale, he would be waiting for them when they arrived.

၁

Many believe there is no such thing as coincidence, and some owe all seeming happenings of chance to Providence instead. I am inclined to agree with these, for it seems irreverent to thank luck for the fact that Snyder chose Philip's stable from which to borrow horses for his journey. It was not the best stable in the city, nor was it the closest to Snyder's home or the police station. Yet, for whatever reason, Snyder chose that stable on the night in question.

Philip, to his credit, did not visibly react to seeing the police captain enter, though he was certain he was about to be arrested. He greeted the man cheerfully, showing no sign of recognition, nor of relief when he realized that Snyder was simply there as a customer, rather than an arresting officer. He drove a fair bargain for the horses with just the right amount of bartering, and even managed to ask a few casual questions about the kind of travel Snyder planned to do and the length of the journey (to ensure that an important Druinian official had the best horse for the task at hand, of course). Finally, he made arrangements for Snyder to retrieve his purchases later that evening, and saw him to the door. Heart pounding, Philip stoically watched till Snyder was out of sight, before allowing his knees to give way somewhat. After taking a moment to collect himself, Philip summoned his assistant, announced that he had urgent business to which he must attend, and raced back to Damascus.

⌒

The Maskies were palpably relieved when Philip delivered his news. Finally, an immediate task called for their attention!

"At last!" said Tobias. "We must follow him of course, and prevent the children's being caught unawares."

"Besides which, he'll lead us straight to Fairy Tale," said Nathaniel, who, having been introduced to that lady's work by Melody, had a great desire to meet her.

In a moment of uncharacteristic sobriety, Percival spoke up. "To follow a party of soldiers over long distances in the mountains is no small task, brothers. It will take all of our cunning to avoid being caught. It will mean staying within sight of their campfire and being unable to light our own."

Nathaniel gave him a scornful look and Percival laughed. No further commentary was needed.

From that point they had only to decide which of them should go. Everyone was restless to escape the confines of Damascus and be useful again at long last. Andrew argued that there was safety in numbers, as Snyder had acquired only five horses. He and four Druinian thugs would be no match for the entire Damascus Guard.

Ultimately, however, he was overruled in favor of a smaller group that could travel less conspicuously. Percival, of course, would lead the campaign. The rest of the Maskies vied for the other slots, but in service of the children, a little team within the team had formed already, and it seemed only natural that they be the ones to undertake the task.

So it was that when Snyder departed the stable a second time that day, this time in the company of his men and in possession of his newly acquired mounts, Percival, Nathaniel, Tobias, and Ava watched him go. When they had seen him ride a safe distance, they set out as well.

21

SIGNS

Searching an entire mountain range for a single person is somewhat difficult, due to the fact that mountain ranges are quite large, and people, by comparison, are very small. This task was made immeasurably *more* difficult by the fact that the two children and one feline who set forth into the heart of the Western Mountains did not know where they were going.

Naturally, over the preceding twelve years, many expeditioners had set out with the same objective, as everyone in Arden knew that Fairy Tale was held captive somewhere in this mountain range. Some had returned defeated, others having enjoyed great adventures and with fascinating stories to tell. Others did not return at all. Seamus was beginning to think it very likely that he and his young wards would join the ranks of this second unfortunate group. The children knew none of this, but as the mountains loomed before them, they both realized with increasing trepidation that they were wholly unprepared for the task ahead.

As they paused in a thick wood, Molly caught a glimpse of a mountain's far-off peak through the trees. She knew there were more and higher peaks beyond it to the north and south.

"We should have brought a map," she said morosely.

Seamus made a noise that sounded like "humph" but Hatch suddenly went deathly pale.

Molly saw his horrified expression and gave a start herself. "Hatch? What's wrong?

"Uh…" he swallowed. "It's just… I forgot until just now. The whole reason we had to go through the Wasteland instead of approaching the mountains from the other side."

Seamus looked up sharply, as if he too, was only now remembering the conversation.

"What? For a map?" Molly looked from one to the other, uncomprehending.

"Maybe," Hatch said. "I'm not sure. Only, Abner said there was something in Arden we needed before we could go looking for Fairy Tale."

"*What?*" Molly gaped at him. "And that didn't seem important to you?"

Hatch bristled. "Things have been a bit busy."

"Oh well if you've been *busy*, then it's perfectly *fine* that we're wandering the wretched mountains without a single idea where we're going, isn't it?" she began gathering up their lunch supplies and savagely hurling them into bags.

"We don't even know if a map was the thing we needed!" Hatch protested, as if it made any difference.

There were times when Seamus felt highly aware of his diminutive size and this was one of them. "There's nothing that can be done about it now," he said, but neither child paid him any heed.

"Oh no, it's perfectly fine, isn't it," Molly was fairly shaking now, "if we never see our parents on *either* side of the wall again and utterly fail our mission, because *Hatch* was *busy!*"

"Well I might have had a chance to ask about it if you hadn't insisted on sneaking off in the middle of the night!" Hatch snarled. "Everything was going fine until *you* got impatient!"

Molly turned on him, furious tears forming in her eyes. Hatch could not have known how her stomach had sunk at his revelation. He couldn't have understood how she'd suffered alone in the Institute, and how it had stung her that he had gone on without her. He could not have known that she already felt like a burden to him. He saw instantly that he had wounded her, but in the moment he didn't care.

Molly spun on her heel and stalked off into the woods without another word. Hatch refused to meet Seamus' eyes for fear of seeing the reproach in them. Quietly, the cat followed her. Grumbling to himself, Hatch followed too.

It was too late to go back to Arden, so Seamus suggested that they try to maintain a southwest course.

"She'll be closer to the Druinor side than our side," he reasoned. "So our best chance is to head into the mountains toward Druinor. When we have to decide what direction to go, we'll let the sun be our guide."

The children both thought this was sound advice, but neither said anything. Seamus took their silence as assent, and the unhappy travelers trudged on, each resenting the company of the others.

By supper, a tentative peace had been reached. Neither child wanted to be the first one to apologize, but neither did they want to maintain their current mood. Eventually, they each allowed Seamus to draw them into conversation with him until things began to flow a bit more naturally.

But as the days wore on, Molly's nightmares increased and her patience deteriorated. The longer they climbed the more ridiculous it seemed to her that they had ever thought they might find one solitary woman hidden by the enchantments of a powerful wizard, in the midst of an enormous mountain range.

Of course, she was quite right, and in normal circumstances, their quest would certainly have failed. Had they set out as they had originally planned, with the guidance and maps of the palace, and followed the course set out for them, their journey would have been as fruitless as all those who had gone before them. That is to say, if they had gone about things like adults.

But as fate would have it, children's eyes, even in your world, have about them a certain magical quality that allows them to see things adults have by and large forgotten how to see. Cats, having much more insight into the human condition than many humans do, are keenly aware of this difference.

Thus, when Hatch casually remarked one day, "We're nearly past the giant", Seamus stopped so suddenly that Molly tread on his tail.

Seamus ignored her and focused on Hatch. "What did you say?" he asked.

Hatch seemed embarrassed. "Er... it's nothing really. I was just noticing... you see those rocks over there? From almost every angle, it looks exactly like a large man." He pointed to a rock outcropping that was nearly parallel with them.

Molly and Seamus looked where Hatch pointed. It took the cat a moment to see it, but Molly saw it at once.

"I'll say! I can't believe I didn't see it before," she laughed, momentarily forgetting to be irritated. Seamus thought she sounded more like herself than she had in days.

"Anyway," Hatch shrugged, "I've been thinking of him as The Giant because... well doesn't it look just as if he's carrying a boy in his hand?"

Molly's stomach dropped suddenly.

"Does he?" Seamus said, straining his eyes. Turning back to look at Hatch, he had a curious light in his eye. "By the heavens..."

"But it's just an illusion... isn't it?" Hatch said, not understanding why the feline was behaving so strangely.

"Yes of course," the cat answered. "But I think we might as well go have a look, don't you?"

"Why?" demanded Molly. "It'll only delay us even more and it's only a bunch of stupid rocks." A sick knot had formed in her gut at Hatch's words, and she desired nothing more than to get as far away from this waking vision of her nightmares as soon possible.

"Well," Seamus said, feeling a little foolish himself, as anyone does whose imagination has been tempered by an irritated realist. "Perhaps it *is* just a rock outcropping, but it's a very remarkable one. And it just so happens, there's a widely known fairytale about a giant and a little boy."

"There is?" cried Hatch. "Oh tell it to us would you?"

"Gladly," Seamus answered. "But while I do, I think we'd better go take a look, don't you?"

This time both children agreed. The giant, once they'd reached it, however, seemed wholly unremarkable. It was, up close, just what it had seemed from afar – an odd, but coincidental result of natural erosion on the mountainside.

Still, Hatch could not shake the odd impression it gave him, as though something there was more than it seemed. He was, therefore, hesitant to resume their previous course even after a thorough examination yielded no further revelations.

It was Molly who eventually found what they were looking for – not a part of the giant himself, but a little behind him and to the right. It was a little path, so narrow and unassuming it could hardly be regarded as a path at all, and definitely not one worthy of such a mighty sentry as the giant guarding its mouth. There didn't appear to be anywhere for it to lead, except straight into the rock face from which the giant protruded. It was unlikely, therefore, that anyone who saw would bother to explore. Yet it had about it that same intangible mystery that had drawn them to the giant, and they all knew at once they must proceed down it, even if it did come to a dead end. After all, they knew from experience that even an impassable wall could sometimes be breached by the intrepid.

The little trail was lined on each side with flowers. These were all very common species you might find in a garden, but all with a very uncommon air about them. Molly almost felt, as another girl in another tale had felt once before, that they might answer her if she spoke to them. But of course, being in the company of others, she was too shy to attempt to talk to flowers. It is probably a good thing too, since the ground around these flowers was very soft, and they were likely too sleepy to talk.

Of course once the path had been spotted, there was no need to discuss what to do. They all felt instinctively that fate had pointed them in the direction they ought to go, and set out at once, flowers dancing about their ankles, knees, and in Seamus' case, ears.

The little troop progressed with a renewed confidence that they would certainly reach their destination, and Seamus made the children swear to tell him anything they saw that sparked their interest, however unimportant it might seem. He guessed that they might come across other landmarks of the same nature as the giant, but the children were at a disadvantage, not being familiar with most fairy tales. He was likewise handicapped by virtue of being a both a Druinian and a cat – thus imminently practical by nature – making it necessary for them all to lean on one another to find the way.

The little path twisted and turned sharply before leading them into a little valley they would never have seen from the vantage point of the giant. It was not very wide, but it was pleasant – full of sunlight and waving heather, with a little creek running through its center. After their tiring climb, the travelers stopped there for a while to picnic and rest.

The little valley felt like a haven from the cold, weary, mountaintop and no one was anxious to leave it. They sat with their tired feet in the brook talking and laughing, and Molly felt more at ease than she had in some time. But the day wore on quickly, and reluctantly they heeded Seamus' urging to take up the journey again.

However, when they followed the little footpath out of the valley, their initial fear was realized: it was a dead end. Cresting the hill on the opposite side of the valley, they came to a plateau covered by a wind-blown sea of waist high grass, and the rock face itself which sprang up before them to an alarming height. At this barrier, the path ended abruptly, and no alternative routes immediately presented themselves.

Still, ever since the giant, they had all felt sure of their direction, and were not as crestfallen as they might have been a day or two before. Instead, they set themselves to problem solving.

"Do you think there's a way to climb it?" Molly asked, peering doubtfully upward toward the cliff's distant top.

"I perhaps could," Seamus said. "But not you two."

"Seamus," Hatch ventured, thinking back over their adventure thus far and remembering his captivity in the dwarf warren. "Are there any fairy tales that take place underground or inside a mountain?"

Seamus thought about this for a moment. "Eldon once told me an account of some adventurers using the dwarf tunnels inside a mountain to find a dragon. But in that tale there was a door which opened to them upon the speaking of a secret word. I see nothing of that sort here. There was another in which a boy discovered goblins living inside mountain tunnels, but he found them by working in a mine."

At the thought of goblins and dark mountain tunnels, Molly shuddered involuntarily.

Seamus began to walk the perimeter of the little clearing looking for signs. After a few moments he darted back to where his companions stood.

"I think I've found something!" He purred with excitement.

Found something he had. Leaving their comfortable little footpath and plunging into the waves of grass, they followed him till they came to a low stone hewn cylinder which could only be the mouth of a well.

"This must be it," he announced. "And perhaps our own Mother Holle lies at the end."

"Mother who?" Molly asked, looking apprehensively into darkness of the pit below.

"She makes it snow, my dear," Seamus said, failing to provide any illumination to the children thereby.

He would be persuaded to tell the tale as they traveled,

but at the moment the cat's attention was occupied by trying to find a way down the well. The pulley and its rope, if they had ever been there, were long gone, but an examination of the stone lip revealed what appeared to be an engraved spindle on its outside. On the inside of the wall, in the corresponding location, there was a groove carved out of the stone. Hatch swung a leg over and lodged one toe into it, feeling further down with his other leg.

"This must be it," he said when his foot had found purchase for the third time. "Yes of course. This is it."

Despite his bravado, Hatch's voice trembled a bit, and Molly didn't like it much either. Watching Hatch descend into that pit, clinging to the walls, made her feel queasy. Seamus, too, seemed to quail. Still, it seemed they had no other choice. Molly invited Seamus to sit on her shoulder and reluctantly began her own descent, though she kept her eyes closed as she felt her way down.

It seemed like an impossibly long climb, but they all reached the bottom safely. The whole party felt shaky after their ordeal, so for a few moments they sat and caught their breath.

In the dim light afforded by the mouth of the well above them, Molly spied a lamp that must have been left for just such travelers as they. Once lit, the lamp revealed a bare tunnel extending out indefinitely before them. Despite a few visible spider webs, the tunnel lacked the frightening, gloomy feeling one would expect in the sort of fairy tale where one meets goblins in the heart of a mountain, so they took courage and began to proceed down it.

As they walked, Seamus told them the story of Mother Holle and the two step sisters.

"But that well wasn't like this one at all," said Hatch.

"There are no sunlit plains, or baking bread, or apple trees here."

"Indeed not," Seamus answered. "But that makes no matter. If my theory is correct, then the path to Fairy Tale's prison is lined with bits and pieces of the stories, but that's all."

"Like fairy tale landmarks?" Molly asked with interest.

"Exactly," said the cat. "Like the stars that lead a sailor home, and which only a sailor knows how to read."

"Then Marlowe won't be able to see them?" Hatch asked.

"I should think not. He hasn't the eyes you have, nor the understanding of fairy tales. He might see one or two, like the giant, but they'd mean nothing to him."

"Why would Marlowe need to see them?" said Molly with a derisive snort. "He's the one who *put* her there. Don't you think he knows where she is?"

"True," Seamus answered. "But I can't help but feel these little signs were placed here for us."

"But what good is that? Marlowe's sure to be waiting for us as soon as we get there," Molly retorted. She had been thinking this for some time now, but it had not previously occurred to Hatch, who looked greatly taken aback.

"I've been wondering that myself," Seamus said quietly. "I don't know the answer. I only know that every time we find one of these little fairy tale markers, it sets us in the right direction, and we must follow it."

Molly was unconvinced, but they knew there was little choice but to keep moving forward, even if they were heading into Marlowe's trap.

﹏

The adults had all felt quite certain that they would catch up to the children before they were forced to split up, and were becoming more and more concerned as they drew near the foot of the mountains.

"They must have the protection of fate upon them," Brogan would often remark, but this brought little comfort to parents twice deprived of their offspring.

Once they reached the mountains themselves, Aodhan theorized, they would be sure to find signs of the children's passage more quickly. There were only a few passable routes, and they must have taken one of them. They chose the three most likely paths, and each party drew straws to determine who would search them. Brogan and Lydia, the straws determined, would take the path nearest by, Aodhan would take one to the north, and Grace and Rowena would take the southernmost route.

It was Grace who suggested that they journey only two days into the mountains before returning to a central meeting point.

"If we see no sign of them at all in two days, chances are we've missed their trail altogether," she said. "If any of us are not back here in four days, we can assume they have actually found signs of the children. The rest of us can set out immediately to catch up."

Thus they shook hands, quickly recited the Entreaty for Divine Protection, and set off on their separate paths.

Aodhan's instinct had been right: the children were much easier to track in the mountains.

Within only a few hours, Lydia stopped suddenly and gasped. "Look!" she said.

Brogan followed the direction of her pointing finger to where a little campfire, now cold, had been stamped out. His heart quickened. Surely they would catch up to them now! After all, he and his bride were on horseback and the children on foot.

They paused to search the area and found other little signs that confirmed their suspicions: the discarded beginning of a carved wood figurine, a piece of a bootlace, and most telling of all, soft paw prints in the ashes.

In truth, they were not far behind the children and they very well might have caught up to them, had it not been for their eyes, which, unfortunately, were those of adults. Thus when they passed a large rock outcropping that looked a little bit like a giant holding a small boy, they thought nothing of it and passed by.

Not long after that, all signs of the children vanished entirely.

⁓

The rest of the journey through the mountains was uneventful, with only a small exception. To Molly's relief and Hatch's disappointment, they did not encounter any goblins or deformed mountain folk who wander the underground warrens of some stories. There were certainly many smaller channels that branched off from the one they traveled, and occasionally they could hear far off sounds of movement from deep inside the mountain. However, they did not sound ominous or out of place, nor did anyone question whether they ought to turn into one of the connecting tunnels. By unspoken unanimous choice they continued along the path of the hall they'd entered, until they found its end.

The only hiccup happened when they'd been several hours inside the mountain and were nearing (though they did not recognize it as such) the place from which they would emerge.

Though the tunnels were not frightening, they were exceedingly dreary and most of their conversation had given way to weary trudging. Molly could not help but recall a similar journey she had taken through the dwarf warren, but her memory omitted the joyful hope she had felt at the time. Instead, it recalled only the loneliness of that trek, the cold and hungry night that followed and the imprisonment in the Institute. She remembered the wicked Professor Dalton, and Captain Snyder's stinging accusations, which returned with fresh potency. She forgot the warm comfort of finding a friend within the school's walls and the relief of escape, dwelling only on the bitter days spent in detention, and the miserable battle with Snyder, in which her victory was more and more beginning to feel like defeat.

She knew in her heart of hearts that Hatch had never abandoned her and never would have. She could have called to mind his pained expression when she had told him, in the light of Ardenian sunlight, of her woes and how he'd wept for his inability to save her. But once the memory has chosen the sour rather than the sweet, it becomes more and more difficult to change directions, and Molly felt her old resentment rise up once again with fervor.

Lost in these dark thoughts, she had slowed her pace considerably. The others were not far ahead of her, but Molly did not realize how large a gap she had allowed to grow between her and Hatch. When she stubbed her toe painfully on a bit of rock jutting out from the floor, Molly reached out to steady herself on his arm and instead found only empty air. She lost her balance and sprawled painfully on the rocky ground.

Seamus rushed back to make sure she was alright, but his concern only humiliated her. Hatch, meanwhile, had just caught sight of a dim glow some distance ahead and was quickening his pace toward it. On hearing Molly's cry, he momentarily stopped and turned halfway toward her.

"Hurry up I see a light!" He shouted impatiently.

It was with wounded pride and a decidedly sour demeanor that Molly endured the rest of that long trek through the mountain.

An hour or so later, the little party emerged into a fresh, starlit night, alive with the sounds of wind in the trees and the scents of wildflowers and pine. By this time, however, the poor girl had drawn too far within herself to find any enjoyment in it, and the bright exclamations of the others only annoyed her.

22

FAIRY TALE ISLAND

L ong before Captain Snyder reached his destination, he became convinced that the children never would. His trek had been a taxing one. Within days of setting out, their horses had either been stolen, frightened off by wild animals or absconded of their own accord. Since then, he and his soldiers had been driven by blizzards and plagued by bitter winds that seemed to blow from all directions. They had hazarded dangerous climbs and narrow passes, and experienced several close calls with wolves, bears, and other mountain dwelling creatures.

Throughout all of this, the Weasel had felt a nagging sense that they were being watched, though no evidence of such presented itself. Occasionally, Snyder thought he could make out ethereal voices on the wind, but thought this was likely a trick of the mountains. He repeatedly sent his men on patrols to search the surrounding woods and caves, but as each expedition turned up nothing, the patrols became more and more perfunctory.

Of the children they had seen neither hide nor hair. Snyder was surprised and not a little disappointed not to have found their frozen corpses huddled in some cave. Of course, there were many places the children could have entered the mountains, and there was always the possibility that, not knowing where they were going, they had become lost somewhere else in the range. However, Snyder knew of Brogan and Eldon's involvement, and assumed they would not have sent two children on such a mission unless they had reliable intelligence pointing them to Fairy Tale's location.

Surely, he thought, *they have been eaten by wolves or died in a blizzard along the way. No mere children could survive a journey such as this.* It never would have occurred to a man like Snyder that the mountains themselves were revolting against his presence, rallying their forces to drive him back and thwart his progress. And it certainly never crossed his mind, not even as a fleeting fancy, that whatever mysterious power pressed back against him was likewise working on the children's behalf to draw them closer to their destination.

◡◠

Tobias returned from scoping out Snyder's camping spot to find Nathaniel, Ava, and Percival huddled together around a feeble fire that did little to warm the alcove in which they camped. They spoke little and shivered much as they attempted to recover from that day's climb and prepare for another that would surely follow.

I wish I could report that the same winds of favor the children and Seamus enjoyed graced our friends in the Damascus Guard as they pursued Snyder and his men, but alas on their side of the mountains the rain fell on the just as well as the unjust. The frigid storms and snarling predators that afflicted our beleaguered villains likewise hunted the Maskies, driving them back and slowing their progress. These perils did serve them in some regard, however. The noise of predatory beasts masked their movements, the freezing rain covered their tracks, and the howling wind chipped away at the vigilance of their foes to such an extent that our heroes remained relatively safe from discovery.

Unlike Snyder, they did not have a map to guide them, and as such, they had no idea that the next day would bring them to their journey's end. They knew only cold toes, weary legs, sleepless nights and unevenly cooked rabbit meat. Still, their spirits were not so damp as they might have been. They knew Snyder and his gang were no better off, and had, within the first few days of the trek, had the pleasure of relieving the captain of his horses while their enemies slept. They had unanimously decided to set the horses free, though they would have liked to keep them. Following on horseback would only have drawn attention, and the terrain very soon became too unwelcoming for mounted travel.

It was nonetheless a cold and tired company that stared absent-mindedly into the fire that evening, each lost in his own thoughts.

"He did it again," Tobias announced, dropping down beside Ava.

"Eh?" asked Percival, rousing himself.

"Snyder."

"Oh right. Strange. Could you hear him at all this time?"

"Not a bit. He's definitely talking to someone though."

"Either that or he's a narcissist," said Ava. "Which I still suspect is the case."

"Sure, but so is Nathaniel and even he doesn't talk to himself in the mirror," Tobias retorted.

Nathaniel was too tired to be annoyed and only smiled half-heartedly.

The "it" Tobias referred to was a mysterious habit of Snyder's that they had witnessed multiple times in the preceding days. Every third or fourth night, the captain would walk a short distance from his own camp until he was out of sight of his men, withdraw what appeared to be a handheld mirror from his pocket, and proceed to have a conversation with it. They could never get close enough to discern the words, but being no strangers to magic, they assumed that the mirror was a communication device of some sort.

"Whatever that looking glass said to him it must not have been pleasant," Tobias mused. "He looked none too pleased."

Ava snorted. "Imagine if you saw his face looking out of every mirror. You'd probably be tempted to curse at it a bit as well."

Percival chuckled but his expression remained dark. "There is something ominous about it though, isn't there?"

They all agreed. The first time they had seen the mirror, they feared it was some sort of magical spyglass which would reveal their presence. After several discourses with the object, however, Snyder had shown no sign he was aware of them. Still, none of them could shake the dark feeling that little bit of glass gave them, as if some sort of evil power radiated from it. Whatever it was, that mirror was bad news.

༄

Snyder was, if nothing else, an obstinate man. He knew of

course that he could never return to Druinor to report that he had turned back halfway, having found neither Fairy Tale nor her would-be rescuers. Better to die on a cold mountain pass than deliver that news to Emperor Marlowe. So, despite the near mutinous grumblings of his men, he did at last reach the place where Marlowe had, 12 years earlier, condemned Fairy Tale to her mountain prison.

It was a marvelous place. Snyder had been picturing a little cave, cold and set with icy bars at its entrance, but it seemed that Marlowe had a flair for the dramatic. The prison was unlike anything Snyder or his men had ever seen or could ever (of course) have imagined.

Before them lay a great, circular canyon. So great, in fact, that when Snyder stood at the edge and looked over, he could only see a sickening drop with no bottom. The canyon's opposite wall was too far away to be visible, and was, likewise, shrouded in mist. From the swirling darkness at the canyon's center, a geyser of rock sprang up, so slender at its base as to appear almost delicate, but widening into a large plateau at the top. The resulting island was flush with the top of the canyon wall on either side. On that stone table, hardly discernible from Snyder's vantage point, smoke rose from a little cottage chimney. This, apparently, was where Fairy Tale had spent the last twelve solitary years.

Snyder smiled to himself as he called his men to a halt. The children could not escape him now.

༄

Seamus' intuition proved trustworthy. Their progress continued to be guided by the most unconventional of sign posts. Some were small, whimsical, barely noticeable – a patch of wildflowers that looked just like little red, hooded capes dancing in the breeze, or a pumpkin which was so shrouded in vines they would have passed it entirely, had not a mouse darted out from behind it. Other landmarks seemed dark, sometimes a little sad, or ominous. They came across a small lake in a little bower one day, whose nearly black waters were haunted by a solitary swan. She slid so silently, so mournfully across its glimmering surface that Molly began to cry without realizing it. In another place, they found a little abandoned cottage with its roof caved in. Its walls were black with soot and its furniture had long since crumbled away, except for a wicked looking pipe stove.

Yet for all their variety, all the landmarks had the same magical quality that reassured the travelers that their course was correct.

Unlike their counterparts, who strove through dangers, driving snows and harrowing climbs on the opposite side of the mountains, our heroes were so enchanted that they barely noticed the difficulty of their ascent, though they traveled long hours and climbed quite as high.

Thus supernaturally led, they too arrived at the edge of the canyon. They too saw the island balanced precariously atop the bizarre stalagmite, and they too knew they had at last arrived.

ᔋ

On Snyder's side of the canyon, the island was connected to the mainland by an impossibly long and delicate railroad track, suspended apparently by nothing over the chasm. From the mouth of a nearby cave protruded the blunt nose of a dangerous looking train engine coated in rust. Various pieces of it were lying in disarray around its wheels.

It looked as though it had been left unmanned not for

twelve years, but a thousand. Snyder could not see how this dilapidated machine had any hope of making it from one side of the chasm to the other. He congratulate himself that he would not need to test it. Evidently the children had not yet arrived, else the train would be on the island (or more likely, scattered across the chasm floor). It clearly had not run recently, and more clearly still was the only path to the island, and therefore the best place to lie in wait for his quarry.

Snyder was cautious and thoughtful in the positioning of his sentries. He created a perimeter around the train station so that it could not be approached unobserved from any side, while the sentries themselves were nearly invisible. Satisfied that he had taken every possible precaution, he now removed the looking glass from his pack and withdrew to a solitary place in which to make his report.

"Et oculus Dei," Synder whispered, his breath mixing with the cloudy tumult within the mirror's depths. After a moment the mirror cleared and Marlowe's own face appeared. The wizard's countenance looked deathly calm, but Snyder thought he saw a raging and dangerous storm behind his eyes.

"Well?" the emperor's slithery voice demanded.

"Your excellency, we have arrived. I have every reason to believe we have beaten the fugitives here, and are now lying in wait for their arrival."

"You have inspected the island where *she* resides, I presume." It was a statement, not a question.

"Er... no, Your Excellency. You yourself told me it could only be reached by train my lord. The train is on this side still and does not appear to have been used for some time."

Marlowe, however, was all too familiar with Fairy Tale's unique powers and did not find this answer satisfactory.

"I was under the impression,' he said coldly, sending a sickening thrill down Snyder's spine, "that I had sent a loyal servant to do his emperor's bidding. I do not remember bidding you to *think*. Only to obey."

"Yes... yes of course Your Excellency," stammered Snyder, in no small distress. "I didn't realize... we'll inspect the island at once sir."

Marlowe did not feel inclined to converse further on the topic and simply disappeared, to Snyder's immense relief.

He then did as small men always do when someone else has made them feel small, and turned his rage on his men, hurling abuse on them for any and every reason. They, of course, were native Druinians and neither knew nor cared from whence this tempest came, though they complained amongst themselves about it with vigor.

His fury thus spent, Snyder recruited two of them to accompany him across the chasm. As much as he feared that trip, the Weasel feared Marlowe considerably more. Besides, there was something a little fascinating about that island, which he was loathe to allow his men to explore without him.

He had less trouble than he thought he would getting the decrepit engine started up. It did not seem to need a driver, and the source of its locomotion was a mystery. Once they were on board, it simply began to move forward of its own accord, slowly at first, but gaining speed until it was hurtling along madly. For the next harrowing hour, Snyder and his companions clung to loose railings and prayed that neither the train nor the track would disintegrate and hurl them to their deaths, as it seemed extremely likely to do.

Their time on the train, however, was not nearly as harrowing as Percival's.

∽

Nathaniel watched from a careful distance as Snyder first positioned his men, then carried on a brief and apparently unhappy conversation with himself in the looking glass and un-positioned his men again.

It had seemed at first that the little posse was going to content themselves with camping out on the cliff's edge till they could be satisfied that the children were not coming, but the tet-a-tet with the mirror appeared to have brought about a change of plans. If Snyder's abusive behavior toward his men was any indication, this change was not a pleasing one.

Seeing that his window of opportunity was small, Nathaniel slid quietly down the gravelly embankment on which he lay, and ran back to where his friends waited.

"They're going over to the island," he whispered. "We've got to go. Now."

Without waiting for further explanation, his companions sprang to their feet and followed him back up the embankment.

When they neared the top, Nathaniel held out a hand to stay them, then pointed wordlessly toward the spots he knew hid two of Snyder's men. Holding a finger to his lips to signal stealth, Nathaniel began to move forward more slowly.

Snyder and the two men he had chosen to accompany him were already gingerly boarding the train. Their window was closing. Percival and Ava split off to the left, Nathaniel and Tobias to the right. On Ava's side, it was the work of a few seconds to disarm the guard, bind him with his own belt, and stuff his tunic into his mouth. The soldier put up very little resistance to this treatment, but the soldier on the other side was even more compliant. Upon seeing the two Maskies, he voluntarily laid down his own sword and shrugged. Clearly, the man was tired of this seemingly useless trek, and thought that if these strangers managed to kill Snyder, his chances of getting home soon and intact were much improved. Loyalty was not a virtue found often among Druinian police officers.

Despite the Maskies' speed, the train's final car was already nearing the cliff's edge when they caught up to it and swung themselves aboard. Percival was the last to make it and had to run out onto the suspended track itself before catching hold of the railing and launching himself into the rickety compartment. In his opinion, though, that was just the sort of thing that made being a Maskie worthwhile, and he was laughing giddily as he skidded to a stop on the dusty floor. Tobias, on the other hand, looked a little green.

"Well," he said shakily when they were well and good on their way. "Assuming this machine is still in one piece when we reach the other side, what is our plan?"

Percival shrugged. "That's at least an hour from now," he said. "I'm more concerned with the immediate future."

"Hang on for dear life?" suggested Nathaniel.

"Regret all of the life decisions that brought us to this point?" Tobias interjected.

"Find out what's in that mirror," Percival answered placidly.

Everyone looked at him.

"Er..." said Ava, after a moment. "How exactly do you plan to do that?"

Percival only grinned. Then, without warning, he reached up to the overhanging roof and swung himself up, to accompanying cries from his comrades checking to see if he was quite sane.

The three of them rushed forward to get a better view, but none followed him to the roof.

"No one wants to join me?" he shouted down at them. They regarded him with stunned expressions but Percival only laughed again.

"Just the sort of thing he's always doing," Tobias lamented to Ava as they watched their friend perch precariously on the roof of the dangerously decayed train car.

Percival shrugged and began to carefully move toward the front of the train. When he reached the end of the carriage on which he stood, he jumped to the next without a moment's hesitation.

"I can't watch," Nathaniel said, re-entering the car. Tobias followed.

Ava seemed at war with herself for a few seconds. Then, with a shake of her head, she too swung herself onto the roof of the carriage and began to follow the Maskie captain.

The next twenty minutes saw the two of them inching across the length of the railcars, each step seeming more miraculous than the last, till they reached the engine car which was occupied Snyder and his men. They appeared to be directing all their efforts to shaking, sweating, and trying not to throw up.

Percival crouched and waited for Ava to catch up, grinning like a schoolboy. When she arrived and ducked down next to him, Percival mouthed, "Remember the school?"

Ava frowned, then her eyes widened as comprehension dawned. She shook her head.

"You're mad," she whispered.

Percival nodded cheerfully, before quietly moving to the edge of the roof.

Ava stared at him for a few seconds, then sighed. "I'd better be the one to go, don't you think?" she said.

෴

The children's view of Fairy Tale Island was not unlike the view from the opposite side. Just as Snyder and his men could not see them, likewise, they could not see the train or its impossible tracks. What they did see, almost immediately, was startling even after the many supernatural signs that had led them thus far.

"Is that... a boat?" Hatch asked, hardly daring to trust his own eyes.

A boat it most certainly was. Just past the edge of the canyon, where no boat could reasonably be expected to exist, a little ferry was moored and appeared to be floating quite naturally on the nothing that held it up.

In its bow stood a short, fat, bearded man, not unlike some of the slave trading dwarves but a good deal bigger, wearing a comical hat and an unfriendly expression.

"That must be the ferryman," said Seamus somewhat unnecessarily. "Uh... good afternoon sir! We seek passage to yonder island."

The man, not remotely surprised to be addressed by a cat, simply stared at him with arms crossed, as if to say, "That much is obvious."

Seamus was momentarily discomfited. "Might we... er... prevail upon you to ferry us across?"

The man looked annoyed. Molly wondered what right he had to look so. Surely he was not constantly pestered with this sort of request.

"I don't see that you have any other option but to try," he

answered unhelpfully.

"If it's payment you need…" Hatch started to open a change purse at his belt, but the ferryman stayed him with a gesture.

"What good is your money to me?" he inquired, looking around sarcastically. "Think I've got a lot of shopping to do out here?"

"What then, good sir, might be your request?" inquired Hatch, mimicking Seamus' courteous tone, albeit clumsily.

The ferryman responded just as you'd expect a ferryman to respond. "If you can answer three riddles correctly, I will allow you to board." He did not, however, seem too pleased at the idea.

"Very well," Seamus said, perking up a little. He was a great fan of riddles. "What is the first?"

"Take off my skin, I won't cry, but you will. What am I?" asked the ferryman.

Molly knew the answer instantly, having grown up in Town West. "An onion!" she cried.

Hatch slapped her on the back appreciatively, but a touch too hard, and she tempered his enthusiasm with a fierce look.

The ferryman huffed. "A harder one then. Alright. What is it that no man yet did see, that never was, but always will be?"

They each thought on this one for a moment, reasoning amongst themselves. "You can't see anything in the dark… perhaps… but no…"

Seamus suddenly saw the answer and cried "Tomorrow!"

The fat ferryman looked more irritated than ever. He thought for several minutes before posing the final riddle.

"I can bring tears to your eyes, resurrect the dead, and turn back time. I form in an instant but last a lifetime.

What am I?"

The little party of questers each mulled this over silently for a long time. Molly racked her brain for clues. What could possibly resurrect the dead? Some magical spell perhaps? What could form in an instant but last a lifetime?

Hatch, meanwhile, had started thinking about it but let his mind wander. He had only known one person in his short life who had died, and he now returned in spirit to the day the hawk-nosed, friendly stranger had appeared in the field behind his house. He remembered discovering that Molly had arrived in Arden and the bitter grief at the news that Eldon had not accompanied her, and that he would never set foot in his homeland again. Hatch hated to cry in front of anyone, but despite his best efforts, tears stung his eyes.

"Memories!" He shouted suddenly, the word escaping before he had even fully realized that he had solved the riddle. "That's it! A memory."

Seeing that he was duly conquered, the ferryman stepped aside, allowing them each to clamber on board his little boat. The travelers did so gingerly, not being entirely convinced that it would not plunge into the abyss the moment they placed their weight on it.

"That'll take care of half the fare," the ferryman announced.

"In what form shall we pay the other half?" Seamus asked.

The ferryman chuckled. "Ah, that's the catch. You must agree to pay it and *then* you may know what it is, once you are halfway across."

"Now, that's hardly reasonable!" the cat protested.

"At no point," the ferryman said in a dignified manner, "did I promise to be reasonable."

The children looked anxiously to the cat to see what he would answer. He, in turn, looked to them.

"What should we do?" asked Hatch.

"That's your decision," Seamus answered. "Fate has assigned this quest to you, not me, children. And it's you, not I, who must decide whether to move forward or go back. You must weigh the cost of turning back against the cost of proceeding."

"But... but we don't *know* the cost of proceeding!" Molly protested. In her panic, it seemed to her that Seamus was shirking his duty as their guardian.

"Well, what is the cost of turning back then?" Seamus asked calmly.

The children pondered this as the ferryman tapped his foot impatiently.

"I think," said Hatch slowly, "that to turn back would be unthinkable. It may be that nations and lives ride on the success of this mission. If it fails, I can't bear the thought that it might have been my doing. And if we turn back now, I will wonder for the rest of my life what would have happened."

Seamus gave no sign of approval or disapproval, desiring not to influence Molly's decision. "And what do you think, Molly?" he asked after a moment.

Molly was visibly distressed. She did not like the ferryman at all, and was terribly frightened about what his demands might be, but she knew that after Hatch's speech, it would seem petty and small to demand that they turn back. Besides, they had come so far. It ought not to be for nothing.

So, hesitantly and with a white face, she nodded. Considering her trepidation, we may safely credit her with even more bravery than her companions. Molly felt a little sick when the ferry pushed off from what she had unconsciously started to think of as the shore. The ferryman sat down in the boat and began to row, heaving just as he might in a choppy sea. Hatch, on the other hand, found this comical. Seamus curled up in the bottom of the boat comfortably, as only a cat can do in such circumstances.

Aside from being entirely, fantastically, impossible, the ride was rather uneventful. The boat rocked mildly, just as one would expect it to do on the surface of a lake. Of course, the children had never been on a lake of any kind, but it felt as natural to them as anything else. The chasm being very wide, it took quite a while to reach the halfway point at which, as promised, the ferryman stopped rowing.

"Now," he announced. "It is time for the second part of the payment. Her!"

The ferryman was pointing triumphantly at Molly, who had turned deathly white.

"Wait a minute!" Hatch exclaimed rising to his feet. The ferryman held out a hand and laughed in an unfriendly way.

"Nay, young master. I don't mean forever. Only while you complete your business on the island. She stays in the boat with me. When you return, I'll take you back over the other side, and she's all yours again."

"But… why?" Hatch demanded, flummoxed. "What could you possibly want with her?"

The ferryman shrugged nonchalantly and picked up his oars to continue rowing. "That's for me to know. You've already agreed, there's no going back now" he said with a chuckle.

Molly looked terrified. What could this unfriendly stranger want with her? Why would she not be allowed to continue with her companions?

"Stay with me!" she begged Seamus.

"Nope," the ferryman answered on his behalf. "No one stays but the girl."

Seamus hissed and gave him the most piercing look a cat can give.

"I have a feeling we couldn't go back on the arrangement now if we tried," he said coldly. "But hear me now. If you lay a single finger on this young lady, if any harm comes to her at all… you will be called to account."

This may seem like a ridiculous thing for a cat to say, but the ferryman answered soberly. "I see by your eyes you mean it, but you need not fear. No harm will come to her."

Hatch, meanwhile, clasped Molly's hands in his own. She looked at him wildly. "Please don't leave me again," she pleaded.

This ought to have been Hatch's most compassionate moment yet, but he only shook her hands off irritably. "Don't you trust me at all?" he demanded.

Molly realized that she didn't. Hadn't he abandoned her before? Hadn't he sent strangers to rescue her in his stead? Feeling her face grow hot, she turned away before he could see the furious tears that welled up in her eyes.

"We won't leave you for long," Seamus promised, glaring at Hatch. But Molly thought resentfully that he could no more promise such a thing than he could swear to pull the sun from the sky.

⁓

It's well for our friends that Snyder and his men kept their eyes tightly shut for the duration of their breakneck journey over the chasm. Had any of them felt the slightest desire to see their surroundings, they would have seen a strange woman with fiery red hair hanging upside down near the open windows, held at the ankles by unseen hands. They would have watched her frantically motion with her hands as the color of her face began to match her wild tresses, and then slide inexplicably sideways as whatever anchored her feet moved toward them. And they certainly would have noticed the woman reach through the window, retrieve Snyder's knapsack, remove the small gilded looking glass from it, and replace the bag.

Had they snuck a single peek at the vast canyon around them, they would also have been surprised to note that the woman's face looked just as startled as theirs as the train lurched and her companion nearly lost his grip. Had they leaned out the window and looked upward, they would have seen the white, terrified visage of the aforementioned companion as he slowly and painfully hoisted the strange apparition back to the top of the train car.

As it was, they saw none of this, and the two companions shakily made their way to rejoin their nervous friends at the rear of the train, uncaught, uninjured and stunned at their good luck.

23

~

WHAT WAS PROPHESIED

Brogan and Lydia did not return to the meeting point as planned. They had lost all trace of the children's trail, but neither of them could bring themselves to turn back. They knew their companions would follow them when they failed to make the rendezvous, however, so they were careful to make their own trail conspicuous.

"They can't have vanished into thin air!" Brogan exclaimed as he remounted after stopping to search an empty alcove along the way. He had found nothing.

Lydia was as frustrated as he, but she could not compel herself to suggest retreat. "Exactly," she said with a confidence that belied her own troubled mind. "They can't have, which means they *are* somewhere, and if they are somewhere, we can find them. We must press on."

Brogan only grunted, though deep down he blessed the stars for her willingness to persist on such a fruitless task.

As their path progressed steadily toward the mountain

peak, a bitter wind picked up, making conversation difficult. Man and wife wrapped themselves in hooded cloaks and rode with heads bent into the wind, teeth clenched against the cold, gloved hands trembling. The furious gale intensified, until it took all their focus to stay upright on horseback, let alone look for signs of the children's passing. The wind reached into their cloaks, raked its icy fingers through their hair and coaxed involuntary tears from their eyes. The sky darkened, and a freezing rain bore down on them. In the fast-approaching darkness, Lydia could just make out Brogan's dim outline ahead of her, motioning her to follow him off the path.

Brogan didn't know what he would find once they'd left the road, only that they needed to find any shelter the mountainside might provide. He saw a shape looming that might be rocks or foliage, but felt that if they could get to the other side of it, they might find some protection against the storm. It turned out to be large stones, but by the time they could wade their way to the other side, darkness had fallen completely and the storm raged just as furiously on this side as the other. He reigned his horse to a stop and slid off, feeling more than seeing, that Lydia was doing the same. In the dark, he reached for her hand and the two of them huddled against the horse's flank, even while trying to soothe the frightened animal.

They imagined themselves to still be on the mountain's upward slope, so it was with great surprise that Brogan shuffled to his right and found that the ground fell away sharply. He lost his footing and, with a cry, slid onto his back and shot down into the darkness as if down a massive laundry chute. Brogan tried to release Lydia's hand but it was too late, and she tumbled down behind him. The ground was so smooth and slick with sleet that they gathered speed as they slid for an impossibly long time. Peripherally, Brogan noticed that the sound of the storm was fading.

Eventually, the angle of the slope began to gently correct, slowing their momentum until they shot out of a tunnel in the mountainside and spun to a sickening stop. They were sprawled across the surface of what appeared to be a frozen pond. Somehow, on this end of the tunnel they found themselves in cold sunlight.

Brogan looked at his wife and laughed in confusion and relief. Wide-eyed, she returned the look and laughed too. The pair cautiously picked themselves up and crawled to the edge of the lake, where they lay to catch their breath.

"Well," said Lydia after a moment. "At least it's not raining."

There was nothing recognizable about the landscape around them. Yet both of them could feel something in the air around them, prickling their skin like cold air after a bath. *Magic.*

Brogan looked across the lake at the mouth of the narrow tunnel from which they'd emerged. "What are the odds they came this same way?" he asked.

Lydia shrugged. "Neither higher nor lower than the odds that we'd fall into a magical trap door in the mountainside," she said.

"I suppose you're right," Brogan answered. "Anyway, I don't see how we could get back. Onward?"

"Onward," Lydia nodded. "Besides doesn't it feel as if there's something… I don't know… *right* about it?"

Brogan knew what she meant, but couldn't articulate it any better.

"I suppose Ealdor has put us on the path we are to take," he said, picking himself up. He reached out to help Lydia up as well, but she was already on her feet.

"It looks like there's a trail," she said, looking around. "It still goes down, but we ought to be able to walk rather than slide at least. Off we go!"

And off they went.

❦

In another hour the ferry had reached the island, and the boy and cat had disembarked. Hatch reassured Molly that they'd waste no time getting back, and Seamus reminded her that the ferryman was an emissary of Fairy Tale herself, and this was the only reason he would even consider leaving her in his care, promise or no promise.

Sulkily she watched them run toward the island's only structure: a quaint looking little hut.

The fragrance of magic that had perfumed each of the little clues which led them here hung thicker in the air the farther inland they got. A little wheelbarrow had been tipped over on its side near the cottage. It was an ordinary wheelbarrow, and there was no explaining how it gave the impression of having been left there in a rush by a young lover off to rescue fair lady, but that is what Hatch saw in it. Seamus, on the other hand, felt sure it had borne some mysterious wounded creature in need of aid.

Everything they saw in that enchanted place likewise declared a dozen stories yet untold. A little column of smoke drifting from the chimney whispered enticingly about secret fireside meetings, the burning of painful memories and hearthside rendezvous. The little flower garden, with its cacophony of colors in haphazard rows, seemed to have been planted by a fairy sprinkling fairy dust as she flew by, or perhaps by a slave girl whose only small pleasure it was, or by a grief-stricken mother adorning the graves of her children. Everything from the thatched roof to the cobbled walk breathed of romance, poignancy, pain, longing, adventure, nobility, and all the thousand things that make up the storyteller's soul. They were utterly bewitched.

For the briefest of moments, Hatch did not feel at all sorry that Molly was missing out, but as soon as this sentiment arose, he was ashamed of it. Still, she *had* been so contrary of late, and had taken some of the pleasure out of the most interesting thing that had ever happened to him.

So palpable was the air of enchantment and mystery, that it felt out of place to do anything so mundane as knocking on the cottage door, but seeing no magical alternative, knock they did.

From his recent and concentrated education in fairy tales, Hatch had unconsciously begun to form a picture of Fairy Tale herself. In his imagination, she was the quintessential heroine. Tall and achingly beautiful, mysterious and aloof, her sparkling eyes betraying her longing to be rescued by a handsome prince (whose role, to his later chagrin, he himself had filled in his imaginings).

So you, dear, readers, will excuse his momentary befuddlement when the door opened on a plump little woman with cotton colored hair fastened in a bun on top of her head. She wore a checkered apron with little apples on it and a welcoming smile, as if there was nothing in the world so likely as a boy and a cat dropping by for a visit to her prison island now and then. Her appearance in the open door was accompanied by the unmistakable aroma of baking cookies.

∽

Another little party was approaching the cottage from its

other side and having a very different experience. Astute readers know already that the fragrance of life for some folks is the stench of death to others and I can think of no more apt description of Fairy Tale's cottage as it appeared to Snyder and his men.

At first glance, Snyder thought the place so desolate that he wondered if Marlowe's prisoner had expired during her years of captivity. There was only one residence on the plateau, and it appeared to be in a dreadful state of disrepair. *But no*, he thought. *There is smoke coming from the chimney.* What Hatch had seen as a herald of a cozy hearth, Snyder saw as black, oily smoke, as though something unpleasant was being cooked over the fire from which it issued. The cottage's one window was dark, the pane cracked and thick with grime.

None of this was terribly remarkable on a prison island whose only occupant must surely have gone mad from despair and loneliness. Yet it was the way the place made them *feel* that was objectionable. It was like the house in some neighborhoods that children will cross the street to avoid passing on their way to school. Every element of the scenery seemed somehow ominous, from the tree which stretched its gnarled, blackened limbs toward them to the jagged edge of the broken spade handle protruding from the rocky soil.

Snyder motioned for his men to halt while he surveyed the bleak, decaying hovel before him. The sense of mystery and magic that saturated the place was not lost on him, but in him and his men it inspired deep foreboding.

The Weasel signaled once again and he and his men began to move cautiously forward. As they drew near to the dwelling, nothing stirred, but this did little to ease their minds. The sense of lurking evil was too potent. Leaving one soldier stationed near the back window, Snyder circled the house from one side while the other soldier took the opposite side. After scoping out the perimeter, they met in front of the cottage, feeling that at any moment some foe would appear out of nowhere and battles would ensue. Instead they only found the front of the house, which was just as bleak and gloomy as its back. An abandoned wheelbarrow was turned over on its side and a pitiful flower bed contained a few wilted daisies.

Still there was no sign of life from within the house and, more importantly, no sign of the children.

But couldn't they see the boat? You may well ask, or was the fog too thick? How could they not see that the children were there already?

It was said once by one of the great storytellers of your world, that at times of great import, evil beings sometimes fall strangely blind. Then again, sometimes it's not so strange.

◆

Upon returning from their dangerous ride atop the train, Ava and Percival presented their find to Tobias and Nathaniel, who examined the mirror with fascination. It was clearly a magical implement of some sort. It had the *feel* of dark magic all around it, and when they looked directly into it, they could see the shadowy motion of what looked like smoke broiling deep under the surface.

Yet try as they might, they could elicit from it no response. They uttered spells, waved it about, looked at it in different lights and different angles, issued commands, even prodded it, all to no avail. So wholly engrossed were they in examining the little talisman that they forgot to be terrified of the disintegrating locomotive, and barely noticed when it began to roll to a stop.

They were, however, suddenly roused when the carriage finally swayed to a creaking standstill. The Maskies peered carefully out of the doors of the compartment and saw at once that they had reached the island, and that Snyder was disembarking. Just as it had to Hatch and Seamus, the island seemed thoroughly enchanting to them. Each immediately felt the stirring of noble adventure in their breast and felt sure they were a part of some great tale about to be told. Each felt as if they could conquer dragons. Tobias was almost ready to leap off the train and challenge his enemies when wisdom prevailed.

"Wait," Percival said. He spoke quietly but his own eagerness was barely suppressed. "There's no cover on this island. We'll wait till they're a little farther away."

"But what if the children are there?" Ava protested.

"We can be there at a run in 45 seconds," Percival reassured her.

"What if they kill Fairy Tale?" Nathaniel asked.

"I doubt she can be killed," Percival said. "Otherwise, why go to all the trouble of having her imprisoned?"

Nathaniel looked surprised that such a simple idea had never occurred to him before.

Ava looked dubious, but consented to wait. They watched as their enemies slowly crept up to the cottage. To them, of course, it was a bright and cheerful place, thrumming with mystery and life. They could not help but wonder why Snyder and his mercenaries approached it with such apparent apprehension.

༄

Hatch, Seamus, and Fairy Tale sat around the table (in the interest of accuracy, Seamus actually sat *on* it) in the cottage's warmly lit kitchen, talking. The delicious smell with which they had been greeted had materialized into soft, warm cookies. Hatch was still overcoming the minor shock of disillusionment at Fairy Tale's decidedly un-princess like appearance, but he was quickly adjusting. To be in her presence was to be at ease. She was a mother to everyone she met, if there was any such thing as meeting her, for it felt as though she had always been there. Hatch knew at once that she was the sort of person a child could really talk to without any fear of being misunderstood or not taken seriously.

She was delighted to see them, but had clearly been expecting their arrival. She was not a seer, in the same sense that Abner was, but sometimes she knew things all the same. Seamus had asked her how she could know, but she could only say that she was a teller of tales and could often understand how they might go.

They had only been talking for a few moments but Hatch was anxious to be on his way, mindful of poor Molly and somewhat conscience-stricken by his impatience with her. The guilt of abandoning her to the boat man, while they sat in the warm glow of a magical fire eating cookies, was beginning to weigh on him.

"The sooner we're off this island the better," he said. "Marlowe's men are after us and surely they must know where we are heading. I can hardly believe they haven't come already."

"Oh they have dear!" said Fairy Tale cheerfully. "They're just outside. Sit down, sit down, you needn't be alarmed just yet. There's a powerful enchantment around this house that's blurred their vision a bit. For now, we're perfectly safe."

"We noticed everything seemed a bit... rich and magical, I suppose," said Hatch, staring anxiously at the nearby window. "But it only drew us *toward* you."

Fairy Tale seemed pleased. "Yes, of course. You've just that sort of mind, haven't you? That's exactly how it should work on someone like you. But on *them*? They're wicked men, with wicked intentions my dear. It won't be at all the same for them. They'll see only darkness and desolation."

"Then it's a conscious enchantment?" Hatch asked with interest. "It knows who it's talking to?"

"That's not a bad idea!" she said. "A conscious enchantment. Fancy that. But no, I would say it's more like a mirror enchantment. It merely reflects what it sees back to each person it encounters."

"Poor fellows," Seamus feigned concern.

"You jest," Fairy Tale said, "but it's truer than you realize. Imagine being the kind of person who *chooses* to be in Marlowe's employ, and seeing all that darkness reflected back at you."

Hatch shuddered.

"Well if they can't see us, what are we waiting for?" Seamus said, rising.

Fairy Tale held her hand up to stop him. "They can't see us as long as we're inside or close to the house, but the enchantment only stretches so far. We don't stand a chance of making it to the boat."

Hatch started, horrified. "Does that mean they can see Molly? She's in the boat!"

Fairy Tale smiled at him warmly, but Hatch detected sadness in her eyes too. "It's alright, dear. Molly couldn't be safer than in the care of the ferryman."

"Oh?" said Seamus, letting a little of that distinctively cat-like disdain creep into his voice. "He didn't seem like the sort of fellow to leave friends with to me."

"Oh, he's alright, love. A little rough around the edges

perhaps, but loyal as a dog." The indelicacy of using such an analogy to ease a cat's mind was apparently lost on her.

"But then… why *did* he make her stay?" Hatch demanded, with sudden color rising in his cheeks, "and now that we've come to it, if you've got a loyal boatman who can row back and forth between here and the mainland, why did you need rescuing at all? Why didn't you leave ages ago?"

"That's just not how fairy tales work, dear," answered Fairy Tale, most unsatisfactorily. Hatch would have pressed the issue further, but Seamus interrupted him.

"We can talk about all that once we've got off this island. Right now, we've got Marlowe's soldiers prowling the premises between Molly and ourselves, and I'd say that's the most pressing issue at the moment."

Hatch could not argue with the cat's logic.

∽

Far away from all this, in the center of the grimy capital city, at the top of the palace's most forlorn tower, Marlowe sat perfectly still.

In front of the old magician, on a black table with cruel looking corners, sat a perfectly round orb, pulsing with a dim light from within. At the moment it was mostly opaque, though if you had looked closely you would have seen a strange, amoebic substance churning slowly in its murky depths.

To anyone watching he would have appeared the picture of control. His face was impassive, his hands loosely clasped. Only his eyes betrayed the seething turbulence of his mind. Had anyone been so foolish as to ask him, Marlowe would have been unable to account for the unease that had risen up within him these past few days. It wasn't the discovery of treachery within his government that troubled him. That was to be expected. Nor was it the discovery that the Damascus Guard were more active than he'd imagined. Political dissidents, as I've said, could actually be quite useful if one knew how to handle them properly in the newspapers. No, it was the children.

He told himself that two worthless children from two nothing towns could not possibly do any lasting harm, besides which, the last report from Snyder had been quite encouraging. Likely as not they had died in the mountains and would trouble him no more.

So why was he afraid?

The truth, dear readers, is that men who come to power by wicked means are always afraid. In fact, any person who gains something through treachery will never be secure in his ownership of that thing. He will cling fearfully to it, grasping and striving to keep that which was never his to begin with. There can be no peace, saith Ealdor, for the wicked.

Still, Marlowe had sunk into relative complacency of late, and did not like to admit how this threat to his sovereignty shook him. *Children!* Marlowe screeched internally. That two stupid children and two house cats could outwit his men was unacceptable. When this was over and the brats had been found, they, and a long list of others, would pay for robbing him of his peace of mind.

With the slow, methodical movements of a spider, Marlowe reached out toward the orb. It lit up at his touch.

Now, as we readers of fairy tales know, every witch or wizard's crystal ball works differently. This one, for example, was not all knowing. Had it been, locating the children would have presented no problem. This crystal ball was more of a hub. It connected a variety of other objects – like

Snyder's mirror – to one another, and it was only where these other objects were that Marlowe could see. No matter where these items traveled, they gave Marlowe eyes. So even though the mirror was tucked safely away in Snyder's pack, Marlowe had a bird's eye view of his exact location.

Or rather he ought to have.

Though the ball lit up as expected, to his great consternation, the swirling mists did not clear. Something was not right. Moving his face so close to the ball that his decaying nose was nearly touching it, he gazed hard into its depths. After a moment, he could see a few indistinct moving shapes, but nothing more. This was maddening. The crystal ball was usually clear as day, allowing him to focus on the smallest grain of sand if he so chose. Now, try as he might, he could only make out a few vague stationary objects, and three hazy, slowly moving figures.

Some interference was obscuring his view. Marlowe, who could not stand to be foiled in the smallest measure, felt rage well up in his chest.

His spidery hand caressed a wicked looking staff leaning on the wall nearby. The time to use it may very well be at hand. Still, he would wait until he was certain.

❧

Molly stared sullenly at the ferryman. At that precise moment, the injustice of everything that had happened since leaving Town West seemed too much to bear.

Why should *she* have been abandoned to the Institute, to abuse by professors and interrogation by brutes, while Hatch was camping under the open stars with Brogan and Seamus? Why should it be she who lost a father in the Wasteland, while both Hatch's real parents lived? Why was it she who was plagued with nightmares while the others slept soundly? And how ungracious they had been to her throughout their trek! How impatient, how boorish! Now this final injustice – that while the boys were rescuing Fairy Tale and receiving her benevolent smiles and thanks, she was forced to sit in the boat with the unsavory ferryman and wait.

The ferryman, it turned out, wasn't really so bad after all. Once he'd moored the boat and seen the boys off, his demeanor had completely changed. The man had given her a friendly smile, said "Shall we have a snack?" and produced, seemingly from nowhere, a plate of sandwiches, which he offered to her. They looked very good and Molly *was* hungry, but she was too intent on sulking to accept any kindness. Instead she crossed her arms and frowned at him. The ferryman merely shrugged, and ate one himself.

Her punishing silence appeared not to bother him, so eventually she broke it. "It's not fair," she announced.

"Sorry?"

"It's not *fair*. Why should I have to stay here with you while all the rest of them get to go onto the island."

"Oh that!" he smiled patiently. "It's just the nature of the magic. The ferry only runs if it has a passenger, you see."

"What?" Molly demanded. "But that doesn't make any sense. Can't you just row back and forth yourself?"

He shook his head. "Couldn't if I wanted to. There'd be nothing to row. The ferry only appears when someone needs passage. If there's no passage, there's no ferry!"

"But that doesn't make sense either! We'd have needed it again after we'd retrieved Fairy Tale. Wouldn't it have reappeared then?"

"Certainly, but on the other side of the chasm. It only has one starting point, you know. It appears exactly where you first found it, and nowhere else. Otherwise Fairy Tale could've summoned it and rescued herself whenever she liked."

"Well that's... that's just ridiculous!" Molly spluttered. "Who makes an enchantment like that? It's just useless, isn't it?"

"Not entirely," the ferryman said placidly, gesturing at the island. "Here we are, aren't we?"

"But why? I don't understand."

"It's the best she could do to counteract Marlowe's enchantments," he explained. "She couldn't cancel them out entirely and just escape – Marlowe made sure of that. So instead, she did what she could to ensure that her rescuers would have the easiest time of it."

This, dear reader, is when something very dreadful happened. Again, I must entreat you to remember the enormous amount of strain that young Molly had been subjected to, and not think too unkindly of her. Frustration boiled up inside her till she could no longer contain it.

"Well I *haven't* had the easiest time of it, have I?" she shouted, rising to her feet. "In fact, I've had a completely rotten time of it! It's not *fair!*" she stamped her feet. "And... and... I don't believe you. Who would design an enchantment like that? It's just plain stupid, that's what it is!"

And, hardly knowing what she was doing, Molly obeyed a sudden, furious impulse, and scrambled out of the boat and onto the shore.

24

DREADFUL CONSEQUENCES

Peering out the window, Hatch was disconcerted to see that Snyder and his men were plainly visible. "I thought you said we couldn't see each other?" he said, drawing back quickly.

"They can't see *us*," Fairy Tale corrected him gently. "The enchantment doesn't blind everyone to the truth, it just shows them what they are naturally inclined to see. If you're the sort of person who loves what's true, that's what you see. If you're not... well then it's not. Understand?"

"Not really, but I'll take your word for it. Anyway, there's three of them," Hatch said anxiously. "I can't fight them. *You* can't fight them. What are we to do?"

"No, fighting is quite out of the question," Fairy Tale agreed. "I'm sure I can come up with something to distract them till we get there. That is, if the enchantment lasts that long."

"What do you mean?" Hatch exclaimed. "Why wouldn't it?"

"Well… it's a bit difficult to understand," Fairy Tale said. "But haven't you noticed that a lot of magic is sort of… well for lack of a better word, responsive?"

Boy and cat stared at her blankly.

"No, I suppose not." Fairy Tale said. "There's no way you could have known that's what was happening, even if you'd experienced it. But it's like this. There are varying levels of effectiveness, depending on the skill of the magician, but nearly all magic is subject to influence by outside sources too. Most notably, by the person the spell is being cast against or for."

Of course, Hatch and Seamus had never known how it was that Molly made her way out of the dwarf warren, but you do, and so you probably understand the concept a little better.

"Do you mean," Hatch said, "like in the story of Lilith and Brutus? The good fairy's spells could only work if Brutus was willing to wear the ring of his own accord, that sort of thing?"

"Precisely that sort of thing!" Fairy Tale rewarded him with a pleased smile. "Haven't you ever wondered why, after twelve years, cracks suddenly appeared in the Wasteland Wall?"

"I don't understand…" Seamus began.

"Don't you? Think about it. Two Ardenian children growing up in Druinor, with imaginations that remained unquenched – that resistance to Marlowe's suppressive magic is what started them! Then, when you had set your minds to the task at hand – that is, to rescuing me and all of Druinor – they widened. The wall didn't disappear, but it became passable."

"*We* caused the cracks?" Hatch could hardly believe his ears.

"You did!"

"But... what does that have to do with the enchantment here?"

"Ah, yes." Fairy Tale once again looked inexplicably sad. "It was my magic, responding to all of you, that brought you here. My little clues, and your noticing them. It sort of paved the way. But it worked because you were all of one heart and one mind to complete the task. If any of you were to betray the others... well I don't know what would happen then. I only know..."

Seamus jerked his head up. "The prophecy?" he asked.

"Though she whose soul you love, traveler, may hold the traitor's knife," Fairy Tale recited.

"What are you saying?" Hatch demanded angrily. "None of us would ever..." but before he could finish, a loud crack split the air around them and the cottage shook a little.

One of Snyder's men shouted in surprise. The warm, cheery, light of the kitchen became sterile and cold, like high noon on the sea. They stared wildly at each other, knowing without having to be told that the enchantment had lifted. They were found out!

Hatch started toward the door. "We've got to make a run for it. We've got to get to the boat!"

"It's worse than you think," Fairy Tale groaned. "The boat's gone."

༄

Ava, Nathaniel, and Tobias gathered around the mirror once more, while Percival watched Snyder and his men from the train window. The wicked little object hummed malevolently in Ava's hand. They all felt instinctively that their theft had caused some disruption in its operation and that it was angrily resisting them, but they felt no fear –

only fascination. What world did Snyder see when he gazed into its roiling depths? What face gazed back? They all suspected the answer of course.

They were startled from their inspection by the same thunderclap that shook the island. The floorboards of the train car quivered beneath their feet. The travelers glanced at each other sharply, then rushed to the door.

It took Ava half a breath to see what she needed to see – the cottage, Molly's small figure, and Snyder and his men between them. She sprang from the train without thinking, dropping the mirror as she went. The others quickly followed. Nathaniel, Tobias, and Percival sprinted toward the cottage and Snyder, while Ava split off and ran directly toward Molly.

∽

To those on the island, hero and villain alike, the change occurred with the suddenness of a thunderclap. From where Marlowe watched, however, it was far more subtle. By now, he had correctly guessed that his mirror was in the hands of an enemy, and had been on the verge of taking things into his own hands when the glowing orb began to give off a faint shimmer. The once maddeningly vague shadows grew sharper by a hair, and a few seconds later, the haze cleared. All was laid bare.

He saw his men surrounding the cottage. In a glance he took in the gardens, the warmly lit windows, the homey curtains and the silhouettes behind them. He saw the train and the Maskies leaping from its rear carriage, their eyes wide in surprise.

Then, his eye caught a movement a distance from the cottage, near the edge of the plateau.

Marlowe jumped to his feet. *Could it be?* Molly Morris

stood on the cliff's edge, looking startled and a little angry.

৽

Molly knew before her feet touched the ground that she had made a terrible mistake. The instant she stepped out of the boat, she saw the world in front of her collapse into another, darker version of itself with a deafening clap.

As the enchanted mist that had hidden her cleared, two Druinian soldiers stared at her, thunderstruck. She knew the one on the left instantly, and saw a flash of recognition in Snyder's eyes as well.

She felt sick. There was no question that the changed landscape was her doing. Her small act of rebellion had lifted the protective cover not only from herself, but from her friends as well. She was gripped with a cold assurance that the boat and ferryman were no longer within reach, though she dared not turn to check.

Snyder seemed indecisive for a fraction of a second, then gestured his comrade toward her and turned himself toward the house to deal with the rebels therein. Molly watched in horror as he swung the door open, pistol drawn, and went inside. She looked about wildly for a way to escape from the soldier running in her direction, but saw none. There was nowhere to run on the island, nowhere to hide.

Just then she saw another figure, much farther away, running toward her at a dead sprint. She knew the runner even from a great distance and her heart leapt. Whether she could make it to Ava before the soldier caught her was irrelevant; it was her only chance. Molly turned and ran along the cliff edge, away from her pursuer and toward her friend.

The third soldier, emerging from behind the cottage, ran ahead to cut off her path. Seeing that she was thoroughly trapped, she turned inland and dashed toward the cottage. She had no plan or thought of what she might do when she got there, she only knew that she would rather be caught than surrender.

And caught she was. The two soldiers made quick work of it between them, and in a matter of moments she was struggling in their grasp as they dragged her toward the cottage, Ava on their heels.

～

The words had barely left Fairy Tale's lips when the door slammed open and Snyder's imposing figure filled the doorframe, gun drawn.

"Drop your sword," he thundered, but a second later his eyes widened as he absorbed the scene before him.

He had expected to be met by Brogan, armed and ready to fight. Instead he saw a boy, a cat, and an old woman, all staring wide-eyed back at him. Snyder adjusted quickly, pointing his revolver directly at Hatch. This was his moment. He was about to make himself the most important man in Marlowe's employ.

"You," he said to Fairy Tale, "will stay here, as the emperor commanded. And you," he motioned to Hatch and Seamus, "will accompany me to the train and face the penalty for your crimes against Druinor. *Move.*"

Seeing no alternatives, they moved. Snyder kept his weapon trained carefully on Hatch and kept a close eye on the cat. He would not be caught by surprise again as he had been outside the school.

The three filed out the door and around the side of the cottage.

(*"You fool!"* muttered Marlowe, miles away).

Upon their exit, Fairy Tale sat down, picked up a set of

needles and some beautiful, shimmering yarn, and began to knit furiously. I regret, a little, that there was no one still inside to find this appropriately shocking.

Snyder marched his captives just outside the cottage, to find Molly and the soldier waiting for them. She had no time or method by which to express her remorse to her friends, but her wretched expression spoke for her.

Turning toward the train, Snyder finally saw the Maskies converging on them. He ducked behind Hatch, wrapped his arm around the boy's waist and picked him up, holding him with one powerful arm like a kicking, struggling shield. His other hand kept the pistol pressed against Hatch's temple.

The soldier holding Molly followed suit and the third drew his own revolver and aimed it at Percival.

The maskies stopped running. Everyone assessed the situation.

"We are going back to the train," said Snyder. "All of us."

The unencumbered soldier motioned to Ava with his weapon. "You first," he said coldly.

The Maskies looked at each other calmly and agreed without speaking. There were four of them and only three of their enemies, besides which, they knew something Snyder didn't: he was without men on the other side of the chasm. There would be plenty of opportunity to turn the situation to their advantage.

To Snyder's great surprise, Percival shrugged. "Alright then," he said.

Percival turned and began to walk toward the train. Ava followed suit, while Nathaniel and Tobias fell back a little, so as to keep the children in their peripheral vision as they walked.

Their little caravan never reached the train however, for

when they had gone about halfway one of the soldiers glanced over his shoulder and made a startled noise. As the others turned to look, they saw what appeared to be a thicket of thorny vines growing toward them at breakneck speed from the direction of the cottage.

Nobody expects that sort of thing to happen, even on an adventure, and everyone gaped at it for a second or two.

"That's interesting," said Percival stupidly.

"What on earth?" Snyder asked the universe.

Had they thoroughly examined the sudden foliage, they would have traced it back to a bit of shimmering thread trailing through the cottage window, but with no time for such investigation, they were forced to accept its reality without context and respond accordingly.

Chaos briefly ensued. Tobias lunged for Molly and had little trouble wresting her from the momentarily relaxed grip of her captor. Scooping her under an arm like a sack of flour, he sprinted back toward the cottage.

Hatch managed to loose himself from Snyder's grip, but had no time to duck around him to follow Tobias. Instead, Ava grabbed his arm and took off running in the opposite direction. In the span of just a few seconds, the vines grew into a thorny wedge that split the island in two, separating Ava, Hatch, Seamus and Snyder on the left from Tobias, Molly, Nathaniel and the two soldiers on the right.

᠅

Marlowe had seen enough. Rising, he grasped the knobby staff, raised it high above his head, brought it down to strike the marble floor with a sharp crack, and promptly disappeared.

᠅

On Hatch's side of the island, the racing flora caught one of

Snyder's heels and knocked him down. He recovered his balance in good time, but did not recover his pistol.

On the other side, the pursuers had better luck and caught up to Tobias before he reached the cottage. Setting Molly down roughly, he bade her get inside, and turned himself to face his assailants, drawing his sword as he did so. Nathaniel, who was swiftly approaching, had likewise drawn his.

"Take your time!" Tobias called to his friend, and the two soldiers turned to see who was behind them.

"Thank you, I will!" Nathaniel grinned and tipped an imaginary hat.

This annoyed the Druinian soldiers. One of them aimed his pistol at Nathaniel. With a lightning quick flick of his sword, Tobias relieved him of the weapon. The ensuing fight only lasted a moment. The Maskies had barely begun to enjoy it when a second thunderclap issued from the direction of the mainland, and the world seemed to collapse in on itself yet again.

There, at the tip of the thorny wedge, stood Marlowe himself in all his grim glory. With him came the almost palpable certainty of doom to our heroes. A deathly silence fell over the whole island. Maskies and mercenaries alike stood with their weapons hanging limply at their sides, staring at him with slack mouths. Inside the cottage, Fairy Tale's fingers ceased their frenzied work. Snyder, Hatch, Ava, and Percival stood as if their boots had been nailed to the earth. Only Seamus was nowhere to be seen, having had the presence of mind to disappear into the shadows of the newly arisen thicket.

This frozen silence seemed to stretch on for an eternity, but in truth lasted only a few seconds. It was broken by Marlowe himself, who defied his own decrepit appearance by springing into action with shocking speed. He chose a course to the left of the thicket, striding toward Hatch.

As he approached, Snyder attempted a bow. Without stopping to look at him, Marlowe pointed his staff in Snyder's direction. A sharp green light shot out of it, hitting Snyder squarely in the chest and propelling him backward into the brambles, by which he was absorbed. Whether he died there or was transported to some other place I do not know. Perhaps he lived a long and penitent life and met his end in later years. I know only that he did not emerge from those enchanted vines for the remainder of our tale, and no trace of him was later found.

Ava dodged a similar shot aimed at her, but Percival was not so lucky. Before he knew what hit him, he was sprawled unconscious several yards away. Marlowe picked Hatch up easily by the back of the neck, carrying him with one hand like a doll, and utterly impervious to the child's struggles. He turned, aiming his staff once again at Ava. This time he hit his mark. Ava saw the flash of light and felt an icy spear pierce her left shoulder. The shot spun her around and she staggered a moment before falling to her knees, pain radiating through her body.

Seeing that the wizard meant to circle around to the front of the cottage, Tobias ran the same direction, casting an agonized glance over his shoulder toward Ava as he did. Seamus let out a hiss and shot out of his hiding place among the vines. He launched himself at Marlowe as he passed, but the emperor easily swatted him away with his staff, and the cat landed in a crumpled heap next to Percival.

The soldiers, on the other hand, were content to keep their distance from the action, now that the emperor had arrived. They had no fear of the Maskies overcoming their master, but they greatly feared the wizard himself, and thought it best to go unnoticed if at all possible. Nathaniel ran past them without so much as a glance in their direction and caught up to Tobias.

Marlowe continued forward until he had neared the edge of the precipice where Molly had come ashore, then turned, Hatch still firmly in hand. "Bring the girl," he said in a voice that was both quiet and clearly audible – as it if were coming not from his mouth but from all around.

No one was quite sure to whom he spoke, whether to the soldiers, Fairy Tale, or the Maskies, but all felt the force of his command just the same. Cold despair gripped their hearts. They had lost. No one had ever conquered Marlowe, and no one ever would – or at least not a ragtag little group of children, cats and old women.

In the back of Hatch's mind a very, very small voice suggested that every great villain in every great fairy tale he had heard in his travels had been defeated in just such a way. But the force of Marlowe's presence was amplified by his physical touch and that little voice could not overpower it.

Trembling, but seeing clearly that she had no other option, Molly emerged from the cottage, Fairy Tale at her side, and advanced toward the edge of the island. Nathaniel, and Tobias formed a protective wall in front of the woman and the girl, but they dared not make a move while Hatch remained in the emperor's clutches. Ava struggled to her feet and began to stagger toward them.

Molly quailed at the sight of Marlowe next to the precipice, one hand cruelly gripping Hatch's neck. All her nightmares assailed her with the force of a hammer blow and had it not been for Fairy Tale's steadying arm, she may very well have fainted. When they were only a few feet from Marlowe, they stopped, and for a moment, all was still.

The reality that all their plans and pains had come to naught after all weighed heavily on each of them – so heavily, in fact, that they could think of nothing else. Marlowe's insidious magic had begun to do its work in each of them, and they began to believe that not only their plans, but all the hopes and dreams of all peoples would meet their death here on this precipice. How foolish they had been to think they could change Druinor, Tobias thought. How naïve! Surely Marlowe had only allowed them to get this far to taunt them with the hope of victory before their crushing defeat.

Molly had the worst of it. Marlowe's voice reverberated inside her head, reminding her that there *had* been a chance after all, and that it was she who had spoiled it. *You thought you were an outcast before* the voice said. *This is all your fault and everyone knows it! They'll never forgive you now.* They all saw the future clearly in that moment. Prison and torture and defeat was all that awaited them, each was quite sure.

Marlowe gestured to the two soldiers, who came forward at once and forced Tobias to his knees, and binding his wrists behind him. In his state of catatonic dread, he barely resisted, though he would never think of that moment again without a twinge of shame. The soldiers repeated the process with Nathaniel and Ava, leaving Molly exposed. Fairy Tale put a protective arm around her shoulders. Only she was not lost to despair. Fairy Tale, of course, knew enough of villains and heroes to not give up so easily. She was older by far than Marlowe, and had seen her fair share of tyrants rise and fall. She saw him as he really was – a desperate, grasping old man.

The wizard gestured to Molly, beckoning her to come to

him. It was time, that gesture seemed to say, to put all this nonsense to an end. She must go, and she would. She and Hatch would be killed, or imprisoned, or sent to the Institute. Which of the three, Molly realized, mattered little.

Hatch had stopped struggling and hung limply from Marlowe's immobilizing grasp. When the soldiers had stepped forward to detain the Maskies, he caught Fairy Tale's eye. She was staring at him intently. He stared back, and as he did, understood with a stab of brutal certainty what she was asking of him. He shook his head slightly. *You*, he told himself, *are no knight. You're no hero.* He felt Fairy Tale's steady gaze, but it made him angry. They were only *tales* after all, not real life. *This* was real life, and the villain in *real* life was stronger than he.

She looked at him with no reproach, which made the furious struggle within him even more intolerable. *Can't you see he's stronger than me?* He willed her to hear his thoughts, to understand. To his surprise, a voice answered him back. *Sometimes, the hero doesn't win.*

From under Fairy Tale's arm, Molly watched him closely, and as she watched, the place on her shoulder where Fairy Tale's hand rested began to tingle. Inside her something else began to stir. The little voice that had suggested to Hatch that dragons can be conquered after all began to whisper to her as well. And suddenly, she too understood. Tale after tale that she had heard from Seamus, from the storytellers in Arden, and even, she realized vaguely, some she had never heard at all, began to appear in her mind's eye.

She saw wicked stepmothers put in their proper place, paupers elevated to royal stations, witches and wizards defeated, giants and dragons slain. She saw Lilith's love for her brutish brother inspiring an act of selfless, sacrificial love.

And it came to her as suddenly and clearly as if Fairy Tale had said it out loud. She understood what the important thing was that Abner had told Hatch they would need – not some object or talisman bestowed by King Mardius. Not the sparkling stones and frocks with which she'd been so enthralled in Arden, but this *actual* treasure buried in the stories themselves. The fairy tales weren't merely fantastical falsehoods, but beautifully decorated platforms on which to display the truth. Suddenly, the potency of Marlowe's seeping despondency ebbed. With one joyous burst of clarity, Molly understood the prophecy and the curse. She saw why of course it *must be* she and Hatch, who belonged in both countries, and neither, who could and must break the curse. And she saw with cold precision how it must be done.

Sometimes the hero doesn't win, Hatch thought again, and it was a relief. His decision was made. It didn't matter if he won or not. What matters, he told himself, is that when you lose, you don't lose because you spent your last moments hanging from his hand like a limp vegetable.

It was now or never. With a furious effort, Hatch suddenly twisted his body around in Marlowe's grasp and began to flail wildly, clawing at anything within reach. Most of his frantic blows met only air, but once he felt the old wizard's face between his fingers, and as he raked his fingernails across the decrepit flesh, he saw the skin tear.

Marlowe screamed more in rage than in pain, and when he did so, everyone saw him as Fairy Tale had seen him already: not as a powerful and malignant wizard, but as a frail and pathetic old man.

Marlowe dropped Hatch and covered his now bloodied

face with both hands. Hatch staggered, and felt a little foolish that all he had accomplished was a scratched face. But it was the chance Molly had been looking for. She lunged forward, and before anyone realized what was happening, wrapped both her arms around the old villain's waist, and flung herself sideways, wrenching the wizard off his feet and plunging them both over the edge of the precipice.

⁓

"No!" Ava shouted too late, crawling toward the edge as fast as her injured body could carry her. Fairy Tale and the other Maskies followed, but the Druinian soldiers remained rooted to the ground, both of their faces a mask of uncomprehending shock.

Hatch screamed. Had Tobias not held him back, he might have hurled himself over the edge as well, so frantic was he at the sight of his friend disappearing into the bottomless chasm before her.

"No, no, no," he moaned, collapsing into Tobias' arms. "Oh no, she can't, she can't!"

But she had.

An extraordinary change, meanwhile, was taking place all around them. It wasn't that the island was returning itself to the more cheerful state in which they had found it. Rather, it was becoming a new place entirely. At first, the changes happened so gradually that those gathered didn't notice it, blinded by grief and shock as they were. An aroma of wildflowers began to fill the air and new blossoms unfurled in a magnificent array of colors and varieties. Behind the cottage, the briars withdrew once more into the earth, replaced by a bubbling stream. Graceful willows and birch trees sprang up along its banks and the sunlight grew steadily warmer. Ava and Percival, who had regained consciousness just in time to see Molly and Marlowe disappear over the edge, felt the cold poison of the wizard's magic drain from their bodies and strength once again rush in.

The cottage, too, was undergoing a transformation. It had been quaint and cheerful under Fairy Tale's care, and desolate and haunted in the eyes of Marlowe's men. Now it became something wild and beautiful. The stone walls took on the form of gnarled wood, growing out of the ground itself. The door that appeared in the wood was ornately carved, its frame adorned with the runes of some ancient magical race. The roof was covered in succulents in vibrant hues of scarlet, purple, and yellow.

Hatch was far too overwrought to see these things, however. Still, Fairy Tale urged him to rise. "Come, my love. This island isn't mine anymore. You've done what you came here for. It is time to leave," she prodded gently.

Hatch only wept helplessly and allowed himself to be prodded along, never thinking to ask how Fairy Tale meant to get off the island. Percival picked up Seamus, who was still unconscious. He himself was wracked with shock and grief, though he'd only briefly made Molly's acquaintance. He paid no more mind to Marlowe's soldiers, nor they to him.

The soldiers, having seen both their commanding officer and their emperor fall, had simultaneously come to the conclusion that their services were no longer required and had quietly turned to leave. The Maskies did not hinder their retreat, but they were surprised to find, when they reached the place where the train had been on the other side of the island, that it had been transformed into a rather large hedgehog. Not knowing what else to do, they eventually took up residence in the cottage and lived a quiet and peaceable life there for some years. One of them did eventually discover a way to leave the island and return home, but the other had decided by this time that it was as good a place as any to settle down, and we can assume he remained quite happy there for the rest of his life.

Our heroes, meanwhile, made their way to the place where the ferry had been moored. Fairy Tale had an idea that it might have reappeared by now and she was not wrong. The ferryman gently guided Hatch into the bow of the boat while the others clambered aboard.

Much to everyone's surprise (even Fairy Tale's) he pushed the boat away from the shore and directed it not toward the mainland, but downward, into the chasm. Percival gave the ferryman a questioning look, but he smiled and shook his head.

"Trust me. You'll want to go this way," he said.

So down they went.

All the ferry's occupants maintained a reverent silence as each processed the events of the preceding half hour. Eventually Hatch's tears ran their course and he began to feel drowsy. He had no right to be drowsy though, he thought. No right to sleep! No right to rest, when his friend lay broken at the bottom of this chasm.

These thoughts helped him fight sleep for a little while, but it *was* a long way down, and the boat was swaying so gently and everything was so quiet…

25

⁓

AFTER THE ISLAND

Brogan and Lydia approached the little cabin before them with no small sense of wonder. They had followed the path from the edge of the frozen lake with relative ease, despite the steep decline that led them ever lower, until Brogan felt sure they had long passed the altitude from which they started at the base of the mountains. Still the path plunged ever deeper into a massive valley at the heart of the mountain range, till at last they had arrived at a wide circular opening, warm with sunlit grass. At the center of the circle, a rock geyser sprung from the ground and proceeded upward so far that it disappeared behind the clouds. It was narrow at the base, but widened as it reached skyward, leaving the impression of a wooden spinning top lodged in the earth. Nestled against the base, was a cozy looking wooden cabin. The windows were flung open and the curtains danced lazily in the mild breeze.

As the travelers approached, the door was swung outwards and a startled looking man with a heavy rope hung over one shoulder regarded them with surprise.

This could hardly be wondered at. Visitors to these parts were no doubt rare, but especially ones so bedraggled and travel-worn.

"Hello!" Lydia called out with a friendly wave. "We're... um..." she paused to consider how to go about her introduction, but the stranger only shot a preoccupied glance over his shoulder into the house as if trying to decide what to do.

The dilemma lasted only a few seconds. At the sound of Lydia's voice, a girl appeared in the doorway, looking every bit as bedraggled as Lydia herself, but shining with joy. Before Lydia had time to recognize her, the girl was rocketed toward her and flung her arms around her neck in greeting. Brogan and the stranger looked on, equally bemused.

"Molly!" Lydia cried, weak with relief. "Molly... oh you, brave, foolish child, what are you doing here?"

"So you, er... know each other, then?" the stranger asked, looking relieved.

"Know each other? We've been looking everywhere for her!" Brogan laughed, having caught on. "But where's Hatch?"

"Well that's convenient," the stranger said with satisfaction. "You see I've got to go, but I wouldn't want to leave her alone with strangers about. Make yourselves at home. I won't be long."

At that, the man conjured a boat out of nowhere, clambered into it, and disappeared.

$\backsim$

Hatch opened his eyes later that same day to the smell of sausage cooking, and the sound of happy voices. His stomach growled but the moment he sat up, the day's events flooded back like a douse of ice water, and suddenly the sound of cheerful laughter was an insult. *How could they be happy? Did they not know that Molly was dead? Did they not care?* Angry tears sprang from his eyes, and he swung his feet out of the bed. Before he could lay them all waste with his hot indignation, however, the door swung open and Fairy Tale's warm face peeked in. She smiled when she saw him

"He's awake!" she called.

Hatch heard the sound of chairs moving and bodies shuffling, and to his astonishment, Molly's head appeared from under the arm with which Fairy Tale held open the door. Her eyes shone as she crossed the room in a single bound and catapulted herself onto the bed, nearly bowling the boy over with her embrace.

"What?" was all he could manage.

༄

Knowing as you do the way that magic works in that world, what happened will make sense to you, of course. Just as Molly's rebellion had lifted the protective enchantments and banished the ferryman, her act of self-sacrifice had the opposite effect.

As soon as Molly flung herself and Marlowe from the cliff's edge, the emperor had grasped his staff and disappeared (much to the Maskies' disappointment) and left Molly falling alone. At the same moment, the ferryman, who as you will remember was only able to appear when someone needed passage to the island, did just that. Only Molly's act had been so selfless, so willing, that it had lifted all of the enchantments Marlowe had originally used to keep Fairy Tale imprisoned on the island. No longer forced to contend with Marlowe's will, Fairy Tale's spells could work without limitation. The ferryman appeared not only when, but exactly where passage was needed, which meant that Molly landed roughly in the bottom of the ferryman's boat rather than plunging to her death.

The ferryman himself (who, it turned out, had not been oft called upon since being assigned to his outpost) had built a cozy little home on the canyon floor, in which he lived when his services weren't needed. It was there that he had taken Molly, who was bruised, but otherwise no worse for the wear, and had only just deposited her there when he found himself once again summoned to retrieve the rest of them from the island. It was there again, that Brogan and Lydia, led by whatever magical force inhabited those mountains, had found her. And there that the two children made their tearful amends to one another; she for the bitter resentment she had nurtured which led to her failure to honor their pact with the ferryman, he for his cold indifference that had made her feel so alone. It was there that forgiveness was granted and all resentments buried beneath warm, grassy earth, hot sausages, friendly laughter, and the telling of a new fairy tale.

༄

King Mardius was in his office, reviewing a new trade agreement with a neighboring kingdom, when the door to his study burst open. The king of Arden was, as you know, a friendly fellow, but for his office to be so unceremoniously intruded upon was still most unheard of. He looked up in no small surprise to see an Ardenian soldier, wide eyed and breathless, standing before him.

"Your majesty!" the soldier exclaimed. "It's gone!"

"Ha! Well that's very interesting!" Mardius beamed back, slapping his desk enthusiastically. Mardius liked to get into the spirit of things. Still, he thought it might be wise to follow up, for clarity's sake. "What, exactly, is gone?"

The soldier's eyes sparkled. "The wall your majesty!"

This time Mardius rose to his feet, genuinely stunned. "You don't mean..."

"I do, sire. I mean just that."

"Are you sure?"

"Quite sure. I saw it go myself. It was like... I hardly know how to describe it sire. It was as if the whole thing came crashing down at once. It sounded like shattering glass but all we felt – the rest of the patrol and I, that is, sir – it felt like a great wind that passed over us once and stopped blowing. And then we walked right out into the Wasteland."

᎙

In Druinor, extraordinary things were happening. I wish I could say that when the wall fell, the dark enchantments over that country dissipated, leaving its populace free, but alas, that was not the case. The Druinians had been Druinians long before the wall went up, after all, and their emperor, though licking his wounds, was by no means vanquished. Still, the crumbling of the wall was felt in every corner of that country, as though its shattered pieces had scattered far and wide into Druinor's streets and byways.

In households and workplaces, people caught themselves smiling over some joke told long ago, or letting their minds wander briefly from their tasks to think of some pleasant memory. The honest and decent folks, like the Morrises and Hollands, felt a nostalgic pang. They did not recognize the call of their long-forgotten homeland as what it was, but they felt it all the same. A restless longing never before felt rose up in Pudge the bartender so strongly that he closed the pub early and went for a walk.

The meaner spirited Druinians, on the other hand, felt a somewhat different sensation. For one fleeting moment, a new kind of fear lurched up in their stomachs. It wasn't the fear they were used to, of Marlowe and policemen and each other, but a fear of losing those things, of change, of uncertainty. This made them all out of sorts and they took it out on each other in very unkind ways.

In Damascus, the effects were felt more potently. Alice, Rob, and Ben, who had been playing cards, suddenly looked up at one another, startled and joyful without knowing why. From that moment forward, they each began to imagine things—just a little at first like tendrils of steam rising from Martha's cooking pot, but the whisps grew until... well, that's another story.

The other residents of Damascus, at the moment the wall fell, felt a joy so high and piercing they could barely stand up under it. Wes wept with his face in his hands. Joel danced a jig. Andrew bellowed "hurrah!" and opened a jug of beer. There were shouts and cheers all around.

Most remarkable of all, however, was Joel, who shot to his feet and stood stock still. His face had gone white as a tombstone. Seeing his stricken look, Raymond stopped dancing abruptly, with one foot still stuck straight out before him, and nearly toppled over.

"My dear fellow!" he cried. "You look as if the wall landed directly on your head."

Joel looked at him with wild eyes and said incomprehensibly, "It did! I remember! It did, my good man."

You see, at the moment that the wall lifted, so did a thick fog that had dwelt so long in Joel's mind, it had become as comfortable as furniture there, which is only seen when it's gone. In one penetrating stab of clarity, he remembered his life before Druinor. He remembered smiling sunny days, pleasant hearth sides, friendly neighbors, stories sung, some even sung by him. He remembered the panicked cry of his neighbor the night the man's daughter had disappeared, and the wild chase he gave across the Wasteland in her pursuit. He remembered seeing the black mist bear down on him and knowing he would be enveloped in it. But he remembered nothing more. Not how he had wandered, dazed, into a Druinian town, nor going from there to the capital with a passing supply coach, nor how he had first encountered the Damascus Guard. To him it seemed as though he had always been with them. He remembered only that he had a homeland, and the longing to see it again was so poignant that he found he could barely breathe.

And let us not forget sweet Melody, that faithful cat who had endured much and for very little glory. Imagine how her heart must have beat. Her dear children, whom she loved so, had succeeded! The day was nearer than she had dared to hope that she might see them again, and in a fairer, freer country than this in which she had labored so long.

It would be many more weeks before either she or Joel would see that country again, and much would pass before they could be reunited with the children, but that is a story for another time, and one that cannot steal even a second of the joy they felt that night.

ᗡ

The journey back to Arden was unlike any of their travels up to that point. It was a long expedition. They started at the bottom of the chasm and hiked upward from there, having been told by the ferryman it would be a more pleasant route than starting at the top of the chasm and climbing down the mountains the way they'd come.

Yet their fellowship was sweeter than it had been, not only because they had succeeded in their mission, but because all jealousies and foolish rivalries had been cast aside, leaving in their place only the affectionate love of brothers and sisters for one another. Molly and Hatch still quarreled from time to time, as weary children do, but their words held no sting and their irritations were fleeting.

Fairy Tale's very presence was a blessing. She filled their time with wonderful stories that captured their imaginations, adorned their paths with enchanted things, and made a friend of every creature they encountered. In this new state and in such company, the weeks that constituted their return trip seemed like no time at all. On Brogan's advice, they found the place where he and Lydia had fallen through the tunnel, in order to pick up the path they'd originally followed into the mountains. Thus they encountered Aodhan, Grace, and Rowena, who were camped at the spot where they had lost Brogan and Lydia's trail. They had been taking turns scouting the surrounding area for signs of either the children or the Borhagens.

The whole party was met, upon entering Arden, with much fanfare. For the first time since leaving the chasm, both children were tempted once again to remember their selfish actions on Fairy Tale Island. When Mardius sang the children's praises to their parents, and at banquets in their favor, their private shame guarded them against taking too much pride in the adulation.

However, they each recognized that sometimes it is a greater act of humility to share in unmerited praise than to reject it for the sake of pride.

"Our adventure together was more than just that hour on the island," Hatch told Molly one day. "I think we've got to keep the whole thing like a treasure... the sum of all its parts... even the bits we're ashamed of."

Brogan was quick to remind the king that Marlowe, though foiled in this particular, had not been vanquished.

"If the account our travelers bring us is accurate, he's not dead," Aodhan had agreed. "Which means that wherever he is, he's livid, and we are in his sights."

Thus the men and women of Arden did not take long to rest or revel in their victory, but set to work at once, planning, strategizing, and bolstering their own defenses. The oppressed people of Druinor were waiting for their aid.

Before long, the fear and pain of the children's adventure had worn off, leaving only the wonders and miracles of it. These were turned over again and again in their conversations like well-loved books with covers worn from much use. Naturally their story was told and retold in a dozen ways by the storytellers of Arden, and now that Fairy Tale was free, new tales could once again be spun. These newly woven stories, and one in particular about two ordinary children whose extraordinary actions conquered a great villain, made their way across the Wasteland, as far as Druinor, and were told in secret to children who perhaps were not quite as dull as we originally suspected.

EPILOGUE

I t was a fine morning – at least as fine as a morning in Druinor could be. The air was cold and crisp – just the sort of morning one wanted to be drinking tea by the fireside, rather than heading to work, yet that was exactly what Martha was doing.

Carrying a large stack of books in one arm and a heavy bag over the other shoulder, she pushed open the heavy door and stepped inside the shining, sterile hallway. She took a deep breath. She never would get used to this place. Martha was born to make homes cozy and hearths warm, not to engage in espionage.

She was not, however, one to shirk a duty, nor one to abandon children in need, and so here she was. The young faces all around her were still dull and sullen, but more and more frequently she was seeing among them sparks of creativity, of curiosity, and even compassion. It was for these little moments of illumination that she and her companions lived.

The Institute had experienced some upheaval that year. Shortly after the emperor recovered from his illness, it had been discovered that Headmistress Bell had been an integral part of the treasonous plot that had resulted in the disappearance of her secretary, Ava Perry, and the embarrassment of capital policeman Steven Snyder. Further evidence, leaked to the Council by a member of Marlowe's palace guard, had suggested that multiple professors, including the notorious Professor Dalton, had also been involved in this treachery. It was suspected that the faculty had been infiltrated by dissidents who plotted to overthrow the emperor. No one knew how far the corruption had spread.

As a result, many of the staff members had been imprisoned, some sacked, and others… well, we may never know what fate they met. This overhaul left several openings in the faculty, and Joel, who you may recall worked at the county registrar's office, was only too happy to furnish a list of possible replacements, and their credentials.

Thanks to a lot of very good planning and impossibly good luck, Martha, Raymond, Luke, Wes, and Andrew all now held faculty positions.

So it was that Martha now found herself entering a classroom full of Druinian children, some of whom greeted her with an enthusiasm she would once have not thought possible.

Every day in this school was a risk. They all knew it. Druinian children like Edith still abounded – children who were wicked and spiteful, who would have sold them out just for the pleasure of doing so, but they had all agreed that it was worth the risk. They used a variety of means, from bribes to enchantments, to protect themselves from such things. Andrew had taught them all how to use the necessary spells, and they had diligently practiced them until they were each experts.

Martha used one such enchantment now, on the classroom window. If any other professor or visiting government official were to walk by, they would see only what they expected to see – a room full of miserable students in uncomfortable desks, and a fat professor droning on about economic policies and the obsolete nature of parenting roles in society. That done, she turned cheerfully to her young pupils.

"Alright children!" she said, beaming. "Let's talk about the story we read yesterday."

"The one about the dragon?" asked a boy in the front row.

"Yes dear, that one. What was the gem in that story?"

ABOUT THE AUTHOR

Kate Ramsey lives with various siblings, nieces, and nephews in Oklahoma where she drinks tea, runs a birth photography business, and writes whatever wants to be written.

Follow Kate's work at TalesMustBeTold.com.

www.ingramcontent.com/pod-product-compliance
Lightning Source LLC
Chambersburg PA
CBHW051955240626
47153CB00005B/1767